M000192382

WHAT READERS ARE SAYING ABOUT *WITH ME IN THE STORM*

"*With Me in the Storm* is a fast-paced, page-turning, plot-twisting tale which leads readers through a journey from despair to determination to hope. It's the story of an unlikely hero, and I loved it."

—Kirk Walden
Author of *The Wall*

"If you like a story that rings true, that captures your heart and mind and holds you there for the duration, look no further!"

—Jola Johnson
Freelance Editor, Librarian

"Maddie's journey caught my heart with the twists and turns of her young life. The people she encountered, both friend and foe, kept me pulling for her. I couldn't put the book down until I had finished it."

—Ginny Graham
Author

"Karen Ingle is a passionate storyteller. From page one I was gripped by the characters and was compelled to keep reading!"

—Carrie Meyers
Pregnancy Center Director

"*With Me in the Storm* hooks you in and keeps you immersed in the story, only drawing you in further with each new chapter. Prepare to have tears of both sorrow and joy throughout the story—it is well worth it!"

—Andrea Trudden
Vice President of Communications & Marketing, Heartbeat International

"Karen Ingle has heard many women's harrowing stories first-hand. This story keeps the pace fast and the tension high while introducing glimmers of hope—a hope based on biblical faith."

—Laura Roesler
Freelance Writer

WITH ME IN THE STORM

by Karen E. Ingle

No fear !
Deut. 31:8
Karen

With Me in the Storm

Trilogy Christian Publishers A Wholly Owned Subsidary of Trinity Broadcasting Network

2442 Michelle Drive Tustin, CA 92780

Copyright © 2022 by Karen E. Ingle

Scriptures taken from the Holy Bible, New International Version®, NIV®. Copyright © 1973, 1978, 1984, 2011 by Biblica, Inc.™ Used by permission of Zondervan. All rights reserved worldwide. www.zondervan.com The "NIV" and "New International Version" are trademarks registered in the United States Patent and Trademark Office by Biblica, Inc.®No part of this book may be reproduced, stored in a retrieval system, or transmitted by any means without written permission from the author. All rights reserved. Printed in the USA.

Rights Department, 2442 Michelle Drive, Tustin, CA 92780.

Trilogy Christian Publishing/TBN and colophon are trademarks of Trinity Broadcasting Network.

Cover design by: Natalee Groves

For information about special discounts for bulk purchases, please contact Trilogy Christian Publishing.

Manufactured in the United States of America

10 9 8 7 6 5 4 3 2 1

Library of Congress Cataloging-in-Publication Data is available.

ISBN: 978-1-68556-555-8

E-ISBN: 978-1-68556-556-5

DEDICATION

Dedicated to my mother, Darlene Patrick,
my first and most loyal fan.

I'm forever grateful that she pointed me to Jesus,
modeled perseverance,
and encouraged me to pick up my pen again and write.

ACKNOWLEDGMENTS

Several compassionate experts assisted me in creating true-to-life experiences for my characters. After days filled with serving hurting people themselves, they took time to read over and correct my early drafts. Any errors that remain are entirely my own. I thank the following people for all that is true about this story:

Suzanne Burns, MS, Certified Family Trauma Professional; founder and executive director, Foundation House Ministries

Brittany Miller, victim advocate with
WoMen's Rural Advocacy Program

Tom Latterell, retired emergency medical technician

Officer Jason Nichols, California peace officer

Andy Merritt, senior pastor of Edgewood Baptist Church (deceased), whose true accounts of transformed lives inspired some key events in this book.

The roughly one hundred pregnancy help servants I have met, interviewed, and worked with—especially one who must remain anonymous—who provided inspiration for the characters of Tricia, Paloma, and the team at the fictitious Dos Almas Pregnancy Center.

Many women's stories have been fictionalized and woven together to become With Me in the Storm. I am in awe of those women's resilience and courage. I hope that Maddie reflects them well.

Of course, this book would not be in your hands at all without the hard work and support of my servant-hearted husband Dennis, my youngest daughter (and fellow writer) Deborah, and my loyal friend Jola Johnson. They gave up a lot to let me write. I love them forever.

Along with Jola, my inimitable friend Heather Smith headed Team KIA to help me build an enthusiastic community of readers and launch team members. Thank you, friends!

Most of all, I thank my Savior Jesus Christ, who alone brings true healing to hurting people.

TABLE OF CONTENTS

CHAPTER 1

Maddie's bare feet crunched across the dried weeds in the patchy backyard. She squeezed the paper sack to her chest, twisting it tighter around the thin cardboard box it concealed. Her heart pounded against her hands. She wasn't supposed to be outdoors while Zach was away. He could return any minute. But she had to make this disappear. Letting Zach see it would be the only thing worse than seeing it herself.

Maddie wrestled with the rusty gate latch. This was trash day, her only chance to get this awful thing out of the house and keep her out of danger. At least for now. Zach hadn't acted like he'd noticed her clothes were getting tighter. But he'd catch on soon. She had hoped there was another reason—any other reason—she was so uncomfortable. But now she knew. And if Zach knew...

The latch scraped open, and she peeked around the gate into the alley.

To the right, the neighbors' trash can overflowed with empty boxes and wads of Christmas wrapping paper. To the left, no can at all. But beyond that, two back gates away, stood old Mrs. Yamamoto's trash can, neatly positioned for the garbage truck. With one last glance in both directions, Maddie shot left down the alley. She slipped her crumpled paper bag of contraband beneath Mrs. Yamamoto's lid and closed it quietly, her hands trembling. Another glance both ways, then she darted back through the gate and across the weedy yard to the sliding door she'd left open. Exhaling at last, she slid the door shut and locked it. The anti-burglar bar dropped down into the slot on its own. There. Everything in its place.

Shaking, Maddie swallowed hard. If she couldn't calm down, Zach would read the whole story on her face. He always knew when she was lying. She took two halting steps into the kitchen. Was it time for her to make dinner?

All she could think about was that paper sack. The truth inside it was shaking her world. Maddie gripped the back of a chair.

A shadow fell across the kitchen floor just as a pounding began on the sliding glass door. Maddie whirled around.

Zach, his face hard as steel, looked huge. Larger than the wiry frame beneath that faux leather jacket. "Let. Me. In," he said through the glass.

Act normal. Act normal. She lifted the anti-burglar bar, unlocked the door. Slid it open. Stepped back. "Hey there. You startled me."

He stepped in, his icy eyes studying her face. "What were you doing out there?"

Maddie swallowed and stepped behind a chair.

Zach swung the chair away from her. "Well?"

"Trash," she whispered. Then, louder, she repeated, "Trash. I forgot to empty the kitchen trash, so I—"

Pushing her aside, Zach crossed to the sink and yanked open the cupboard below it. He whipped out their cracked plastic trash can and shoved the stinking thing under her nose. "Try again."

"I just... I just needed... some fresh—"

Zach tossed the trash to the floor and grabbed her by the arm. His free hand reached into his jacket pocket and pulled out the crumpled paper bag. He held it up to Maddie's face. "You dropped something."

It was pointless to argue. Except arguing meant she might live a few seconds longer. She fought to keep her voice steady. "What are you talking about?"

He shoved her backward, growling, "You know exactly what I'm talking about." He ripped open the bag, sending the pregnancy test and its packaging skittering across the floor.

She backed farther away, running up against the refrigerator. "What's that?"

"Give it up, Maddie," Zach said, his voice ominously low. "I watched you pitch this into Mrs. Yamamoto's can."

She couldn't milk this much longer. He knew. And she was about to die.

Zach's voice turned syrupy. "All of Mrs. Yamamoto's garbage was tied up in tidy white trash bags. But there on top sat this odd paper sack. And inside, a little pregnancy test." His head lowered like he might charge. "Your little positive pregnancy test."

In one swift move, he lunged and grabbed a fistful of her hair. She screamed just as his other fist slammed into her cheek. "What kind of fool are you?! Geez, woman, it was your job to make sure they wore protection! That's all you had to do. Was that so hard?"

"I tried," she whimpered. One arm went up to protect her face, the other her belly. "But not all of them—"

Zach's phone alarm rang. He snorted and shoved her to the floor. Then he yanked the phone from his hip pocket. He swore at the screen, then at her.

"I should have guessed," he said. He kicked at her, flinging her sideways into a kitchen chair. "Look at you! You're fat as a horse. If I didn't have this coke coming today—" Zach rubbed his hand across the stubble on his sharp chin, making a sanding sound in the silence. At least he wasn't high, wasn't acting on impulse. She just might live through the day.

Maddie said nothing, only sat up, making her arms and legs a cage around her pregnant belly. Her chin trembled, but she bit down on her lips to keep Zach from seeing it.

Finally, Zach smacked his hand against the wall. "Of course, I find this out just before I have to pick up my shipment. My biggest yet. I can't take care of this right now."

Take care of this. Maddie shivered and tried to hug her knees tighter against her bulging tummy. Horror stories crept from the back corners of her mind—Zach's stories about "taking care" of his previous girls' pregnancies.

Zach bent and gripped her chin. He hissed in her face, "So, your mistake, your fix. I'm going to make *you* take care of it. Don't move."

She squeezed her eyes shut as he stomped to the back of the house. The closet door opened, there was a pause, then the door closed. She shuddered. For months she had bottled up this fear, ever since she first suspected she might be pregnant. Uncertainty let her keep hoping she was wrong. Finally, she'd secretly asked Tanisha to get her a pregnancy test. Now she wished she hadn't.

He entered. "Here."

Something hit her shoulder and fell to the floor. Her old cell phone.

Zach flipped a silver key like a coin and slapped it onto the back of his hand. He gave her a mocking smile. "Now, a little game, Maddie. Heads, you go get an abortion." He looked at the key with fake surprise. "Well, whaddya know? Heads."

Abortion. Better than she feared.

"Or—" he suddenly straddled her, pressing the jagged edge of the key against her neck, "—tails, you'll be sorrier than you are now."

The key dropped to the floor. Her heart pounded. *It's only a key. Not his knife.* Not this time.

She let the key and the phone lie with the trash on the linoleum, afraid to move her protecting arms. She knew Zach wasn't through.

He crouched directly in front of her. "You understand, right? Get it done and be back by the time I return with my shipment. Think you can remember *that*, Stupid?"

Maddie nodded, tears building behind the face she strained to keep impassive.

"Good. 'Cause this is my biggest deal yet. I'm not letting the big guys down for you." He stood, towering above her. "Mess this up, you know, and I'll just replace you with that cute blonde I've had my eye on. You're disposable. But without me—"

He waited, half a grin on his thin lips.

"—I am nothing," Maddie muttered, completing his mantra.

The last ice cube in the freezer did little to help keep the swelling down on Maddie's cheek. Not surprising. Help wasn't anything Maddie expected anymore. She tossed the dripping washcloth into the bathroom sink and dried her hand on her pants.

Eyeing the front door, just in case Zach came back unexpectedly, she sat on the toilet lid and reached for her phone. Her hands shook. She had to type in her search three times to get it right: "Abortion near me."

Her old phone felt like a familiar friend. And a faithless enemy. She hadn't had control of it for…ages…Ever since Zach snatched it away the day he informed her that he was her boss, not her boyfriend. He only kept the phone paid for and charged so he could give her orders when he sent her out to "work."

The search results appeared. Maddie closed her eyes, breathing a mute apology to her mother, who was probably watching from heaven, shocked. Her own daughter getting an abortion. And on a New Year's Eve, no less.

She tapped on the first search result. Dos Almas Pregnancy Center. A website appeared, filled with images of women her age. Some looked just as confused as she felt. Some—happy and free. Before and after, maybe? Maddie scrolled to the phone number. She looked up, listened. No sound of Zach's car sneaking back to check on her. No sound at all, except the dripping faucet beside her.

It was time. Just call them and get this over with. She tapped. There, it was ringing… And ringing again… No answer.

She watched the faucet drip. Zach never fixed anything. She once thought he would fix everything. That's what he promised when they connected over the internet. And when he drove out to "date" her back in Minnesota. Moving away together, he said, would fix everything. The dark past would disappear into a bright future here in sunny California. She cringed, remembering how easily she had fallen for his smooth talk and his scruffy good looks.

Another ring of that distant phone.

Of course: New Year's Eve. Dos Almas Pregnancy Center had the day off. Just when she needed them.

She didn't know if she could muster the strength to call another abortion place.

Zach wouldn't understand that. He'd come back and hammer her for being too stupid. Then there'd be no baby, and probably no Maddie Clouse. But maybe that would be best, after all. She wasn't much of a Maddie Clouse now.

Another drop fell from the faucet. The faucet he had slammed her face down on when she didn't want to wear the makeup he demanded. Soon she had to wear it all the time just to cover the bruises. She had to look good then, good enough for all his friends and even some of his enemies. They had all come and used her. Creeps. Creeps who had left a permanent layer of creepiness all over her. It never washed off. And one of them—or maybe Zach—had left her with a little something more.

Another ring, far away. Still, no one answered.

She leaned her elbows on her ratty yoga pants and cry-laughed a choked sob. For a split second this morning, holding that pregnancy test, she'd felt a crazy, fleeting hope. Maybe she could keep this child—a little person who loved her. Dumb idea. She really was as stupid as Zach said.

She didn't deserve love. That's why nobody loved her. Nobody cared.

Come on, Dos Almas. Please. Somebody.

Mid-ring, a voice interrupted, "Hello, this is Dos Almas Pregnancy Center. I'm Tricia. How can I help you?"

Her mouth opened, and the words dried on her tongue.

"Hello? May I help you?"

This time Maddie forced out a hoarse whisper: "I…I can't keep this baby."

The voice paused. "You sound a little scared. Do you feel safe right now?"

She blinked. Not the words she expected. "Um…no." Glancing at the front door, she hurried on. "No. If he gets back and I'm still pregnant, I don't know what he'll do to me."

"I see." The voice fell silent for a moment, then went on, "Let's think through the best way I could help you."

Like there's more than one? Maddie scoffed silently.

"May I help you connect with someone who can help you get away to a safe place?"

Speechless, Maddie stared at the faucet, where one drop hung dangling from the very edge. Get away? That had never entered her mind. That was too wild, too impossible. Where would she go? Who would help her?

The woman started speaking again before she could track with her.

Maddie rubbed her forehead. "I'm sorry, what?"

"Do you know how far along your pregnancy is?" the woman repeated.

"I really—I have no idea." She could never tell this stranger how little she knew about pregnancy. Mama had said it would all be explained when Maddie was engaged to be married. Then came cancer, then went Mama. Now this.

The woman continued, unruffled. "I see. Life must be pretty chaotic there."

Maddie covered her eyes and pressed against them. "Chaotic. Yeah."

"Do you think it would be easier to figure out how to deal with your pregnancy if you felt safe?"

"Oh, God, yes." She hadn't meant to blurt out a prayer, but there it was. Something about that wild dream of safety and this kind-sounding stranger was piercing her shell. Her eyes watered.

The woman continued, "I have a friend who's an expert at helping women who want to get out of dangerous situations. Would you like her number?"

Somebody did that for a living? Maddie said, "Well, yeah, I guess so. Um, just a sec." She reached into a jumbled drawer and found an eyeliner pencil and some kind of paper wrapper. "Okay," she said. "Ready."

The woman's voice carefully read her a phone number, then added, "Avery Caine is her name."

Maddie stared at the name and number. Could she ever—

The lady went on, "Speaking of names. I've told you my name is Tricia. Can you tell me your name?"

"Well, um…it's…Lizzie." She'd always liked that name. Then her breath caught. "Wait, your name's Tricia?"

"Yes."

Her Mama's name. A bittersweet ache rose within her chest. Don't go there, she told herself. But she could feel her shell cracking, her heart softening toward this stranger.

"Now, Lizzie, I want to be really upfront with you. Dos Almas provides information about abortion, but we don't perform abortions. Nor do we refer women to abortion clinics."

"Oh." Somehow, she was relieved. A tiny new nugget of hope started making itself at home in a corner of her mind. Now it cast a pale, young light over her thinking. If she could get away…

But could she trust this woman called Tricia? Maybe she was like Mama in more than name—mentally unstable and the whole nine yards. But still… What if there really was a way out of this horror story?

No. Zach had told her to get an abortion and soon. Why was she even talking to this woman if she couldn't help her get an abortion? A sound outside gave her the excuse she needed.

"I think I hear something," she said. "I'll have to call you back."

"Please do," Tricia said. "I'll keep my phone with me all night. I'll be available for you."

"'kay." Maddie tapped the disconnect button. Suddenly exhausted, she leaned an arm on the cold porcelain sink and rested her forehead on her hand. Folded over like this, it was hard to breathe. It made her need to pee. She forced herself to sit up.

The faucet dripped. Dripped again. Not much time. Zach would be gone two, maybe three hours.

Maddie cranked hard on the cold-water handle. A new droplet grew, swelling in slow motion. Like her. Hanging, suspended between where she'd been and the terrifying fall into whatever lay ahead. If she obeyed Zach, she'd fall back into the cesspool where she lived every day. If she listened to the stranger with Mama's name, there was a slim chance she might get away from this mess. But away to what?

Something moved in her belly. She placed her hand over the moving thing, the lump sliding along beneath the surface of her skin. She pushed on it gently. The moving thing pushed back.

Maddie eyed her phone, felt the poke of her key in her pocket. Breath filled her lungs as realization filled her mind. She was not alone. There was someone else with her. Someone else affected by her next move. Someone else she had to defend from Zach.

One of those strange tightenings she'd been having arced across her belly. She stretched backward against the toilet tank, trying to wait it out. Her fingers squeezed tight around the wrapper she'd written on. Would this spasm be a single or one of those clusters she'd had once before?

Either way, when it was over, she would call that Tricia with the kind voice. Then, just maybe, she'd call Tricia's friend.

Tricia Prescott paced her office area, a half-empty box of screws in her left hand. Still, her cell phone lay silent. Had that been a real call? Or just another one of those "fake clients" with a phony story and a scheme to twist her words in the media? Tricia massaged her forehead with her fingertips, replaying the exchange in her mind. *Assume it's real.* A real woman, a real baby, in real danger. Tricia's mind raced through all the scenarios that might be playing out for Lizzie right now.

She returned to her desk and laid down her box of screws to wake up her computer. Repairing that old bookshelf would have to wait. There was a desperate woman—and a child—at risk. If only the girl would call back. Or at least call Avery.

Tricia drummed her fingers beside the keyboard. Avery Caine, an advocate at the local domestic violence relief agency, was one clever professional. She had pulled women out of some horrendous situations and landed them all in safe places.

But what if this girl wanted to stay put? Tricia had heard stranger things in her short three years at Dos Almas. Desperation coupled with coercion could wreak havoc on a woman's sense of identity and intrinsic value.

Tricia opened the file of agency contacts, watching the names of her network partners scroll past. If only Paloma were here. Paloma, with her years of experience, could have rattled off fifteen different people who could be of help to this girl.

Her eyes landed on a maternity home contact. Of course: if the girl left her abusive situation, she'd need refuge. Tricia jotted down the name and number. Those could be useful. *If* the mother let the child live. And if she was nearby. Tricia noted the emergency number for a national network of maternity homes, just in case she lived out of state. Or she fled out of state.

"Please, please call again," Tricia whispered toward the phone. *Help her, Lord. And if I can be part of how you do that, I'm here.*

If Lizzie had called just five minutes later, Tricia would have been heading home for the holiday. In fact, if Tricia hadn't come in to do these messy repairs when the office stood empty, there would have been no one here to answer the phone at all.

Sure, the trained counselors who picked up off-hours calls gave excellent help. But if this young woman was real, and in real trouble, right here, right now—then Tricia was right where she needed to be. "Please, please call back," Tricia whispered, scanning the list on her screen while her fingers kept time on the desk.

This wasn't helping. Tricia stood, pocketed her phone, grabbed the screws, and returned to the rickety bookshelf, talking out loud to the only one who really knew what was going on with that caller.

Several minutes later, Tricia had the shelves secured and all the educational DVDs back in place. Someday, the whole decrepit thing would probably collapse, pancaking like an old apartment building in an earthquake.

Tricia sighed. If she were a better speaker, a better fundraiser, she could afford better office furnishings. Then she caught herself. "Sorry, Lord," she muttered aloud. "I keep questioning your provision. You know our needs here. Just keep us open. For women like Lizzie."

She sent her screwdriver clattering into her toolbox and lowered the lid, smiling ruefully. Who knew Executive Director not only meant Public Face of the Organization, but also Chief Handywoman and Head Toilet Scrubber? If she had known what was ahead, would she still have taken this position?

Her phone rang, displaying Lizzie's number.

Oh, yes, she would. In a heartbeat.

"Are you still there?" Maddie began.

"Yes," the woman's voice said. "Like I promised."

Standing in the dim living room behind drawn curtains, Maddie felt a flicker of hope, like the flicker of movement in her belly. Something about this woman at Dos Almas made her feel like she could talk to her about anything.

The woman asked, "Are you okay?"

"Mostly. I was having some... like, cramps, in my belly," Maddie told her.

"How often do they happen?" she asked.

"Well—" Another one of those spasms tightened her belly so hard it took her breath away. As the woman said something else, Maddie's eyes clenched shut, and it felt like her ears did too. But in a moment, the pain eased. What was going on? Maddie found her voice again. "What did you say?"

"I asked if it's possible you're having contractions."

"Contractions? What are contractions?"

After a moment's pause, Tricia said, "Contractions are the work your muscles naturally do to deliver a baby."

Maddie gasped and reached out for the ragged arm of the sofa beside her. Could she be *that* pregnant? Or had Zach done something to trigger these... contractions?

Tricia's voice was calm and firm in her ear. "Do you have a way to get to a hospital?"

"A hospital? No, he keeps my—" Maddie said, but then she felt in her jeans pocket. "Oh, wait, yeah. I do."

"Do you think you can drive yourself?"

"Maybe. But I'm scared, Tricia. I'm really scared. He told me to get an abortion. What'll he do if I have this baby? I just—I just don't know what to do." She couldn't keep her voice from coming out high and squeaky.

"Stay calm. Listen to my voice," Tricia said. Maddie bit her lips and nodded. The lady went on, "It's important to get somewhere safe, where someone can help you. Somewhere like a hospital. Are you in Colson County, like me?"

Once again, Maddie's mouth opened, but her brain shut. She shouldn't give away too much.

After her long silence, Tricia said quietly, "If you're not okay with telling me, that's all right. But is there a hospital you can go to?"

Maddie's thoughts raced as quickly as her rapid breaths. "I don't know where to go. He knows people everywhere. I'd have to be pretty far away for him not to find me..."

Footsteps outside the door froze her words.

An instant later, somebody rapped a familiar rhythm on the front door. Maddie crossed the tiny living room and peered through the peephole.

Outside, her friend Tanisha beamed a wide smile at her. She held up a colorful plastic shopping bag and shouted to be heard through the door. "Hey, girl, you gotta see this!"

Maddie sighed. Not now. Tanisha didn't really understand the situation here, with Zach. What awful timing.

Maddie spoke quietly into the phone, "Tricia, my friend's at the door. Sorry. Just a minute."

Maddie pressed the phone to her chest, determined to send Tanisha away. She unlocked the deadbolt, opening the door just enough to say, "Hey there. I'm—"

Tanisha brushed her aside and entered, opening her shopping bag. "You are not gonna believe the sale I found—"

She pulled a pair of bright yellow stiletto-heeled sandals out of her bag. Holding them in Maddie's face, she said, "Aren't you so jealous? I got them for only—" Suddenly, she tilted her head, eyeing Maddie. "Girl, you don't look so good."

"I don't feel so good." Maddie lowered herself onto the lumpy brown sofa, trying not to show the discomfort building in her belly. She pointed to the phone still pressed against her chest. "Look, I'm on an important call right now. Can you—"

Tanisha plopped down on the torn, rust-colored La-Z-Boy across from her. "Oh, sure. I can wait." She slipped off her platform shoes to strap on one of the new ones.

Maddie rolled her eyes. This wasn't working. "Tricia," she said into the phone, "I'll have to call you back in a few minutes." She hung up and frowned at Tanisha.

"What?" Tanisha said, one shoe on and the other in her hand.

Maddie only shook her head. Maybe it was time Tanisha knew. She might even have some good advice. After all, Tanisha knew a lot more than Maddie did about "the ways of the world," as Mama used to say.

She took a deep breath and launched in. "Tanisha, I've got something to tell you."

Tanisha frowned and stood, silencing Maddie with her intense stare. She pointed to Maddie's cheek. "How'd you get *that*?"

Maddie shrugged. "Oh, you know me, The Klutz. Slipped in the kitchen—"

Tanisha, hoop earrings swinging, planted her hands on her hips. "You did not. Seriously, you can't let that man push you around that way. One of these days, he's gonna go too far, and then I'll have to come pick up all the little pieces of you."

"Yeah, yeah. I know. Tanisha, sit down. Let me talk."

Tanisha, still standing, crossed her arms. "So. You're pregnant, right?"

Maddie's mouth fell open.

"Madd, I've been around. You asked me to pick you up a test. Now you're chillin' in these yoga pants and a hoodie that could hide a circus. Not like you're showing much, but I guessed. Wondered when you were gonna tell me." She tipped her head sideways. "So, am I supposed to be happy for you? You're not exactly partying."

Maddie looked down at Tanisha's stilettos. "I'm not. Neither is Zach."

"So, you gonna take care of it? Soon?"

Maddie nodded. "I was trying to… um… get an appointment when you came in."

Tanisha glanced at her phone. "Well, you go call them back, girl. If they're still open. New Year's Eve, you know."

"The woman said she'd wait for me."

Tanisha frowned. "Right. They don't do that. My first abortion, I called over the Thanksgiving weekend." She shook her head. "They were locked up tight."

"Zach wants me to get it done before he gets home tonight. He's… He's really ticked off."

"Tonight? It's New Year's Eve." Tanisha shrugged. "Whatever. You call, I'll drive you." She tossed her platforms into the plastic bag, then turned when Maddie groaned.

"Tanisha," she grunted, "wait. Something's happening." She squeezed her eyes shut. This kind of pain was new, and worse. She exhaled hard and said, "The lady said… I should go… to the hospital…"

Tanisha looped the bag handles over her arm and reached out to take Maddie's hand. "You got this. Wait 'til this passes. Then we'll go."

Maddie's fingers clenched around Tanisha's. It was so intense this time. She felt like a water balloon being squeezed in a vise. When the worst pain passed, she let Tanisha help her to her feet.

"So, how far along are you?" Tanisha asked, reaching for her bag.

Maddie just stared at her. How was she supposed to know that? Suddenly, a strange warmth flooded her legs. She looked down and watched a puddle spread on the carpet. "I think I peed."

"Girl, that ain't pee." Tanisha's nose wrinkled. "We're taking *your* car."

CHAPTER 2

Tricia's phone buzzed over her children's laughter. Lizzie's number. She laid down her fork and stood to her feet. Her husband, Reece, asked if she was okay.

"Sorry, honey. I'd better take this. It's on the work line." She smiled at her family around the dinner table. "Sorry, guys."

Drake said, "Sure, Mom," just as Joey flicked a pea at him. Reece gave her a quick thumbs-up before reaching to catch the pita bread Drake frisbeed across the table at his brother.

"Sorry, girls. I hope I won't be long," she said to the twins, whose eyes spoke disappointment in matching languages. She pushed her chair up to the table and hurried off to the privacy of her bedroom.

A deep breath, a quick prayer for help, and then she said, "Hello, Dos Almas. This is Tricia." She sat on the edge of her bed.

"Tricia. I'm on my way to the hospital. My friend Tanisha is driving me." Lizzie's voice was hoarse.

"Are you having more contractions?"

"Uh-huh." There was a pause while a voice in the background spoke words Tricia couldn't make out. "Yeah. And my water broke."

Tricia smothered a gasp. She said simply, "Then you're headed to the right place."

The happy sounds of her family drifted her way. Reece and the kids were preparing for a fun night of games and special snacks to welcome the dawn of the new year. But she knew what she needed to ask. "Do you want me to meet you at the hospital?"

"You would do that?" The poor girl sounded like she might cry.

"If you want me to, Lizzie."

There was a long silence. Then her voice came, small and child-like, "I'm scared, Tricia."

"Oh, dear girl. Of course you are. Having a baby can be pretty intense. But you're going to be okay. Lots of women have done this before you."

She whimpered. "Here it comes again." Now Lizzie was moaning.

"Lizzie, listen to me. This will help. Breathe in deeply through your nose, blow it out slowly through your mouth," Tricia said firmly. She made exaggerated breathing noises into the phone. "Breathe with me, Lizzie. Breathe in... blow out, slowly."

Lizzie was trying to comply, she could tell. Tricia could hear her softly moaning, attempting to control her breathing along with the prompts Tricia gave.

When the girl's voice lost its fearful edge, Tricia said, "Good, Lizzie. You're doing it."

The small, childlike voice came back, "Really?"

"Lizzie, you're amazing. Just do the same thing again whenever the pains start up." She paused a moment, then decided to press in just a little. "Which hospital are you going to?"

"Saint Something. The one with the statue of kids out front."

Tricia nodded. St. Catherine's Hospital, then. Several Dos Almas clients had delivered there. She could be there in twenty minutes. But Lizzie hadn't asked her to come. She would have to respect that unspoken "no."

Barely audible over the background engine noises, the girl whispered, "So, Tricia, I've been thinking. This friend of yours, with the phone number? If I call her, you really think she can help me... be safe?"

Tricia guessed Lizzie didn't want this question overheard. "I know she has done that for many other women, Lizzie. She will do her very best for you. Do you have a place to go? Family who will take you in?"

"Not really. I came from…another state." After a moment's pause, the girl released a flood of words. "Tricia, have you ever done a stupid thing—you know, like a big stupid thing—that you thought would solve all your problems, but it only made things worse?"

"Well, I've certainly made my share of mistakes. But I've made it through the fallout, with help."

"You're lucky to have someone to help you."

"Lizzie, you do have someone now. You have me."

A stifled whimper. "Tricia, um… I should tell you… My, my name isn't Lizzie. It's really Maddie. For Madeline. Madeline Clouse."

"Maddie." Tricia repeated the name silently to herself. "Thank you for trusting me with your true name. That means a lot to me."

Behind Maddie, the other voice spoke again, then she said, "We're here. I'd better hang up."

"Okay, Maddie. But please know you can call me—or text me—at this number anytime. *Any* time." Tricia cradled the phone with both hands, wishing it were this girl's hands.

The call ended. Tricia lay back on her bed, trying to slow her racing thoughts. She doubted Maddie thought to bring Avery's name and number with her. And Tricia couldn't risk texting the information without permission. If the wrong person saw the message, Maddie's life could quickly become even more frightening.

As soon as the nurses took over, Tanisha jetted out those hospital doors.

She stopped in the breezeway to gulp in the fresh, damp air. Hospitals always freaked her out. And she was not going into that baby birthing wing, even for her best friend. No way. She had heard all about women screaming bloody murder in there. Just the thought of feet in stirrups and the mess and the pain gave her flashbacks. Still… Curiosity tugged at her. What was it like to go in and come out with a baby? Maybe she should go back inside to support Maddie. The girl was terrified. She was so clueless…about so much.

Tanisha shook her head. No, thank you. She would wait right out here. Assuming that was what Maddie wanted. It had all happened so fast, she wasn't sure what she should do.

There wasn't much for seating here by the front door. So Tanisha hiked across the tough Bermuda grass, punching holes in it with her heels, hunting up a bench or something.

She finally dropped onto a painted metal bench next to a bank of spindly lilies of the Nile, all wet from the fog. Nice view of the parking stack. "Huh," she grunted, crossing her arms. From here, she could just see the roof of Maddie's old green Malibu above the half-wall around the first level. Tanisha's eyes narrowed. That whole car ride was wack. Maddie on the phone with some lady at that place she had called. Maddie whispering about someone to help her be safe. Safe from what? Zach?

Tanisha slid her own phone from her hip pocket and scrolled through her photos. There. And there. Two pics of Maddie and Zach going out on the town, Zach looking mighty dappa, and Maddie dressed to kill. But not happy. Not happy at all. What was up with that?

Seemed like he was always taking her out. Maybe Maddie was getting tired of the party scene. But who'd be like that? Maybe she was homesick for small-town life back in Missouri, or Minnesota, wherever she was from.

"I'd take that boy off her hands," Tanisha mumbled to herself. A dude with that much cash would be a walking party. But maybe that wasn't enough for Maddie. Loyal as she acted to him, she didn't want to have his baby. Of course, it could be Zach who didn't want her to.

Poor Madd. That was it. She wanted to settle down, but Zach loved his fun. There now, see? Fun was Tanisha's middle name. Seemed like the answer here was for her to find Maddie someone more her speed, and then Tanisha could have a turn with Zach herself.

Tanisha slapped her knee. "Listen to me. The girl's in there having Zach's baby, and I'm out here splitting 'em up. Some friend I am."

She stood, chilled by the January damp, and pulled up the heavy zipper on her denim jacket. She paced the sidewalk between the bench and the road. A strap on one of her new stilettos cut into her pinky toe. And the annoying puzzle of Zach and Maddie only made it worse. The thought of that weird car ride with Maddie kept crawling around in her head like a cockroach. She wasn't sure she wanted to think about it much more.

Just as she swung back toward the bench, a voice called out, "Yo, Tanisha!"

Her head came up. Slipping up to the curb in front of her came a sweet black Corvette. The window lowered, and Tyson Bates flashed her a smile from the driver's seat.

"Hey, baby!" she said, "What's up?"

Tyson rolled his fine gym body out his door and onto his feet. He grinned at her across the roof of his car. She leaned forward to rest her arms on her side of the roof. His eyes went right where she wanted them to.

"'Nisha, it's New Year's Eve, and I'm looking for someone to go with me to a party at Jada's." He grinned. "You busy?"

Tyson's throaty, velvet voice and full lips made her mouth water. Even better, she knew Jada never threw a party where she didn't provide the means to feel real good. Tanisha raised an eyebrow. "Am I ever too busy for you, Ty?"

"Then climb on in here, woman." He flicked the unlock button.

She threw a quick glance back toward the hospital. "Hang on, now. I got me a little dilemma, Ty. I drove a friend here in her car, and I've still got her key." Tanisha worked the key free from the pocket of her skin-tight jeans to show him.

Tyson said, "So? You know where the car's parked?"

She stood back with her hands on her hips. "I ain't one of those 'now where'd I parked my car' chicks."

He spread his hands. "So, leave the key under the floor mat and text your friend where to find it."

Tanisha slid her cell phone from her hip pocket and flapped it at him. "Tyson Bates, you are one brilliant Black man. I'll just walk over there and be right back."

She made sure to give him something to watch as she walked to the parking garage. Behind her, he cranked up his sound system while she found Maddie's sorry-looking Malibu and hid the key inside. When she came back out into the twilight, Tyson coaxed the Corvette across the garage driveway to meet her.

When he shoved the door open for her, Tanisha climbed in next to him.

"Ooh," she crooned, letting her words stretch out with her legs, "I do love these seats."

Tyson chuckled, a low husky sound like the rev of his engine.

Pretending she couldn't feel Tyson's eyes sweeping over her, she sent Maddie a short text. There, done.

Tanisha returned Tyson's hungry look and swiveled her shoulders toward him. "Let's go, baby," she said.

This new year would be starting off right.

At home, nearly asleep in bed beside Reece, Tricia jumped when her cell phone rang on the nightstand. She snatched up the phone.

"It's her, Reece."

He squeezed her hand. "We prayed earlier. I'm praying now. You stay. I'll slip out." He kissed her cheek and climbed out of bed. Snatching a book from the dresser, he left the room to her.

When she answered, rhythmic beeping and swooshing lub-dub sounds accompanied Maddie's voice to her ear. Tricia had had three rounds of experience with those sounds. They'd led to four children she wanted very much. Now Maddie was heading toward delivering a baby she wasn't sure about.

"Hello, Maddie. Sounds like you're settled in at the hospital." Thank God for that girl, Tanisha.

"Yeah. Tanisha drove like a crazy woman to get me here." Another woman's voice gave instructions in the background. Maddie mumbled an answer. In a more subdued voice, she continued, "Tricia, I really like your name."

Tricia raised an eyebrow. "You do?"

"It was my mother's name."

Tricia blew out a breath away from the phone. "What a lovely coincidence. But I take it she's no longer here?"

"No. I wish she was. I wish she was here right now." Sniffles and a groan.

Tricia waited a moment. She needed wisdom. "What would your mother do if she were with you, Maddie?"

"She would pray for me. She always prayed. After she died, I stopped praying."

Tricia took a deep breath. "Maddie, I like to pray too. I am a Christian, and I believe that God loves you very much. Would you like me to pray for you while we're on the phone?"

"Wait—" Maddie responded to the distant woman's voice. The fetal monitor's swooshing heartbeat sped up while Maddie moaned softly. The sounds slowed and dimmed. "Whew! That was a big one... So, um, yes. Please. Pray for me. I'll listen."

Tricia closed her eyes and spoke from her heart to the God of life, asking him to stay close to Maddie throughout her child's birth and beyond, and to bring her baby safely into the world. Silently, she added a plea for protection from her abuser.

"Thanks, Tricia. No one has prayed for me in a long time."

Another contraction came and went, and Tricia waited.

When it was over, Maddie said, "So, how do you know God loves me?"

This girl really cuts to the chase, Tricia thought. "I know it because he sent his Son Jesus to die in your place, to pay the price for all the things you've ever done wrong. He must love you an awful lot to do that for you."

With something between a whimper and a sigh, the girl said, "I used to believe all that."

"Did something change, Maddie?"

"I did." She moaned, and the fetal heart monitor swooshed faster. She stayed silent longer than before, and the woman's voice spoke quietly near the phone.

Minutes later, she picked up the story. "I used to go to church. But then...my mom died. She had cancer. God healed other people in our church, but not her. Why not her, Tricia?"

Tricia sighed. "That, I don't know."

"Well, that was the last time I went to church." Maddie's voice was hard and flat now. "I gave up on God. Obviously, he'd already given up on me."

Tricia never imagined having this conversation with a young woman in labor. She said gently, "Just because our lives turn out differently than we would like, that doesn't mean he has given up on us."

"Well, it's too late for me, anyway. I've made a rotten mess out of my life."

"But, Maddie, that can't stop God from loving you."

After the silence that followed, the girl's next words came with effort. "Are you... Are you sure?"

"I am, Maddie," Tricia told her quietly, "because 'God demonstrates his own love for us in this: While we were still sinners, Christ died for us.' God doesn't wait for us to deserve his love. He just loves us and does what it takes to save us. Period."

The girl was moaning but fighting it.

"Breathe, Maddie, in through your nose, out through your mouth." *Oh, dear God, hold this girl. And her baby.*

The monitor sounds revved, then subsided. But only momentarily. The distant woman's voice was closer now, calm but firm.

"No," Maddie said to the voice. A muffled "yes" replied.

Tricia said, "Maddie, do what the nurse tells you. I will keep praying for you—"

A loud groan made Tricia hold the phone away from her ear. "Tricia!"

"Maddie, focus on your baby now. You can do this." She paused. "And when you're all done, feel free to call when you want. I'll still be here."

The fetal heart monitor raced, Maddie groaned, and the phone went dead.

CHAPTER 3

Avery Caine stood waiting by the floor-to-ceiling windows of St. Catherine's Hospital lobby. Outside, the January mist rolled in sluggish waves across the parking lot. Fog. That just about summed up stories like this one. Confusion, doubt, love, hate, dependence, fear…

Logistically, getting a woman away from an abusive relationship was a whole heck of a lot easier than convincing her she *needed* to get out. But this one was ready. So ready. And it was some sort of miracle that she had a place to go.

Avery checked the notes on her phone:

- Referred by Tricia P. at Dos Almas PC.
- Family back home in MN: none.
- Friends in MN: Chris and Lena Nelson. Might come take her back with them.
- Hometown: Jefferson, MN

The girl had called Lena Nelson already. Sounded pretty sure they would come right away. Just waiting for confirmation from Chris. Shortly, if all went well, the girl would be safe in a secure hotel room. In a couple of days, her friends should arrive and pick her up. For some reason, she turned down Lena's offer to move into their home. Instead, she opted for a maternity home Tricia Prescott recommended to her. Interesting.

To kill time, Avery scrolled down her phone notes to her info on the Nelsons. Next-door neighbors in childhood. Yet there was something the girl wasn't telling her about them, and that bugged Avery. Understandably, the girl had major trust issues—she hadn't even wanted to tell Avery her real name at first. Maddie would only say the Nelsons were loyal friends and neighbors, church-going folks. They stood by her when her mom died. But what was up with that couple? Even promises of confidentiality hadn't opened the door any wider on that front.

Well, this maternity home plan might just turn out to be the best option. Clueless as Maddie was about life with a kid, she could benefit from their structured program for getting new moms on their feet. Job training, emotional support, family-style environment. Avery had checked them out, online and by phone, and they were legit. She hoped Maddie would stick with the program. Far too many women just defaulted back to the life. They would end up singing the same song, second verse, a little bit louder and a whole lot worse.

She had no doubt Zach Jarvis could dish out much worse than Maddie had been through. Probably had, to some of the women Avery had heard from only once. She ground her teeth. One of these days, she and her buddies in law enforcement would find a way to nail that animal. And she would be there to watch him go down.

Avery lowered herself into a padded chair and glanced at the canvas tote of transition supplies she'd brought for Maddie. It was tempting to dig into one of those granola bars after a long day of making arrangements to resolve this girl's situation. Once again, she'd gotten so wrapped up in the calls and paperwork she'd forgotten to eat lunch. And dinner. Avery's phone said 7:35 p.m. That hospital case worker was taking her own sweet time.

"Ms. Caine?"

Avery stood as a woman in business casual strode across the lobby, the obligatory clipboard clutched to her fitted blue blouse. She extended a manicured hand toward Avery. "Hello, I'm Monica Sanchez. Social worker on this case."

Avery pulled a business card from her hip pocket and handed it to the social worker.

"Perfect," the woman said, clipping the card onto her board. "It's nice to meet you. My supervisor told me you're exceptional in this field. Shall we head on up to the patient's room?"

Avery nodded toward the elevator. "I'll follow you," she said and bent to retrieve her canvas tote.

Monica Sanchez held the elevator door as Avery entered. This was one social worker Avery had never met. The woman's sidelong scan, once they were inside the elevator, was almost tangible. Avery let the woman stare. Her half-pink hair and majorly torn jeans were meant to put clients at ease. Professionals like Ms. Sanchez could like 'em or lump 'em. They hadn't stopped her from finishing grad school nor from helping dozens of women escape from their own personal hells.

Avery watched the floor numbers light up overhead and chuckled darkly to herself. Her husband Rocky liked to joke that she was a woman's Get Out of Hell Free card. Avery wished it were that easy.

The silver doors slid apart on the fourth floor. Avery stepped into the maternity ward and waited for Monica to point the way.

"Down here," Monica said, turning left down the hall. "Room 418."

Avery followed Monica into the half of 418 closest to the window. The bed near the door was empty, thank goodness. Privacy was always a plus.

"This is Avery Caine, from Domestic Advocacy," Monica said to the slim redhead in the bed. In the pale blue room, the girl looked pastel pink. Pretty healthy for a brand-new mom.

"You're Tricia's friend?" the girl asked. Her head turned slightly away, but her eyes never left Avery.

"That's right." Avery stayed at the edge of the space. "Tricia and I have worked together a lot. Mind if I draw this curtain for a little more privacy?"

"Okay."

Avery dragged the drape further closed along its curved stainless-steel rod. Now it would be up to her ears to notice if anyone entered the outer half of the room.

"How are you feeling?" she asked the girl, wondering how someone so slim could have recently delivered the one-day-old baby that slept in the tiny bassinet between the bed and the window.

The girl's hand went to the bassinet rim, a subtle protective move. "Sore. But okay."

"Good. Glad to hear it." Avery saw little emotion in the girl's eyes, eyes that kept her in range without quite looking into her face directly. This girl had major walls. Avery's connection to Tricia was her only street cred here. As always, she would be walking on eggshells.

"So, do you feel up to talking some more about your plans?" Avery waited for the girl's hesitant nod before continuing, "As we talked through earlier, you wanted to be in a safe hotel. I'm here to help you and your baby get there. That hotel is where your friends will come get you. I'm just waiting for final confirmation from them. Does that still sound all right?"

"Yes." The girl's eyes tracked Avery as she pulled the paperwork folder from her canvas tote.

"Great. You and Lucas have a reserved room at a Best Western across the county line." She laid some forms on the rolling bedside table. "And here are some things you may want to consider. May I show you these forms?"

Maddie tried to push herself upright in the bed. The case worker gave Maddie the bed controls so she could raise the head further. Good move, Avery thought, giving her a taste of autonomy. Every little step helps…

Avery rolled the table to the bed and showed her the top two sheets. This took some delicacy. "Maddie, you can choose whether to let the people helping you talk to each other about your case. Now, I know you're leaving our area for another state, but is there anyone here—someone who has helped you already, perhaps—that you might want me to be able to communicate with about your case?"

"Um…" Maddie looked at the confidentiality waiver. She started a slow shake of the head, then stopped. "Yes. Tricia. At the pregnancy center."

Relieved, Avery said, "Okay. I'll just fill in our names on both of these…"

"So, that means you can talk to her, and she can talk to you?"

"Yes, that's right." Avery put a pen on the table and watched the girl sign, all curlicues with circles dotting her i's. "Thanks. Still, everything you tell us is confidential. If we ever tell each other anything, it would only be if we thought it served your best interests."

Maddie nodded. "What's this other one?"

Avery began cautiously, "This is the paperwork we can fill out if you would like to file for a restraining order on Zach."

Maddie pulled her hands from the table. "How does that work?"

"If you choose to file, I would call it in to the judge this afternoon, and he'll issue an 'ex parte' order, effective immediately. That means that Zach could be arrested if he tried to give you any trouble."

Maddie's whole face swung toward Avery. "Forever?"

Avery shook her head. "The 'ex parte' is only good up until a court date the judge would set in the near future."

"Court date?" Her eyes widened. She had the blanket bunched up in her hands.

"To make a restraining order last longer, the law requires both you and the party you want protection from to speak to a judge," Avery said. Maddie was breathing faster, twisting that blanket into mush. Before the girl could get too worked up, she added, "You can 'appear' in court by phone, though, so Zach wouldn't be able to see you or learn where you are."

Maddie stared at the paper. Big breaths pumped her rib cage several times before she spoke. "And after that? The, um, restraining order will keep him away from me?"

Avery wished that were true. "It can't keep him from trying to bother you, but if he did, he'd be guilty of a crime."

Maddie lifted her face to Avery again, with childlike pleading in her eyes. "I don't know…"

Avery nodded. "It is completely up to you. No pressure either way."

Maddie stared across the room. Avery could swear she was shriveling into the bed. In a barely audible voice, she asked, "Could I do it later? From Minnesota?"

"That's definitely an option." Avery pulled a bright green index card from the folder. "If you're interested, here is the contact info for a domestic violence advocate like me in Jefferson. She could help you file from there."

Maddie took the card. Then she glanced around and shriveled smaller still. She whispered, "I don't have anywhere to—"

Avery reached for the tote. "You can stick it in here. This is for you."

Maddie peered over the brim. "What's in there?"

Avery spread the handles of the bag. Inside were all the things the girl had said she needed. New phone, clothes, toiletries, baby things. She tipped it toward Maddie and said, "New stuff for your new life."

The girl looked in the bag, looked up at Avery, and for the first time, her lips wore the start of a smile.

"He's in here!" A stout, middle-aged woman beckoned to Chris Nelson and his partner as they scrambled from the ambulance.

Chris pulled their jump kit from the rig and shouted back, "Yes, ma'am. Here we come." He and Brent navigated the icy front walk up to the house and followed the woman inside.

In her high-pitched frenzy, she threw words over her shoulder while hurrying along the hallway. "I don't know what happened. One minute, Kyle was in here singing away, happier than I've seen him in some time. Then I popped in to tell him something, and suddenly he could hardly talk. He sounded drunk. He tried to sit on the bed, but he just collapsed. Here. Here's his room."

She stopped abruptly and pointed to a small bedroom plastered with auto racing memorabilia. Chris stepped over a toppled pile of magazines to reach the man sprawled on the floor. He looked maybe thirty, tall, slim, and pale, bordering on blue. He reeked of one of those strong, musky body sprays. Chris forced himself to work right through it.

Chris pulled on a glove and gave the patient's shoulder a firm shake or two, saying loudly, "Kyle? Kyle, are you all right? Kyle?" No response. No eyelid movement. Nothing.

He felt the carotid for a pulse. Faint. Way too faint. Uncovering the back of his hand, he touched it to the man's skin. Cool. Clammy.

Brent had already connected the pulse oximeter to the man's forefinger. The readout never topped 89.

Chris listed observable facts, "No sign of external trauma. No bleeding."

The woman whimpered in the doorway. "Is he going to be okay?"

"We'll see, ma'am," Brent answered. "Anything else you can tell us about Kyle's condition? Recent injuries? Changes in medications?"

Chris said quietly, "OD?" When Brent looked at him, Chris pointed with his chin to a baggie of tablets on the bedside table. He continued his report. "Respiration slow, shallow. Pulse faint."

Brent ran the penlight test. "Pupils constricted to pinpoints, unreactive."

Chris wrapped the blood pressure cuff around Kyle's arm and pumped the bulb while Brent asked the frightened woman, "Does Kyle take pain medication regularly?"

"What?" Her gaze darted to the ceiling, then came back to rest on Kyle. "Oh, not regularly. He took painkillers for a while after his accident. But that was four or five years ago. Now and then, he would take them again. But only if the pain came back, he said."

Chris lifted the baggie of tablets to her. "Is it possible he was taking these?"

She pulled her lips in and stepped back, covering her mouth. "Not again…" She looked at Chris through tears. "It's possible. He said he'd stopped… But—"

"I understand, ma'am. Thank you. This shows us how to help Kyle." He asked Brent, "Naloxone?"

Brent nodded and pulled the blunt syringe from their kit, prepped it, and administered the dose nasally.

Within a minute or two, Kyle's vital signs were normalizing. Chris rose and headed to the door, stopping only to address the mother. "Kyle is breathing better now, and his pulse is stronger. But he needs to go to the hospital for complete medical care. He's still unresponsive," Chris noted.

The woman sniffed and exhaled as if it was the first time in many minutes. She nodded, her face blank. "Okay."

He stayed a moment longer. She obviously had a lot to take in. He moved into her line of sight and said, "Ma'am, I'm going to get the stretcher now. You may want to prepare to follow us to Jefferson Regional Hospital. It's a cold January day out there."

She blinked a few times and nodded again. After one more glance at Kyle, she trotted off down the hall to another room.

Within minutes, Kyle and the stretcher were stowed in the back of the ambulance with Chris seated beside him. Brent, built like a bear standing on his back legs, threw a good-natured barb in around the doors: "See ya there, Shorty."

Chris grinned. "Hey, shut the doors. You're letting all the heat out."

Kyle remained stable but unconscious throughout his short ride and admittance to Jefferson Regional Hospital. As Chris and Brent finished their report, staff showed Kyle's mother to his space in the ER.

As they crossed the parking lot toward the ambulance, Brent shook his head, exhaling a cloud into the frigid air. "What a way for a guy to start the new year, huh?"

"Not my style, that's for sure," Chris said, climbing into the passenger seat. Just as he shut the door, his cell phone rang. He intended to ignore it, but it was his mom's number. Strange. She knew he was working this shift. He turned to Brent. "Mind if I get this?"

Brent waved dismissively as he steered out of the driveway. "Better than me having to talk to you all the way back."

Chris grunted and took the call. "Hey, Mom. What's up?"

There was a moment's hesitation on the other end. Then his mom's gentle voice said, "Chris, it's about Maddie."

His mouth tightened. A dose of equal parts fear and anger pumped up his heart rate. He sucked in a long breath, then let it go. "What about her?"

"She wants to come home."

Fear evaporated. Anger alone clamped down on his chest. Home? What did that mean—now? He sat silent. Waiting.

"She has asked if we would go get her."

Chris glanced down at his fist balled up against his thigh. "And you said...?"

"I said I would ask you."

His mom was equally good at silent waiting. She probably knew he was sitting there wanting to kick something, wanting to hijack the ambulance to California, wanting to punch somebody, wanting to give in to hope. If only he'd been able to forget Maddie, to stop measuring every other woman against her. If only she hadn't slashed his heart and left him bleeding. But he hadn't. And she had.

"I don't know, Mom."

His mom's quiet voice barely rose above the ambulance heater and engine noises. But he could guess what she was going to say, anyway. "What would you do for any other friend, Chris?"

He ran his hand up his forehead and over his short hair. Fortunately, most of Kyle's gosh-awful body spray had washed off.

He sighed. "When do we leave for California?"

Tricia smiled as Paloma Cisneros tucked a soft brown teddy bear into a basket already brimming with gifts for Maddie. Paloma looked like a happy little grandma with her long, silvery braid and wide smile.

Nodding her thanks, Tricia looped her jacket and purse over one arm while shouldering her cell phone up to her ear. "Yes, Joey, Drake will make pizzas for all of you. I'll be home a little late—"

"Oh." Joey sounded disappointed. "When will Drake get home?"

She frowned. School ended over an hour ago. "You mean he's not home yet?"

Tricia hardly heard Joey's reply as Paloma added the basket handle to her arm, opened the pregnancy center door for her, and whispered, "Good luck."

The misty evening air chilled Tricia almost as much as knowing her three youngest children were home alone. She set her armload on the hood of her faithful old station wagon and dug for her keys. "Just a minute, Joey. Let me think." Where had Drake gone to this time? Maybe he was with a friend, like Jamie, or that girl he liked—Laci—and forgot he had promised to be home for Joey, Aly, and Lydia. Reece's on-site client meeting wouldn't wrap up until 5 p.m.; then he'd have a grinding commute home. That made her the closer parent. But what about delivering these gifts to Maddie? Once Maddie moved away, Tricia would probably never hear from her again, let alone get to meet her.

Glass shattered on Joey's end of the call.

"Joey? Are you okay?"

"Um, Mom, you know that vase with the flowers Dad gave you?"

Decision made. "Joey, I am coming home right now." Tricia got the rusty car door unlocked and tossed her things onto the front seat.

"'Kay. Sorry, Mom. But, Mom—"

Jerking on her seat belt and cranking the key in the ignition, she went on, "Make sure your sisters stay clear of the broken glass. Use lots of paper towels so you don't get cut—"

"Mom? Hey, Mom!" Joey's voice finally cut through her babbled instructions and the protesting of the car engine.

"I'm sorry." She seemed to say that a lot these days. "Yes, Joey?"

"You know that history test? I passed! I got a B!"

She sighed and let her head tip back. "And you were so worried. Good for you! Sounds like we'd better ask Dad to pick up a treat on the way home tonight to celebrate, don't you think?"

"Could we have chocolate ice cream?"

"Chocolate ice cream it is." The engine almost turned over. She tried again, "Joey, I should be home in about twenty minutes. I'm looking forward to sharing that chocolate ice cream with you tonight!"

Joey was silent a moment. Then he said softly, "I love you, Mom."

The engine started as Tricia wilted in her seat. She wanted to fly home magically, right now, and hug that tender-hearted boy. The one she sometimes overlooked. "Thanks, Joe-Joe. I love you, too. And I'm enormously proud of you." She could easily picture his grateful smile and his squinched-up eyes as he hung up the phone. It was so easy to make that boy happy. She needed to focus on doing that more.

Tricia turned left out of the Dos Almas parking lot, flinging one arm in front of the basket of gifts to keep it from tipping over. Smiling, she decided to name the brown bear Chocolate. Chocolate like the ice cream she would be privileged to serve her family tonight. Too bad she would never know how Maddie handled the privileges—and challenges—of motherhood. And whether she ever found a good man to share her life with.

Maddie stared at Avery's text, lighting up the darkness of her hotel room. "They're here," she whispered. "Lena…and Chris." After a moment of stunned shock, her heart started flipping around in her chest. She needed to repeat the words to believe them: "They're here."

What were they thinking about her? How would they look after four years? How did she look? She slid to the edge of the bed, wincing a little when pain reminded her she'd just had a baby a couple of days ago. A baby. A baby boy. She'd named him Lucas. Just because she liked the name.

She leaned over the rail of the crib. Little Lucas. He lay on his back, head turned toward the one little fist he had raised. He looked like a fighter who had fallen asleep in action. Best of all, he looked nothing like Zach. Beyond that, she didn't need to know more. As long as he wasn't Zach's, Lucas was all hers. And she would do whatever it took to protect him.

Was he warm enough? Maddie tried to remember what Tricia had taught her over the phone. Safe Sleep Class, she had called it: all about what should and shouldn't be in the crib, how to dress a baby for sleep, and about some horrifying thing called SIDS. She watched Lucas carefully, biting her lip, and only relaxed when she saw his steady breathing. Lucas was fine. And so cute! Pudgy face all smushed up in a pout, dark hair as soft as feathers. Looking cozy in a pale green sleeper from Avery. He was doing fine. A smile tugged at the corner of her mouth. Maybe she wasn't going to be a wreck of a mom after all.

She tiptoed away from the crib, softly closed the bathroom door behind her, and only then flipped on the light. Squinting against the white glare, she ran her fingers through her hair. The old bright red dye job was fading from the natural red roots. Great. Two-tone hair. Huge dark circles under her eyes and a flabby baby belly. She looked like a red-headed zombie. She leaned her arms on the bathroom counter and took a deep breath. If Tanisha were here, she'd be saying, "Girl, get a grip! Don't rag on yourself. You just popped out a baby, and now you're heading off on your own? Ain't just anyone could do that. You go, girl!"

Her chest tightened, and tears pooled in her eyes. Tanisha, the one good friend she'd had here in California. Now she would never get to really say good-bye. That one short text before switching to the new phone didn't count—it was barely more than "going home to Minnesota, thanks for the ride, don't tell Zach." Tanisha had promised not to say anything. But she couldn't possibly know how important it was to keep that promise. Zach could lay on the charm when he wanted to. Tanisha always said Maddie was lucky to have such a hot boyfriend. If only Maddie had dared to set her straight.

Maddie pressed her hand to her chest. Her heart was hammering. She closed her eyes and willed Tanisha to read her mind: *Stay away from Zach. Don't tell him anything.*

Her new phone buzzed again: Avery would usher Lena and Chris upstairs to the room after she had checked them out "just in case."

Maddie typed, *OK Tell them I can't wait to see them.*

Not quite true. She could wait to see them. Because now they were here, she felt how far apart the three of them really were. Lena and Chris had stayed the same, she was sure. But she had been dragged through the sewer.

And she looked it. Avery's "bug-out bag" included some basic makeup, but Maddie decided to skip it. It wouldn't fix this mess. They would see her face, naked, which was the way she felt. Exposed. Nothing to offer, needing everything. Her only clothes Avery had provided. Loose-fitting stuff, good at hiding her size and shape. From anyone. Her old clothes, Avery had promised, would disappear, along with her car. There would be nothing in Colson County to clue Zach in to her whereabouts. Only Tanisha knew. And Tanisha wouldn't tell. At least not while she was clean and sober. *Bye, Tanisha...*

Avery texted, *Ready for me to bring them up? Maybe 5-10 minutes?* Maddie breathed out slow and hard. *I think so. Just washing my face. See you soon.*

Maddie shivered. Five to ten minutes. After four years.

She ran soothing warm water over her hands. Then she raised them to her face, her closed eyes seeing pictures like an old movie... pictures of Lena and her mom laughing together, of a summer day detasseling corn with Chris and the field crew, of Lena singing in church, of Chris and his deadly aim with snowballs...

Chris. There may have been a time when the two of them were meant to be. But then Mom had died. Chris kept believing all those things about God, while she... did not. No matter what he had said back then, she knew God no longer cared. God let cancer eat her mother alive. It had been easy for Chris to keep believing. He still had his mother. But Maddie had no one.

"You still have me," Chris had said. Those maple syrup eyes and that gentle way he held her hand… But she had pushed him away.

Her own words still echoed in her memory. "I don't want you. I don't want anything to do with you or your phony faith! Go away and leave me alone!" She had never shouted at him before. But anger had boiled up behind her eyes until they watered. She was wild with a sense of power. This was *her* choice. She was deciding. Not her mother, not Chris, not her deadbeat father. Not some God who didn't care. Just her.

And look where it got her. She raised her dripping face to the mirror. It got her into this mess. The California nightmare that was Zach. Zach, who used what seemed like love to twist her around his fist, twisted everything until she believed she was crazy. Maybe she really was crazy. But if *this* was being crazy—this taking a chance on a new life—it sure felt sane. The sanest thing she had done for a long time. Even though she owned nothing but what Avery had given her, and she had no one she trusted, except Tricia. Maybe Lena.

Chris probably hated her.

But he had come.

Maddie had carefully told him and Lena part of her story. How would they feel if they heard the rest?

Maddie shut off the water and dried her face. The dark circles still hung below her eyes. But otherwise, she didn't look as bad as she felt. A quick brushing and a blue scrunchie improved the look of her two-tone hair. She straightened her extra-large gray T-shirt and turned to go face her former friends just as she was, with a flabby belly, a black-and-blue cheek, and a baby.

Three knocks at the door matched Avery's pre-arranged signal. Lucas was fussing himself awake. Maddie bent and picked him up, hoping she was holding him right. It felt good to have something to do with her hands.

She walked to the door.

Here goes.

CHAPTER 4

A soft "come in" passed through the hotel door to Avery, where she stood in the hallway with the Nelsons.

When Avery's key card turned the latch light green, she pushed open the door and peered around it. "Your friends are here," she said to the wide-eyed girl inside.

Maddie nodded, looking freshly scrubbed. She held the baby protectively close to her chest, looking like a natural with infants. Avery stepped inside. The young man Chris and the woman Lena—whom she had expected to be his wife, not his mother—followed.

The guy could hardly look at the girl, but once he did, he couldn't stop. Wrestling with a boatload of strong feelings, Avery guessed. He stood silent behind his mother, a good six inches taller, with an expression that flickered like flame behind his brown eyes, intense enough to either scorch or melt a heart of stone.

The girl darted glances at him, apparently feeling the heat.

So, that was the deal. Love that got lost somewhere in the backstory. Avery pursed her lips. This was going to be awkward.

Lena broke the silence with a gentle, almost unwavering voice, "Maddie. It's so good to see you again." She made a tiny move forward, then drew herself back again. "And is this your new baby?"

"His name's Lucas." After a moment's hesitation, Maddie held the baby out toward Lena. One tear escaped and raced down her cheek.

Lena took the baby and turned him to face her. With professional-level mothering skills, she nestled him in her arms and touched his puckered face with her forefinger. "Oh, Maddie, he's adorable."

She cooed to him and stroked his head beneath the light blanket, one Avery recognized. Lena smiled at Maddie. "I feel honored to meet him so soon after his birth."

Maddie wrapped her empty arms around herself, looking even smaller in her baggy clothes.

Lena turned to her son. "Look, Chris, how he wrinkles up his nose. Isn't that cute?" Lena turned the baby toward the young man. He lowered his eyes from the girl to look at the baby.

He touched the tiny hand, which wrapped itself around his finger. A smile raised one corner of his mouth. Lena gently placed the baby in his free hand, and he didn't resist. In his muscular arms, the infant looked like a midget football.

"Hey there, little guy," he murmured.

A long pause followed. The girl sniffed and rubbed her nose.

When Chris raised his head, a gentle warmth lit his eyes. He said, "You have a beautiful baby here… Maddie."

Maddie ducked her head briefly and folded her hands tightly together.

Lena opened her arms. "We've missed you, Maddie."

Maddie inched toward Lena and awkwardly gave her a hug. Then stifled weeping shook her body. Lena stroked her back, and it subsided.

Okay, then, Avery thought. Her gut told her these were the right people to transport this girl home. She seemed to trust them. And she'd been wise enough not to move in with them. Maddie would be okay, eventually. She hoped.

Avery moved to the far corner of the hotel room to give the reunion a little space. She pulled a couple of forms from her messenger bag and laid them on the desk with a pen.

The girl and the guy were talking now, a couple of words here and there. Letting their eyes meet for a second or two before darting away. It was a good start.

Lena left their conversation to walk over to the desk. "Are these the papers you wanted us to sign?"

Avery pointed. "Yes. Here, and here. I'll need Chris's signature, too." As Lena bent to sign, Avery watched the couple at the other end of the room. Chris still held the baby, and Maddie had moved a step closer to him, her timid gestures hinting that she was describing something about her son.

Straightening, Lena said, "We'll do all we can to help Maddie, you know."

This was one of the rare occasions when Avery believed that. She nodded and shifted into handoff mode. "Now, when we go downstairs, I'll want to transfer some stuff from my vehicle to yours. Like an infant car seat donated by the pregnancy center. I'll take care of checking her out of the hotel after you're all safely away."

Lena stepped closer to Avery, her voice low and her face earnest. "Thank you for everything you've done. Without all this help from you and the pregnancy center... I don't know how she would have been able—" She left the words hanging as her eyes followed her son and Maddie.

Avery crossed her arms. "She's a rare one, this Maddie. It takes a lot of courage to leave 'the life' once you're caught up in it. No matter how bad it gets."

Lena caught her breath and turned inquiring eyes on Avery. "'The life?'"

Avery, chiding herself, backpedaled. "This life. A tough situation." She should have known Maddie wouldn't tell her friends the whole story up front.

Lena nodded silently. Then she murmured, "Sometimes, all a woman's choices are hard ones."

Avery studied Lena's face. "Maddie's lucky to have you for a friend."

Lena smiled at her and then called to Chris, "Let's sign these papers and be on our way home."

"You bet." Chris handed the baby back to Maddie and walked to the desk. After his initial discomfort at the door, the guy seemed happy to be with Maddie. But would she ever be equally happy around him? Avery wished she would be around to find out.

Tricia didn't need Reece to shake her awake. The whole world was shaking.

"Get into the doorway! It's an earthquake!" he shouted, just a bit louder than necessary.

The bed rolled beneath her as she clambered to her feet and stumbled toward the door frame. Reece came to join her. Drake was up and bracing himself in his own doorway down the hall. Through another doorway, Tricia spotted both Lydia and Alyssa in their matching nightgowns, hiding under their identical desks.

"Joey!" Reece called. "How can he sleep through this?" He crossed the hall and pulled their younger son out of his bed, which lay directly below a window. "Come on, Joey, stand in the doorway." Reece hugged the sleepy boy and leaned over him, bracing his back against the door frame for both of them.

"Mommy—" Lydia whined. A pencil jar slid off her jittering desk and clattered to the floor. Alyssa yelped. The earth rumbled on.

"Just a moment, girls," Tricia called back in an almost matter-of-fact voice. "You know how these earthquakes are. It'll all be over in a minute."

And sure enough, the house quit riding the ground wave seconds later.

"Everybody okay?" Reece called.

"Yeah," Drake replied, his hands already free of the door frame. "I like those rolling ones. It's the jarring earthquakes that creep me out."

Tricia thought she heard a distant and deep growl from beneath her feet. "Aftershock! Stay where you are."

The girls squealed as the house shuddered for several seconds. Reece called to them firmly, "Hang on, girls. Just a bit longer." That was the voice the girls always calmed to. Their whimpering subsided. But Drake's nails dug into the doorframe down the hall until the shaking stopped.

Tricia winked at her son. "Good one, huh?"

He wore a sheepish grin as he unlocked his fingers from the wood. "I'd say a 3.8 on the Richter scale." He grabbed his phone to look for news reports. "Crud. Internet's down."

"Let's hope that's all that's down," Reece said.

Joey looked up at his dad and yawned. "Can I go back to bed now?"

Reece shook his head. "Not by that window of yours. Come on, you can sleep in my bed, Joey."

He gave him a piggyback ride into the master bedroom and tucked him into the big bed there, tousling his light brown hair.

Reece slipped on some jeans and told Tricia, "I'll go check the gas and water lines." Then he leaned into Drake's room and said, "Come on, Drake, let's check everything out. Bring your flashlight; it's still a little dark out."

A groan sounded from Drake's room.

Reece countered in his radio announcer voice, "It's what we Prescott men do!" then headed for the garage and the toolbox.

Tricia walked into the twins' room. Kneeling by their desks, she said, "Girls, you can come out now." Just then, one of Alyssa's plastic horses that she used as a bookend tipped over, and a tall storybook clapped down onto her desk.

Both the seven-year-olds squealed at identical ear-splitting pitches. Tricia winced. "It's just a book, girls. Come on out. You're okay." She sat down on the floor nearby.

Drake passed the door. "Don't be such chickens," he told his little sisters.

"Drake…" Tricia cautioned. He kept clucking all the way down the hall.

Alyssa crawled out first. Tricia opened her arms. "It's okay, Aly."

Alyssa climbed onto her mother's lap, where Lydia joined her. Tricia gave them the brightest smile she could. "There you go, Lyddie. What a surprising morning we've had!"

Tricia snuggled with her girls, glad to be together, unharmed. They were still snuggling together, giggling, when Reece returned. His mouth was a grim, straight line.

Tricia tried to frame a question that wouldn't scare the girls. "Is all well with the house?"

"Yes. We're good here. Even the internet's up again. But—"

Drake plowed into the room with his eyes riveted to his phone. "Mom, guess what? The epicenter was like a half mile from Dos Almas! Look at this!" He thrust the phone screen into her face. Once held at a readable distance, the phone showed red hazard signs filling the map, like a pool of blood surrounding her beloved center.

"Better call the landlord," Reece said, gently taking the phone from Tricia. "He'll probably want to have an inspection done before you open again."

Alyssa placed her little hands on either side of Tricia's face. "Mommy, we better pray."

Tricia smiled. "You're right, Aly. You want to do it?"

Alyssa squeezed her eyes shut and pressed her hands together. "Dear Jesus, help Mommy's center be okay so the other mommies can still get help. Thank you, amen."

"Thank you, Aly." Tricia kissed her daughter's silky blond head. "Now that the important work is done, I'd better go make a few calls." She stood up and set the storybook upright, a plastic horse on either side. She hated to think what the rickety bookshelf at the office looked like right now.

"I see… Yes. I understand. Well then, Mr. Underwood, I'll see you on Monday at the building." Tricia ended the call and laid her phone face down on the table.

Reece sat down beside her and pulled her close for a hug. "Not good, huh?"

"Right now, things are rather bleak. They've turned off all the utilities for safety until they can get an inspector on site. But the whole front wall is leaning westward, and there's a major crack in the rear of the building. The roof is compromised. And I'm worried about looting. We've got computers, a printer, client files…" She wilted into her husband's embrace. "This may not be something we can recover from. Our finances were so tenuous already…"

Reece remained silent, just holding her. She knew Reece was a realist. He had to be. As a freelance draftsman, he depended on generating a steady stream of clients or securing long-term retainer contracts. He knew his numbers. And he knew his God. His silence steadied her.

"Meanwhile," she said, "Paloma and the rest of our crew are all safe. We have that to be grateful for." Her mind added, *Because it'll take every last one of us to pull through this.*

"Hey, Dad," Drake blurted as he barreled into the kitchen, "since school's called off, a couple of guys and I wanna go to the beach."

Reece leaned forward, wearing a smirky smile of feigned exuberance. "Sure, Drake, you could take your boogie boards and try to catch a tsunami!"

Drake opened his mouth, then closed it. "So that's a no? C'mon, Dad. You know you would have done it when you were my age."

Reece snorted. "Done what? Ride a tsunami? Uh, no, Drake-and-Shake. Sorry to disappoint you. Even back then, I erred on the side of caution."

Drake fired off one of the curse words he'd been trying out lately. "Ahem," Reece said.

Drake didn't even glance up, just frowned and punched a short text into his phone. Tricia braced herself for the cold glare of disdain that she expected him to shoot at them. But instead, Drake muttered, "Sorry," and pocketed his phone. Then, with the hint of a grin, he pantomimed surfing out of the kitchen, his head of dark curls bobbing as he caught imaginary waves. "Maybe next earthquake, then," he said over his shoulder. "Later, dude."

Reece's chuckle percolated deep into Tricia's soul. Relieved, she lifted her mug in a toast: "To riding the waves!"

Ugly goblin faces in horrible colors pressed up against Maddie on all sides. She couldn't scream. They pressed against her mouth. And her breasts, and her legs, and—there behind them was Zach, laughing with his head thrown back. Maddie tried to move away, but something held her tight. Now Zach was running toward her, hands out. And though he never touched her, she fell and fell, and the concrete steps came rushing up at her—

Frightened awake, Maddie rubbed her eyes against the searing daylight. A radio newscast. Engine sounds. She was in a car. *Oh, no. Not another car.* A green digital clock read 9:19. A man's outline to her left. Who was he? Where was he taking her? What would she have to do for him? Heart racing, she tightened every muscle. Her eyes watered no matter how fast she blinked them clear. Fear pounded inside her ears.

"Hey, Sleeping Beauty," the man said. That voice… She swiped at her eyes, and his profile sharpened into a familiar face. She covered her eyes, squeezed her legs together. It was forever until she could speak. "Oh, Chris. It's you. I forgot where I was."

"No wonder. We got going pretty early, and we've hardly stopped moving. Except when you needed to feed the little guy back there." He tipped his head toward the back seat, where Lena snored softly beside a baby car seat draped with a light blue blanket.

She had a baby.

A moment later, Maddie caught familiar words over the radio. "Did you hear what they said about Colson County? Something about an earthquake?" She leaned forward, listening.

"Yeah. I think they gave it a 5.1. Wasn't that where you were living?"

She leaned closer to the radio. The newsman was still reciting names of familiar streets and neighborhoods, detailing the damage and the casualty count. Was it wrong of her to wish that number included Zach Jarvis?

When the announcer moved on, she released her ponytail and dragged her fingers through her tangled hair. Zach's face still intruded on her thoughts. She might have to run forever to keep him from finding her. "Where are we?" she asked.

"We just crossed into Utah." Chris turned his eyes her way just long enough for her to need to look away. "Ready for a break?" he asked.

"Well—" Now that she could relax enough to stretch, she yawned, watching the cotton-covered countryside roll past her window. Snow. She'd almost forgotten what snow looked like, how it sparkled some days and turned several shades of blue on others. "A break would be nice."

Lena spoke up from the back seat, "Did someone say we're stopping?"

"Then it's unanimous," Chris announced. "We'll pull off at the next promising off-ramp."

Delicate baby grunts rose from the car seat. Maddie sighed. "Yep, unanimous."

CHAPTER 5

Tricia wiped her hands on a dishtowel when her cell phone rang—an unfamiliar number. "Hello, Dos Almas Pregnancy Center. This is Tricia. How can I help you?"

"Tricia, it's Maddie. I heard about the earthquake. Are you okay?"

Tricia blinked. *Maddie is calling—still? And asking about us?* "What a sweet surprise to hear from you! I'm fine, Maddie. Thanks for asking. As for our building, only time will tell. But anyway, how are you? Where are you?" She bit her lips. *Oops. Too invasive.*

"I'm good. Somewhere in Nebraska." A long pause followed. "By tomorrow, I'll be back in Minnesota."

"Minnesota?"

"Yeah. That's where I was from before I… moved to California. So I'm kinda going home. Kinda."

Tricia relaxed into a chair at her kitchen table and propped her legs up on another. "You sound happy about that."

"Yeah, mostly. It's good to be with… friends again. And I've missed the snow."

When Maddie remained silent for a long moment, Tricia spoke up, "We certainly don't get much snow here. I'm glad to hear your friends could come and pick you up. That was a really long trip—in two directions."

"I know, right? They're… really amazing."

"And how's Lucas doing?" Tricia tried to picture a newborn traveling cross-country like this in the middle of winter.

"He sleeps a lot. Seems okay, though. We're all about ready for a stop when he is." She made a cooing noise, and Tricia imagined her playing with her baby's tiny hand. Then Maddie said, "Here, I'll let you listen to him. Isn't it cute?" What had been a distant chirping sound grew louder.

Tricia waited, listening, then said, "Ah, he's talking to his mommy. What a sweet little sound."

"So, Tricia, I can't talk long on this phone—it's one Avery gave me. And I think it needs charging. But I want to say thank you, for the car seat and for connecting me with Avery. You gave me a whole new start." Her voice softened as she said, "When I called you, all I could think was that I couldn't be pregnant around Zach. You helped me find a better way—a way out. And I have Lucas. I'm so glad I called you."

"I'm glad you did, too." Tricia held back tears as she cleared her throat. "Before you go, Maddie, is there anything you want me to know in case we can be of further help to you? Like where you and Lucas will be staying next? I don't want to invade your life. It's up to you."

"No, that's totally good. I—I would like to stay in touch if we can. I don't know where I would be right now without you. Before you, I felt totally abandoned. So, um—" Paper rustled before she continued. "Here it is. Me and Avery liked those maternity homes you recommended. I picked the one in Jefferson, my hometown. It's called The Harbor. I think it's near the lake."

A snowy lakeshore—quite a contrast to the sunny, succulent-lined concrete patio outside Tricia's sliding glass doors. She said, "I've met The Harbor's director, Emily Radner. I think you'll like her."

"I hope so. Avery said she sounded nice, but no-nonsense. That's probably what I need." Her voice grew fainter. "Most of all, I need to feel safe. I want to be so far from Zach that he'll never come after me."

"Do you really think he would?" Tricia's brow tightened over her eyes. "What reason would he have to make that long trip?"

"Not much, I guess. It's not like I'm really worth anything to him now." Several seconds went by in silence. "He's probably like, 'out of sight, out of mind.' He always said he could replace me."

Tricia answered, "I bet your true friends feel very differently. There's only one of you, Maddie. You're irreplaceable. Now you can just focus on starting fresh and enjoying being a mother. Lucas will change quickly, so soak up every moment."

"Yeah, I will. Oops, battery's dying. Gotta go. Thanks again, Tricia. I'll get back in touch soon."

"Please do, Maddie. We're all praying for you here at Dos Almas."

A brief hesitation. "Thanks. Hope it helps."

The phone cut out. Tricia laid her phone down on a placemat, absently watching a sparrow hop across her patio beyond the sliding glass door smudged with fingerprints. Would Maddie ever see God's fingerprints all over this "new start" she felt Tricia had given her?

As she rose, dishtowel in hand, to clean the glass, Tricia asked herself, *Will I ever see God's fingerprints on the earthquake damage to Dos Almas?*

The building inspector affixed a notice of condemnation right across the Dos Almas logo on the office door. Tricia's shoulders drooped as she watched from beside board chairman Mike Benson and their dejected landlord, Al Underwood. After fifteen years of serving here, Dos Almas had one week to clear out their remaining valuables. Then the building would be torn down—torn down before it fell down.

The inspector pulled three sheets of paper from his metal box-style clipboard. "These instructions are guidelines only," he said, handing the sheets to Al. "If you must enter the building to remove equipment, I cannot guarantee your safety." The inspector looked at each of them in turn, nodded, and left for his gleaming white pickup truck.

Mike stuffed his hands into his khaki pockets. "Al, I'm awfully sorry for this loss. I know it hits you the hardest."

Al, all eighty of his years evident in his slumped shoulders, ran a shaking hand across his thin white hair. "I thought the old office had another five years in her, at least." He glanced up, attempting a bright smile. "Well, we made the most of her, didn't we?"

Mike shook Al's hand. "Yes, sir, we did. It's been a pleasure to rent from you."

Al looked from Mike to Tricia. "What will you do now?"

Tricia's mouth opened, but she had no words to speak. Mike took over in her silence.

"We have a very resourceful team. We'll find creative ways to keep caring for clients. And we still have our online presence to help people find us."

Al waved a hand. "Sure, sure. All that social medium stuff."

Tricia had to smile. "We'll be okay, Al. God will provide. He gave us you, you know."

"And now he 'taketh me away.'" He threw one last look at the sagging building and said, "Welp, guess that's all for today. I'll get those forms together for you, and we'll meet up soon. Good luck to you." He headed for his oxidized red Mazda with a slow shuffle.

Behind Tricia, another car crunched to a stop curbside, and the driver's door opened.

Paloma came toward them, tsk-ing and shaking her head. *"¡Qué triste! Después de quince años, y—"* she snapped her fingers, *"—todo se acabó en un instante."* She studied the building a moment. "What about the computers? The DVDs? And the boutique items? Our clients will need supplies soon. Many of them live in the damaged apartment buildings on the west side."

Mike rubbed a hand across his chin. "Right. We're going to have to go in and retrieve all we can. I suggest we get some of the board members and a few volunteers here to help us. Do you think we could round up enough people to tackle that tonight?"

"Let's do it," Tricia said. "We don't want to leave salvageable items to the looters."

"Okay. I'll make a few calls. Any idea where we might get some hard hats?"

Tricia thought for a moment. "Reece was meeting with a client today—Slayter Construction. They might loan us a few. I'll have him ask." She texted him just as Paloma's phone signaled an incoming message.

Paloma glanced at the screen and said, "It has begun. This woman needs formula. A father texted earlier about diapers. I'll let them know we hope to have some tomorrow. I can make deliveries. *Bueno*. What time tonight?"

"Seven?" Mike suggested.

"Sounds good," Tricia agreed. Paloma nodded and walked back to her car, texting.

Tricia surveyed the building once again. "Thanks for coming, Mike. I really wasn't up to hearing this news on my own."

"We're all in this together. See you tonight?"

She glanced at her phone. "Yes. And Reece says we've got hard hats."

Mike gave her a thumbs-up, and they parted ways. Tricia leaned against the hood of her old station wagon, texting Drake to send her a picture of the grocery list she'd forgotten. His reply was a long time coming.

While she waited, trying not to dream up trouble for him to be in, a young Black woman strolled along the sidewalk, stopping in sight of the center's sign. She looked from the sign to the building and finally approached the door, stepping carefully over the new, gaping crack in the walkway. She read the condemnation sign, one slim finger running along the words. Was she pregnant? Did she wonder if she was? Tricia straightened and walked toward her.

"Hi. Are you looking for Dos Almas Pregnancy Center? I'm Tricia, the director. Can I help you?"

The young lady in her cropped top, skin-tight leggings, and yellow stiletto heels turned, her huge gold hoop earrings swinging. "Oh, so you're Tricia. A friend of mine said she's been talking with you lately. She was gonna end her pregnancy but changed her mind after she talked to you. I'm not sure what you said to her, but—I've never seen her so… I don't know… brave, you know? Confident."

Tricia, ever protective of client confidentiality, gave what she hoped was a noncommittal smile. "And what's your name?"

"Tanisha." When she held out her hand, Tricia shook it. So, this was the girl who drove Lizzie—Maddie—to the hospital. Tricia wanted to hug her. Sometimes protecting clients' confidentiality really bridled her natural warmth.

"Tanisha, it's a pleasure to meet you," Tricia said. "I'm always glad to hear that we've been of help."

Tanisha looked back at the condemnation notice. "So, are you all closed down?"

Tricia cast a glance toward the office door. "We won't be able to work from this building anymore. But we will continue serving people remotely. Until we find a new home."

"Ain't that the way?! I'm looking for a new home myself. My apartment building's got the same sign on the front door. One week and I gotta be all outta there."

"Do you have somewhere to go?"

"Oh, I've got options, all right. I can always find a way to stay off the streets. Know what I mean?"

Tricia was afraid she did know. She slid one of her business cards from the case that backed her cell phone. "Say, Tanisha, if you or any of your neighbors can use some extra help right now, we can have lots of resources and partners we can connect you with. Just text this number. Or call. We'll still be around to help."

Tanisha frowned at the card. "Yeah. You're good people. Thanks." She waved the card at Tricia as she followed the uneven sidewalk to the curb. After pausing to tuck Tricia's card into the thin sequined purse that hung from a long cord at her shoulder, Tanisha crossed diagonally in the middle of the street and disappeared around the corner.

Tricia headed back to her car, shaking her head. "Girl, stay safe."

Emily Radner stood beside the bedroom doorway, gesturing inside. "And this is your room, Madeline."

Maddie held Lucas closer as she walked past the lady. She could almost touch the peace in the room, from the lacy curtains at the window to the thick quilt draped across the foot of the twin bed. On the other side of the room stood a new crib with a smooth white sheet on the mattress, beside a low chest of drawers topped with a padded surface, probably for changing diapers. Everything was soft colors and gentle light. Like hot cocoa for her soul.

Hot cocoa. When was the last time she had thought of it, let alone tasted it?

Emily entered after her, bringing along her canvas tote of possessions. It looked awfully small when Emily placed it on the desk beneath the window. As if she sensed Maddie's thoughts, Emily picked up an envelope from the desk and handed it to Maddie. "Here's a little something to welcome you to The Harbor. Inside are gift vouchers for our thrift store, where you can pick out some special items for yourself. We carry baby clothes, too, if you would like some things for Lucas."

"That would be great," Maddie said, a new warmth rising in her chest. She hadn't gone shopping for clothes *she* liked in years.

Judging by Lucas' steady breathing and sealed eyes, he was ready to lie down. Maddie started for the crib, then stopped to ask, "Okay if I put him down here?"

"You bet. That's Lucas' bed now."

Maddie placed him gently on his back, just the way Tricia had taught her. Meanwhile, Emily slid open the top desk drawer and pulled out a device that matched a larger one sitting on the desk. "Here's your baby monitor handset, Maddie. This is the part you can carry around in the house," she said, "to let you know when he wakes up or gets fussy."

Emily explained the settings. Then the two of them stood back to watch Lucas sleep.

"Looks like he's comfy," Emily said. "Soon, I hope you will be, too."

Maddie gave Emily a sidelong glance. Nice as this place was, Maddie felt like she'd been in a blender for the last several days. The best she hoped for was that things would stop changing so fast.

Emily checked her watch and said, "Well, I suppose your friends are about ready to leave. Would you like to come downstairs and see them off?"

Maddie's heart sank. After three days with Chris and Lena, she was about to be left all alone with these strangers. She knew Chris and Lena weren't there to be her guardian angels or anything. They had done her a huge favor by driving all the way to California to get her. But they were just being nice to an old friend. Maddie was no longer the church girl they used to know. Not by a long shot.

So, staying at The Harbor was the right move. That way, when Chris and Lena learned the truth and bowed out of her life, she would still have a place to call home. For now.

"Okay. I'll come down," Maddie said at last. She started to pick Lucas up again, then hesitated.

Emily smiled and pointed to the monitor. "You'll be able to hear him if he needs you. And there's no one but us Radners and Clouses here right now. The other moms are out at a movie with Cindy, our community life volunteer. Lucas should be okay here if you're comfortable leaving him."

Maddie picked up her baby. Comfortable was a long way away.

That night, Paloma's favorite phrase seemed to have become, "*¡Qué triste!*" In every room within the damaged walls of Dos Almas Pregnancy Center, she said it again. Over and over: "How sad!" Tricia could only agree.

Panels shaken down from the hanging ceiling had fallen onto whatever lay beneath. Powdery white dust covered most surfaces. Two of their three computer monitors were shattered, thanks to a toppled cabinet. The computers themselves, buried under heaps of spilled files, were badly dented. At least all their digital files were backed up off site.

Broken lines to the emergency sprinklers had doused everything in the reception area, including the front desk. Nothing there could be salvaged. Ironically, while the educational DVDs had avalanched from their shelves, the rickety old bookshelf itself was still standing. Dripping wet but still standing.

Paloma emerged from a counseling room with something in her arms. *"¡Míren! ¡Mis bebés!"* She held out the plastic display box filled with life-sized fetal models. "It's a miracle. My babies survived!"

Tricia, relieved to find *something* intact, said, "Thank you, Lord, for saving the babies."

Paloma caught her eye. "And we will keep saving babies—and their mamas!"

"Just from somewhere else," Mike Benson said, his voice trailing away as he passed with two plastic totes of maternity clothes.

As the last useful items were loaded into the available cars and one small trailer, the clean-up crew removed their hard hats and laid them on the small front lawn outside the shell that once was Dos Almas Pregnancy Center.

As a few gentle raindrops hit the cracked walkway at his feet, Mike Benson removed his Dodgers baseball cap. "Why don't we gather 'round and pray, folks?" The crew formed itself into a ragged circle and took each other's hands, bowing their heads. Mike nodded to Tricia.

Tricia began, wondering if she would be able to finish. "Father, thank you for giving us this building for fifteen wonderful years. Thank you for the families we have served and are serving still, for the children who live today and the relationships that are healthier because of your work through this ministry."

Paloma sniffled.

Tricia's voice broke as she said, "What now, Lord? Where shall we go? How will we find a new home? How can we keep serving our neighbors in need?"

Several murmurs circled the group.

She pushed on, "Tonight, we are full of questions. So many questions. Help us find the answers you have for us. Please, God. We are completely dependent on you." She struggled to get out a hoarse, "Amen."

Mike placed his cap back on as he and the others spread out toward their cars and trucks.

Tricia paused on the curb beside her station wagon. In the unsteady drizzle, streetlights shone on shop fronts and sidewalks, alleys, and avenues. For Dos Almas, for all their neighbors, Tricia murmured again, "What now, Lord?"

Tanisha pulled open the door to Rico's and hurried inside, away from the cold. Blaring music and a drunk in a Lakers T-shirt who almost made her wear his tequila reminded her why this wasn't her favorite bar. Tanisha had to elbow her way through a cluster of rude dudes to find a table for two near the tinted front window. Before trusting her skinny jeans to that seat, however, she used a nearby napkin to wipe her chair dry, then plunked down to wait for her roommate Mariela.

Inside her sequined bag sat a handful of dollar bills. She frowned. *Only one drink*, she told herself. *None on the card.* She had barely enough money saved up to cover her half of first and last month's rent on the new place she'd found. Once Mariela saw the pictures of it, Tanisha just knew she would love it too. She pulled out her phone and cued up the realtor's listing. *Sweet...*

High-pitched giggling told her Mariela had arrived. But when Tanisha turned, her smile faded. Mariela wasn't alone. Her chunky boyfriend Manuel had come along.

"Hi, 'Nisha!" Mariela squealed. Manuel grinned.

Tanisha gestured across the table. "Sorry, only one chair."

Manuel sat himself down and swung Mariela onto his lap. "No problem." He smiled at his petite girlfriend like he'd just done something hilarious. She giggled like she agreed.

A waitress tossed three coasters onto the table. "What can I get you tonight?"

Tanisha ordered a rum and coke. "Separate tabs."

Mariela and Manuel giggled their orders, and the waitress pushed off into the crowd.

Tanisha took a deep breath. She would make this quick. The plan: get Mariela to agree to the new place, slam down her drink, and ditch this craziness ASAP. She leaned forward with her phone facing her roommate. "So, I found us the perfect place…"

Mariela fanned her false eyelashes across her dark eyes and held up her Electric-Pink-tipped fingers. "Oh, 'Nisha, wait. I, um… Well, Manuel asked me to move in… with him."

Tanisha looked from Manuel's pudgy bulldog face to Mariela's makeup-ad face. She laid her phone down and crossed her arms. "And you said yes, huh?"

"Don't be mad, 'Nisha," Mariela said. "Be happy for me. I'm in love again." She twisted to give Manuel a smile made of Red Corvette lips curved across flashing white teeth.

The waitress set down their drinks, so Tanisha didn't have to answer.

Mariela sipped her tiny straw and then picked up Tanisha's phone. She squealed, "This place is so cute! Look, Manuel, isn't it cute? Won't Tanisha just love it?"

Tanisha slid her phone out of her ex-roommate's hand. "No, I won't. Can't afford it by myself."

"Oh," Mariela squeaked, shrugging. "Maybe you'll find someone else to room with. You have a ton of friends!" She chattered on about others they had known in the old, condemned building.

Tanisha hardly listened. *Ton of friends. Right.*

When the two across from her started to giggle at each other's whispered Spanish secrets, her stomach churned. Tanisha raised her glass, ready to bolt down her drink and leave, when a thin guy in a leather jacket sauntered past the window. *Maddie's man.* Tanisha made her free hand a visor covering her face, and watched Zach from between her fingers. But he hadn't seen her. His eyes were on something across the parking lot, something near her car.

Mariela giggled again. "We've gotta go, 'Nisha. Manuel's sister's *quinceañera* is tonight, and we have to get all dressed up." She hopped from his lap and wiggled her fingers at Tanisha. "Thanks for the drinks!" They disappeared into the crowd, leaving Tanisha with her mouth open and her purse running on empty. She shook her head, eyes rolling toward the ceiling.

Tanisha dragged her phone closer. So much for that apartment. She slumped in her chair, frowning as she clicked back to the site's home page and typed in a rent she could afford. The photos that came up depressed her. The addresses even more. She really didn't want to go back to *those* neighborhoods.

She flipped the phone face down and stared out the window. A long, slow drink felt good, burning its way down. Down, down, down. The burn almost kept her from thinking. But then her gaze drifted toward the corner where Maddie had been sitting the first time she met her. Right under that light, where her red hair could shine like fire. Almost like Zach perched her there to catch attention. Tanisha had been with…some guy, she couldn't remember who, and Maddie was there by herself at first. Tanisha's date tripped over something and nearly landed on their table. While he went to clean himself off and replace Maddie's spilled drink, she and Maddie got to laughing and talking, found out they lived near each other, and became friends. Just like that. Too bad the guys had to come back so soon. They changed the whole mood. But a friendship had begun.

Tanisha's heart twisted. Maddie had been gone, what, a week? But it felt like the sun had dimmed or something. A week without seeing each other wasn't unusual, but this was going to stretch on forever. This time Maddie was *gone*-gone. Now Mariela had bailed out on her too. Tanisha felt as empty as her glass.

Behind her, someone started shouting. She raised herself to see over the far end of the partition. The drunk Lakers fan boy yelled, "I said, 'What're you crying about?'"

The bartender moved to intervene. "Hey, dude, why don't you just move a few seats down and leave him alone, huh?" He pulled a bowl of pretzels out from behind the bar. "Here, over here. Fresh pretzels. Okay?"

Tanisha couldn't believe that worked. But the Lakers fan followed the pretzel bowl along the bar until he found an open stool. She glanced back at the guy he'd been shouting at. At the same moment, the guy glanced over his shoulder at her. *Bad timing*.

Zach nodded and gave her that smoldering look of his. She felt a guilty pleasure at the shiver it sent up her spine. Then she remembered: Maddie didn't want him anymore. Zach was available. No guilt, then. She tipped her head and let her lips lift at the corners. He took the bait.

She lowered herself back into her seat, adjusting her tank top for ideal male viewing. Zach stepped up to her table. "Tanisha, right? Mind if I join you?" He waved his tumbler toward the empties on the table. "Or is someone coming back?"

Tanisha shook her head, sliding the glasses aside. "Just some friends who stiffed me for their drinks. Please, have a seat." The night had just shifted in a fine direction. This was a game coming on, a familiar one. Could she lead the guy on without giving away something that she knew, but he shouldn't find out? Fortunately, he didn't know that she knew it.

"Stiffed you, huh?" Zach said with a sympathetic grin. "Well, then the next one's on me." He beckoned the waitress over. With a warm smile, he said to Tanisha, "What'll it be this time?"

Tanisha gave a helpless little shrug. "I don't know this place well. What do you like?"

A slow grin spread across Zach's lean lips. Without taking his eyes off Tanisha, he told the waitress, "I know just the thing. Give her my favorite margarita."

"Sure thing. And for you, Zach? Same as before?" When Zach nodded, she left them eyeing each other.

"You must come here often." Tanisha put on her little girl pout. Guys loved it.

Zach shrugged. "Often enough." His gaze drifted away, and apparently, his thoughts did too. "Used to bring Maddie here a lot," he said quietly.

Poor guy. But he was about to find someone who could make him forget his sorrows. She reached across and touched his hand, where it rested loosely around his empty glass. "I heard she... was gone," she said. "Are you okay?"

He glanced at her hand, then up at her with sad eyes. "I didn't even know there was anything wrong. She just... left me. Did she ever say anything to you, Tanisha? You were her best friend. Surely..."

The waitress set down a broad-rimmed glass sparkling with salt in front of Tanisha and a second drink for Zach. Tanisha used the excuse to pull her hand away. She had to be careful. Maddie *was* her best friend, true. She couldn't go breaking her promise now. But this heartbroken boy was just begging for a little feminine comfort. Tanisha took a sip of her margarita. A second later, she set it down while the alcohol etched a trail to her stomach. She pursed her lips at the glass.

Zach asked, "Something wrong?"

Tanisha shook her head. "I must be turning into a lightweight. More of a bite than I expected."

Zach looked around for the waitress. "I can get you something else if you don't like it."

Tanisha lifted the stemmed glass again. "No, no. It just caught me off-guard." She was gonna like what this guy liked if it killed her. She took a longer second drink. That went down more easily.

Zach lifted his glass. "To good friends gone."

Tanisha clinked hers against his. "To good friends." The next swallow was even better than the last. This bar wasn't so bad after all. So many happy people. And such great music.

It wasn't long before that drink was gone, and Zach made sure she had another, right away. He was so nice…

Pretty soon, they were talking and laughing like close friends. Why had Maddie kept this dude to herself for so long? He told the funniest jokes. Like about the time Maddie surprised him with the news that she was pregnant—or something like that.

"Well, sheesh not pregnant anymore," Tanisha smiled knowingly. She blinked, trying to clear the weight from her eyelids.

"No? How do you know?" Zach's face seemed to ebb and flow, like an ocean wave.

All that weaving in and out made Tanisha feel seasick. She looked out the window, where things stood more still. "'Cause I drove 'er to the hoshpital. In her car. 'Cause, no way…" She waved her hand toward her jeans. "She was a messsh."

"So that's why I saw your car—"

"Yep. Parked it there while sheeee… went to have the baby."

Zach's face wrinkled in a weird way. He said, "She went to have the baby."

Tanisha said, "Is there an echo in here?" and laughed. But Zach didn't. Tanisha got the vague feeling she might have said the wrong thing. She squeezed her eyes closed, then opened them again, but a strange haze still filled the bar. Zach was getting blurry.

"Where did she go after that?" Zach said, doing that wavy thing again.

Tanisha shrugged. How was she supposed to know?

"Did she come back home? Like, to pick up some stuff?"

"I dunno."

Zach leaned into her face and stayed put. "Tanisha, it's important. There's some valuable stuff missing from my house. Did she come back to get it?"

"I dunno. I went to a party. With Ty. You know Ty? No? Nishe guy. Drove me back to get—get my car the neksht day." Tanisha slurped the last of her margarita. She set down the glass and licked the salt off the corners of her mouth. "All gone. My drink ish gone, and Maddie'sh gone... all the way home."

"Home?"

Tanisha nodded and burped. She pointed into the air. "Home to the frozhen north. Mmminn-e-shoda." She worked hard to lift her elbow all the way up to the table and let her cheek sink into her hand. *Wish I had a home...*

"You okay?" Zach asked loudly, over the pretty music and the dancing lights.

"I don't feel so good," she said, burping again.

"Poor kid." Zach stood and helped her to her feet. "Need a ride home?"

"Home?" Tanisha blew a laugh into his face. "I'm out on my butt." She tried to smack that part of her but couldn't find it. She twisted around and still couldn't find it.

His arm around her waist kept her from tipping over. "Well, then, why don't you come home with me? Two lonely people... We could cheer each other up."

Those words were magic. Magic, sparkly fairy dust, all over that secret she was supposed to hide from him. That secret about... what? Oh, well. Didn't matter. She needed a place to go. Mariella let her down. Zach was a place to land... for now.

She smiled, hoping her little girl look was still working. Couldn't quite be sure what her face was doing. "Oh, Zach, you mean... move in with you?"

Tanisha thought he nodded, but her heavy eyelids made it hard to tell. She reached for her purse. Again, his arm kept her from tipping onto her chair. She patted his shoulder when she regained her footing. "You know, I've kinda had my eye on you for a long time, baby."

"Of course you have." Zach propelled her through the pretty music and the dancing lights, out the door into the night.

CHAPTER 6

Paloma Cisneros, her smooth gray braid shining silver and her citrus-striped poncho golden in the January sunshine flooding Tricia's front step, opened her arms the moment Tricia opened the door. "*Amiga!*"

Tricia bent to give her a hug. "Come in, Paloma! Come in. I miss seeing you every day."

"It seems like we've been without our office for weeks instead of just days," Paloma agreed. She followed Tricia into the kitchen, lugging her laptop case. "Today, I met with a new client at her high school. Tomorrow, I'll be at the Evangelical Free Church conference room for our New Hope and Healing group, and then I run home to meet another client there."

"I don't know how you do it." Tricia cleared a space at the table for Paloma amid a sea of papers. Her friend pulled a diet cola bottle from her case and planted it on the table. Paloma's hands went to her hips as she scanned the table. "Is all this for our insurance claim?"

"Most of it," Tricia said, filling her favorite mug full of fresh, hot coffee.

Paloma shook her head at the paperwork piles. "Couldn't we just send them a picture? It would be worth a thousand words." She seated herself in a kitchen chair and opened her diet soda for a long drink.

"Apparently, they prefer the thousand words." Tricia took a quick sip of her coffee and passed Paloma a pen. "Thanks for coming over to help with this. I was feeling overwhelmed. And I'm just sure one of my kids is going to spill apple juice all over it. I've got to get it done and mailed off soon." Before picking up her own pen, Tricia noticed Paloma's eyes darted toward her and then away. Something lay heavy on her friend's mind.

Paloma took her time capping her bottle and setting it down on the table with care as if it might explode if not handled properly. She spoke as she powered up her computer, "Tricia, there is something I think I should talk with you about. Regarding today's client."

Tricia folded her hands to listen. She couldn't imagine what this client could have brought up that Paloma couldn't address on her own.

Paloma pulled up her file of notes on the client meeting and scanned them. "You will find this part encouraging: the student asked for an appointment because she heard one of our presentations at her school—last year. She remembered that we offered free pregnancy tests and that we had given 'good advice on relationships.'"

Tricia thought of all the faces she and Paloma had seen in those classes. Which were paying attention? Which of them would remember what they heard when they needed it? It was anyone's guess.

Paloma went on. "You may know this client in a capacity other than your role as director. That's why I felt I should speak to you."

Tricia could tell nothing from Paloma's composed face except that she was weighing her words carefully.

"This student came to me with two concerns. One was about the health of her relationship with a young man. The other was about whether or not she was pregnant. The student's name is Laci DeWitt."

Tricia sucked in air. *Laci.* The girl Drake planned to ask to prom. The one he'd brought to church once or twice. And taken to dinner with a group of friends. Tricia sat up straight in her chair, her folded hands now clenched tight. Softly, she repeated, "Laci DeWitt."

Paloma nodded slowly. "I remembered you asked us to pray about Drake's relationship with her during a staff meeting sometime last fall. Is he still seeing her?"

"I... I think so." Tricia's mind went rummaging through her jumbled memories, all shoved aside in the aftermath of the earthquake. When was the last time Drake talked about Laci? At Christmas time, he had seemed evasive when Reece mentioned her. And what about that afternoon a week ago, when he didn't show up to watch his siblings? His excuses afterward left her far from satisfied. Every muscle in her body tightened. "Did Laci mention Drake's name?"

"No. In fact, she didn't want to talk about the father."

Tricia swallowed, hoping her voice would stay calm. "And her test was… positive?"

"Inconclusive. I sent a second one home with her and asked her to get back in touch with me when she was ready to talk again. I believe she will. At least, I think so." Paloma leaned back in her chair. "I usually remember students. But Laci has changed dramatically since last spring. Then, she was a shy and quiet blonde in glasses, dressed modestly. Today she was heavily made up and wearing… a very different style of dress."

Tricia rubbed her eyes with a thumb and forefinger. "Did she say much about her relationship concerns?"

"She said her parents divorced when she was young. So until our talk, she didn't know much about how a man should treat a woman. But before she could go on, the passing bell rang and—" Paloma whistled and flicked her fingers, "—she scooted out the door."

Tricia crossed her arms and let her gaze drift to the sliding glass door. After a moment's pause, she said, "I think it may be time for my husband and me to have a heart-to-heart with Drake." Tricia bit her tongue, holding back a rush of self-accusation. But the words still went slithering and hissing about in her head.

Paloma reached out to pat Tricia's hand. "Remember, my friend, make no assumptions. You may find this has nothing to do with your son at all."

Then Paloma's phone buzzed a notification, which she took in at a glance. "Text line. I'll check it on my computer."

"Thanks," Tricia murmured, still dazed by what she had heard. Once again, she had been negligent in keeping up with her children's concerns. Drake used to be so open about his inner world. His recent reticence was strange. And painful.

"Hmmm…"

Tricia caught Paloma's frown. "What is it?"

"New number. Somebody asking for you. Look." Paloma rotated her laptop toward Tricia.

"Do you know a 'Tanisha'?" Paloma asked.

Tricia's brain snapped back to focus on work. "I just met her last week. Right after the earthquake. She's the friend who drove our mystery client to the hospital. I'll reply." Tricia dug her phone out from under the insurance papers. She picked up one paper. "Here's the list of damaged and lost items I started. Could you see if I forgot anything?"

Paloma nodded and took the sheet.

Tricia signed onto the text line and typed a reply. *Hi, Tanisha. This is Tricia. How can I help you?*

I think Maddie is in danger.

Tricia closed her eyes. She needed wisdom here. How did she maintain confidentiality—for someone who was not technically a client—while addressing what might be a real threat to that someone?

Did you tell her?

Tried. Couldnt get thru.

Of course. Maddie had a new number. *Why do you think she is in danger?*

Cause I xdentally told her exBF where she went. Got drunk, said too much.

Tricia frowned, mentally translating Tanisha's shorthand. She typed, *What do you think he will do?*

Go find her. Said she is worth big bucks. Plus he thinks she stole his coke.

Drugs and trafficking. Two sources of income, all tied to one girl. But was that enough to send a man on a thirty-hour trek to the Midwest in the middle of winter? How would he know where to look? Tricia knew too little of the backstory. This was getting too complicated to continue by text. *May I call you? Are you in a safe place to talk out loud?*

Yes & yes

Amid the clatter of silverware on plates, Maddie passed the ceramic bowl of mashed potatoes to Ariel, the tall, pregnant blonde to her left at the dinner table. Ariel accepted it without a word and dished a small helping onto her plate before passing the bowl to Emily.

"Thanks, Ariel." Emily served herself and set the bowl down. "Did the roast beef make it all the way around?"

The other women nodded, forking food into their mouths at a healthy rate.

Jake, Emily's balding husband, sat at the end of the table to Maddie's right. Maddie had subtly scooted her chair closer to Ariel on the left when she sat down. She began the meal breathing quickly, head down, watching Jake out of the corner of her eye. But he seemed intent on not upsetting her, and she relaxed bit by tiny bit.

Jake lifted a forkful of green beans. "Ladies, this is delicious. What a treat to come home to a meal like this after a cold day in town! Thanks."

"Glad you like it," said the chubby black-haired mom whose name Maddie kept forgetting. "I found that green bean casserole recipe online. We had all the stuff for it, so I gave it a try."

"Pass the butter, Monique," Ariel said.

Monique. That was the chubby one's name. Monique passed the butter to Ariel and chattered on for a few minutes about her favorite online recipe sites. When she paused to take a bite, Emily spoke up.

"Was the snow blowing very badly when you drove home, Jake?"

Jake tilted back in his chair to look out the kitchen window. "Not as much as it is now. Glad I left the clinic when I did. I'd hate to miss game night with you all. And spending the night at the office stinks. Literally. All those animals."

As Jake pretended to swat away invisible animal smells, Maddie felt the corners of her mouth lift. Just a little. Gripping her fork and knife for courage, she asked him softly, "Have you often had to sleep at your veterinary clinic?"

"Only once or twice," Jake replied. "I'm more likely to get snowed in way out on some farm after an animal check. But those farm families like to stay on good terms with their vet, so they always make me feel right at home. Not bad places to stay. And I'd rather stay put than drive in conditions that worry Emily."

Emily gave an exaggerated shudder. "Driving home in blinding snow is too dangerous. Especially with those deep dredge ditches on either side of the road. If you went off the road, you could disappear for days in one of those things. Even in your big pickup truck." She drove her hand off the edge of the table to make her point.

Jake winked at Maddie. "See what I mean?"

Maddie wasn't sure what to do with that wink. The last man that winked at her—she curled lower in her chair.

Monique shot a quick glance over her shoulder at her baby monitor. "I'm just glad it was early fall when we had to make all those car trips to St. Olaf Children's Hospital for Tyra."

Hospital? Maddie looked up, buttery mashed potatoes caught in her mouth.

"What was she in the hospital for?" Ariel asked.

"She had a weird growth that my pediatrician wanted checked out."

Maddie reached for her water glass and gulped down several swallows.

"So, I—we—" Monique corrected herself with a squinty-eyed smile at Emily, "took her to St. Olaf's for testing. Turns out it was all okay." She dug her spoon into her potatoes for a heaping bite.

Emily nodded. "St. Olaf has the Midwest's best neonatal on-cologists, and they're right here in Jefferson." She paused, studying Maddie's face. "An oncologist is a doctor who—"

"Oh, I know what oncologists do," Maddie said. She knew it all too well. Tyra must have been okay. At least she didn't have a heart defect. Maddie had probably passed hers on to Lucas. Along with all her other flaws and defects. She was such a wreck. Was there any part of her that wasn't broken?

Maddie stared down at her dinner plate. Her insides had gone hard and tight, clenched by an old fear. What if she *had* passed on her heart defect to Lucas? Lucas could die in his sleep or need super-expensive surgery. She could lose the only truly innocent person in her life. Monique's chirpy voice cut through her darkening thoughts.

"That doctor may be the 'best,' but he sure wasn't the nicest," she said. The glint of Monique's waving fork riveted Maddie's attention. "He could learn a thing or two about customer service, that doctor! Rude? Arrogant? I thought doctors wanted to help people, not boss them around. I was relieved that Tyra didn't need any help from Dr. Megamind Murphy after all."

Jake coughed down a chuckle. "Now, Monique. No name-calling necessary."

Monique looked at Ariel and Maddie, marking out a basketball-sized space between her fork and her free hand. "No, seriously. Big head—and probably getting bigger every day, he's so stuck on himself."

Ariel exhaled loudly and continued cutting perfect one-inch squares of roast beef.

Emily cleared her throat and said in a playfully formal tone, "Thank you, Monique, for reminding us why we stress customer service in our vocational training here at The Harbor."

Monique shrugged and reached out to spear another slice of roast beef.

Careful to avoid others' eyes, Maddie reached behind her to the kitchen island where her baby monitor stood. "I think I heard something. I'll go check on Lucas real quick."

Before she had crossed the darkened living room to reach the stairs, soft footsteps caught up with her. Maddie found Emily at her side.

"Madeline, is something wrong?" Emily tipped her head and looked at Maddie with her gentle green eyes.

A lot of things were wrong. Too many things to talk about. Especially to someone she barely knew. Maybe someday…

"I'm just going to check on Lucas," she replied, turning her eyes to the stairway ahead. "Medical stuff… bugs me." She wanted to go be alone with her baby, but she felt rude just walking away while Emily was still there.

Emily accompanied her to the foot of the stairs and flipped on the light switch for the upper hallway. "Okay. Let me know if you want anything. Come on back whenever you're ready."

"Yep." Maddie hurried alone up the single flight of stairs, glad for the soft carpeting. These stairs sounded nothing like the ones at that motel where Zach—Whoa, not going there. She dialed the baby monitor off and finished her climb. In the bedroom, Lucas made soft, soothing purring noises in his sleep, bringing Maddie's pulse rate down a half-notch.

She pulled the bedroom door shut behind her, closing herself in with her baby and the soft glow from the nightlight. She lowered herself onto her bed. Her soft, comfy bed. Leaning left, she curled into a fetal position, her arm under her head. From here, she could watch Lucas sleep. Maybe this would be a good time to call Tricia. But she really didn't want to move right now. Right now, everything was okay. Emily and Jake seemed like good people. Ariel was quiet and uptight but not weird or anything. Monique was chatty, but friendly.

Lena wasn't too far away. And Chris—Chris wasn't too close. It was all good.

Right now, she could almost believe what Tricia had said, that God had never given up on her. Almost.

Tricia felt like a vulture perched on the sofa where she and Reece waited for Drake to come home after his robotics team meeting.

Reece turned another page of the newspaper and finally gave up pretending to read it. He folded it and laid it down on the coffee table. Standing, he asked, "Want anything from the kitchen?"

Before Tricia could answer, headlights shone through the front curtains. The old station wagon coughed to a stop in the driveway. A door creaked open and slammed shut. Drake's shadow crossed the front window. Tricia wished she'd asked for a glass of water when her mouth went dry in the split second it took Drake to unlock the front door.

"Hey," he said as he stepped inside. He hung up his jacket in the hall closet and turned to head to his room with his backpack, then stopped, looking from one parent to another. "Something wrong?"

"We're hoping you can help us figure that out," Reece said. "Can we talk?"

Drake shrugged and set down his pack. "Yeah. Sure," he said, cracking his neck sideways once, a sure sign of tension he wanted to disguise. He sat on the recliner across from his parents, feet on the floor.

Reece returned to his seat next to Tricia. "How's the robot coming?"

"Programming glitches, and a part broke. The usual." He waited. "So, what did you want to talk about?"

Reece shot a quick glance at Tricia. "Some news reached us... about a friend of yours. We wanted to hear your take on it."

Drake leaned his elbows on his knees, folding his hands. "Okay. What news? Which friend?"

Tricia said, "Laci may be pregnant."

"Oh, no."

Tricia's heart dropped into her slippers.

Drake sat up, hands on his knees, eyes toward the carpet. "Laci. It's been a while since I would call her a friend."

Tricia didn't know if that signaled her to feel relieved or upset. If he had been intimate with a girl and then discarded her...

Drake took a long, slow breath and blew it out. "I've been wanting to talk to you about this for a while. Something... happened, and I wasn't sure how to handle it. But you've been so busy..."

Tricia reached for Reece's hand.

Reece said, "Sounds like it's good we're having this talk, then. What do you want to tell us?"

Drake rocked the recliner a few times, then began. "In the fall, I thought Laci...you know, kind of liked me. She even came to youth group with me that one time and seemed to have fun there. But toward the end of basketball season, there was this guy who kept showing up at her games, just hanging around, kind of watching the girls. All the girls, at first. Then he sort of zeroed in on Laci. He'd come up to her after games and talk to her, wearing his cool leather jacket. He's older, college age maybe. And me? I'm just a nerdy sophomore, so I felt like there went my chances.

"Anyway, Laci started changing after that. I always thought she was pretty in a sort of simple, straightforward way. And shy. Like, painfully shy. But after this guy started hanging around her, she started dressing—You'd call it sleazy. Lots of makeup, low-cut tops, expensive clothes. She had told me things were tight at home, so it seemed weird that she would have all this new stuff. By Christmas break, she wouldn't even talk to me in the halls anymore. She was too busy flirting with every *other* guy at school."

The mother side of Tricia started relaxing. But as Drake cracked his neck again, looking down at his hands, her pregnancy center director side stayed on high alert.

Reece said, "I'm sorry to hear that, Drake. She seemed like a nice girl the one time we met her."

Drake nodded silently. "She was a nice girl. But now...There's something—I think she's in real trouble, Dad." His head came up, his face grim. "Mom, you remember that day I was supposed to watch Joey and the girls so you could visit your client? But I didn't show?"

Tricia nodded. Drake's troubled eyes make her heart ache. "What really happened that day?"

"You know my friend Jamie from robotics, right? Well, he sometimes studies up on the bleachers while he waits for his mom to come get him after team meetings."

When he hesitated to go on, Reece prompted, "And—"

"That day, he said he wanted to show me something that he thought would make me feel better about Laci ignoring me. Only it made me feel worse."

Tricia stilled her hands by tucking them under her legs.

Drake sighed. "We kind of hid up in the bleachers and watched Laci meet that guy—the older one, with the leather jacket—out behind the old concession stand. First, the guy gave her a pill, and she took it. But that wasn't all. In a few minutes, someone else came, and… gave the guy a bunch of money. Then the other man and Laci went off together to his car."

Reece cleared his throat. "You saw money change hands?"

"Yep. A wad of bills."

"Did you overhear their conversation at all?"

Drake's gaze fell to the carpet again. "A little. Enough."

Reece frowned, silent for a minute or two. "I don't want to put words in your mouth, Son. What would you say was happening there?"

His answer came out hard and rough. "Trafficking. Sex trafficking. The guy in the leather jacket was pimping Laci to… the other man." Drake looked away, as if his parents couldn't see his chin tremble.

Tricia felt tears rising in her own eyes. All her confidence in her son's integrity settled back into place while grief for Laci flooded her heart.

Reece turned to her. "You have any suggestions for Drake?"

"You need to report this, Drake. There's a number to call—"

"But calling that number—won't that get the local police involved?"

"I believe so."

"And see, that's a problem."

Tricia pursed her lips. "Why? Are you worried about negative consequences for Laci?"

"Not exactly. The problem is the man who, um, paid for Laci. I recognized him from the Career Fair. He was Steven Cobb. Policeman Steven Cobb."

As the other attendees gathered their papers and the remains of their sack lunches, Avery scanned her sparse notes from the inter-agency meeting with Child Protective Services. Short list of cases this week. Always a good thing. And this time, none of them involved her clients.

Avery shoved the notebook into her backpack and looked up to find Tricia Prescott standing beside her. "Hey, Tricia." Her smile died away. "Uh-oh. Looks serious."

Tricia nodded. "If you have a moment, I have a couple of things I'd like to talk to you about."

"Sure." Avery tipped her head toward the rear exit. "It's quieter on the back lawn."

Once outside the courthouse, Tricia wasted no time telling her the bad news from their mutual client's friend, Tanisha. Avery swore to herself. Why did these cases have to be so complicated? Things could have gone really right for Maddie. Now Tanisha's loose lips could sink her whole ship. And the poor kid was barely settled into her new place. But it sounded like Tricia agreed that for Maddie, staying put meant staying right where her pimp would expect to find her. If he was serious about hunting her down.

Tricia sighed as they walked. "I'm just sorry Emily Radner's maternity home isn't set up as a safe house. Her whole program sounds ideal for a new mom getting a fresh start. But not ideal for this."

Avery stopped and shifted her backpack further up on her shoulder. "Well, one of us should let Maddie know. And personally, Tricia, I think you're the woman for the job. She trusts you way more than me."

Tricia glanced up, her face grim. She had probably hoped for a different answer. She said, "I suppose I should. These things are so hard over the phone when I don't have her body language to tell me if I'm triggering her trauma response."

"Hey, you'll do fine, as usual." Avery turned away to watch a car go by, knowing her face must be saying, *Good luck with that.*

"I just wish she had agreed to get a restraining order."

"She can still get one in Minnesota. I gave her a green card with the number to call there. Or she can look it up. But she'll have to act fast. Meanwhile—" Avery hesitated, then added, "—I do know law enforcement is just itching for a chance to lock Jarvis away. Over the last year or so, that creep has skated free of so many charges he could win a gold medal. But one of these days…"

"That's, um, interesting." Tricia's face took on an odd expression. Avery began to regret pushing the limits to share that little tidbit. There was a long pause, then Tricia finally said, "Which leads me to the other question."

Avery waited, watching Tricia scan the entire area outside the courthouse. At last, Tricia faced her and said. "Someone came to me, an eyewitness to a particular kind of crime. But this person feels unsure how to report what they saw."

"Because—?"

"The crime they witnessed—A police officer appeared to be involved. As a perpetrator."

Avery's eyes locked with Tricia's. "So, your witness wants to make sure they report it to an honest cop."

"Exactly. Avery, you know our law enforcement officers much better than I do. Who would you trust with information like this?"

Avery slid her backpack off and dug out a card as she answered. "Pete Sherrill. Straight as an arrow. I'd trust him with my life. Here: his regular hours, his extension. Best man our little city's got, in my humble opinion."

Tricia took the card and slipped it into her purse. "Thank you. This has shaken up my…witness deeply. They will be glad to know there are still trustworthy officers on the force."

Maddie heard the tapping on her door but ignored it, hoping it would stop. She was panting, elbows digging into the desk, hands pressed over her eyes. In the blackness, she saw Zach's icy glare, the way he looked when he found her pregnancy test. *"Let. Me. In."* Always watching her. She would never escape him.

Again the tapping. And then Emily's voice, "Maddie, are you all right?"

No, she wasn't. She was terrified. So creeped out that she imagined Zach standing behind Emily in the hallway, ready to pounce on her and beat her to within an inch of her life. Then he would turn to Lucas—

"Maddie?" Emily's voice said through the door.

She pushed back her chair. Lucas was sleeping quietly in his crib. Maddie forced herself to stand. She braced her feet and opened the door a crack. Nobody there but Emily. She exhaled and stood back. "Sorry. Come on in."

"No need to be sorry," Emily said, entering and closing the door softly behind her. "When you didn't come down for class, I thought I'd check on you. Did something... come up?"

"Yeah." Maddie dropped onto the bed. She could hardly get the words out. "He—Zach knows where I am. And that I have a baby." She clutched the quilt in curled fingers, hardly breathing.

"I see." Emily went silent, but Maddie's mind was screaming. She could just barely hear Emily ask, "May I ask how you found this out?"

Maddie looked down at her hands. In spite of her new wool sweater, she was getting colder by the moment. She said, "Tricia called, from Dos Almas. Zach ran into my friend Tanisha in a bar. She was homeless, and he offered her a place to stay, along with lots of drinks. She got so sloshed she finally told him my whole escape story."

"Mm. What do you expect him to do next?"

Maddie started shivering. She mumbled, "Come get me." To keep her teeth from chattering, she started talking fast. "Which is really kind of funny, because he always said he could replace me without any trouble. So maybe it's just his missing cocaine that he's worried about. He left to go pick it up the day I...went to the hospital. Then I stayed away. Then they had this big earthquake.

His coke was stolen from the house. He thinks I came back, stole his stash, and ran."

Emily's eyebrows rose.

"Which I didn't do, just for the record."

"I believe you, Madeline."

"Thanks." Maddie glanced up briefly. "Anyway, he's got two reasons to be mad at me. And with Zach, one reason's more than enough."

Emily nodded. She said gently, "What would you like to do next?"

"Tricia and I talked about a couple things," she said, heaving herself up from the bed and retrieving the green index card and her phone from the desk. Her hand shook as she showed the card to Emily. "Avery said this lady could help me file for a restraining order if I ever felt like I was in danger. And Tricia gave me some names, people she had met in Sargent who might help."

Emily asked, "Did she mention a couple named Nick and Flora Dahlgren?"

Maddie hadn't even opened her notes app, but the name was right. She looked up. "Yeah. Do you know them?"

"I do. Jake and I met them at a maternity housing conference a few years ago. We've been friends ever since. I have a picture of them. Would you like to see it?"

Maddie shrugged, mute.

While Emily was gone, Maddie did a search for Sargent, Minnesota. Looked like a two-hour drive farther west. Another move. Another car ride. Always more car rides. Rides she never wanted to take. She dug her hands into the hair at her temples and pulled. Would it ever stop? Would she never be safe? Her scalp started to throb.

Emily tapped on the bedroom door and let herself in. She entered and sat on the bed until Maddie released her death grip on her hair and looked up. "I'm sure this is very hard for you, Madeline. Maybe this will help." Holding up a framed photo, she said, "This is Nick and Flora Dahlgren. They're what we call a shepherding family. They are trained to help young mothers in transition, just like you.

Their home also has extra protocols and security features—outside cameras, motion-sensing lights and such that we don't have here." She handed the photo to Maddie. "Nick and my Jake hit it off immediately. They're both quiet, protective men with warm hearts and steel in their spines."

Maddie nodded, her eyes still focused on the strawberry blonde next to Nick in the photo. "And what's his wife's name? Flora? What's she like?"

Emily smiled up at the ceiling like she saw a happy memory there. "Flora is pretty much everybody's favorite aunt. I like her. She could be an excellent ally for you, Maddie. She is soft-hearted and sweet, but she can be as strong as a mama bear when she has to. Nothing scares Flora."

"They look nice," Maddie said softly. *If you can trust looks.*

"Sargent is a smaller city. Actually, it's more of a town. Large enough for you to have access to the services you might need, plenty of job opportunities. An easy place for you to blend in. Yet it's small enough that if Zach did ever go there, local authorities could easily track him."

Maddie longed to believe that. Longed to find a place where Zach—or one of his "connections"—wasn't hovering in her blind spot. He could charm his way in anywhere, it seemed. Or buy his way in by selling drugs…or her.

She knew Emily wanted her to say something. She had to make a decision. Another decision. Another chance to do the wrong thing.

She forced herself to take long, slow breaths. In and out, like Emily taught her. In and out…

Sargent would be two hours farther from Lena. And from Chris, which might be a good thing. But it would mean a strange new town, filled with strangers. Emily's talk of "job opportunities" frightened her. Could she emerge from hiding to walk in the open among normal people? She would be like a blind person crossing an intersection, always wondering if she was about to be mowed down by someone she couldn't see coming. The thought of Zach coming after her, sneaking up on her when she least expected him… Demanding something she didn't have…

And now there was Lucas. One more innocent person Zach could hurt. That didn't even count the people she would be staying with.

Lucas stirred in his crib, squirming, fussing. Hungry. Maddie handed the photo back to Emily and went to pick him up. Lucas blinked up at her from within his sleeper. Something about the trusting look on his soft little face made her tear up. Living with kind people who weren't afraid to take in someone like her, with all the crud she'd be dragging along—maybe that's what she and Lucas needed.

Emily's voice reached Maddie as if from far away. "Maddie, why don't we pray? God can help you know what to do."

God. Maddie frowned. If he cared, why was this happening? How could God have let Zach trick Tanisha into telling him everything?

Maddie gave Emily a polite nod and bowed her head but didn't hear a word she prayed. She was praying a prayer of her own. Of sorts.

God, you must not care about Lucas and me if you let Zach hunt us down. But you know what? I don't blame you. I'm the one who got mad at you and turned away. I was an angry, stupid kid, and I got myself into this mess. I don't expect you to get me out of it. Just don't let me hurt anyone else. Especially Lucas.

Emily's voice grew stronger, "And Father, please show Maddie how much you love her. Even through this frightening time. I ask all this in the name of Jesus, who died to save each one of us. Amen."

Maddie pulled in a deep breath. Zach would come looking for her. If she stayed here in Jefferson, he'd find her for sure. One way or another. But in Sargent… maybe she had a chance. That was it, then. She had nowhere to go but the Dahlgrens' house. If they couldn't protect her and Lucas…

Her whole body shook, and fear snaked through her core. Lucas grunted and nuzzled her chest. She raised his little hand to her lips. Then she lifted her weary eyes to Emily. "I'll go. Just tell me when."

CHAPTER 7

"The destination is on your right," the GPS voice said. Through the windshield, Chris spotted the two-story tan house with white trim, just the way Emily Radner had described it. 348 East Oak Street. But he drove on past, ignoring the electronic warning to "proceed to the route." At the end of the block, he turned right.

"Chris?" Maddie pointed back over her right shoulder. "That was it, back there."

He worked his jaw loose. Must have been clenching his teeth the whole time. Ever since Maddie started talking, an hour out of Jefferson.

He forced himself to be calm before he spoke. "I know. We're early. I need to stretch my legs." He didn't look at her. Just drove two more blocks, pulled to the curb, and parked. "You're free to join me. Or not."

His mom spoke his name in that tone of hers, something between a warning and a question. He didn't answer.

His mom asked Maddie, "May I wait here and keep Lucas company?"

"Um… sure…" Maddie said. She sounded subdued. Like maybe it had just dawned on her that spilling her guts about what had happened in California wasn't such a good idea. What was he supposed to feel about all that? She had chosen to dump him, chosen to hook up with this wacko. Chosen not to take his calls when he tried to check on her. But had she chosen all the rest? Not directly, maybe… But bad choices have consequences…

He needed to get out. Get some air.

Chris shoved his door open and pulled his coat out with him. He slammed the door before he could stop himself. Inside the car, the baby started wailing. He sighed. *Nice job, Nelson.*

He jammed his arms into his coat sleeves and trudged alongside the dirty plowed snow filling the gutter. Footsteps from behind told him Maddie had chosen to follow. He wished she hadn't.

The crushing ache in his chest and the roar in his head made it hard to think straight. All this time, he'd thought she had this one boyfriend, and when he turned mean, she left. But this—This was trafficking, sex trafficking. His Maddie—He choked on something acrid. His Maddie had slept with so many men she didn't know which one got her pregnant.

His mom opened her door to call after them, "Don't be long. I think he's hungry again."

At the moment, Chris had a hard time caring. Didn't like to admit it, but it was true. The stuff he had heard in the last hour made him want to vomit. Only the sharp, cold air kept him from hurling in the gutter. He stared straight ahead through the uncertain twilight. Focused on the sting of his freezing ears. The crunch of icy snow beneath his boots. The mist from his breath forced out through tight lips.

Maddie was having a hard time keeping up with him. Tough. He had his eyes locked on the dead end ahead.

He hadn't seen this news coming. It was like a war zone all over again. You're rolling right along, and—*blam*—an IED takes out the vehicle ahead of yours. And you're the medic who's gotta pull what's left of your friends from the wreckage. Chris shivered, shook his head clear.

Why did Maddie tell him all this right now, right before he had to leave her again in a whole new place, where he couldn't—? Was she trying to push him away? Again?

She was succeeding.

Chris stopped to let a car back out of a driveway. Its front wheel sloshed into the gutter, sending a spray of dirty slush across his shins.

A wordless epithet spewed from his mouth. He shook off what water he could, but the cold still penetrated.

"So, are you mad?" Maddie asked, catching up with him.

He exhaled hard and punched his hands into his pockets. "Mad? Are you kidding? I don't know what I am. You just dumped the whole truck on me, Maddie. It's a lot to process."

Maddie stepped back. She circled her mittened hands around her mouth and blew on them. "I'm sorry. I never pictured having one short car ride to break all that to you. I thought—" She kicked at a snowbank. "Well, nothing has turned out the way I thought."

For a long minute, the only sounds came from traffic in the distance. Chris snuck a glance at Maddie, head hunched down between her shoulders, eyes trained on the ground at her feet. He knew that look. Her world was caving in on her. Four years ago—heck, even this morning—he would have done everything in his power to keep her head up. To stand with her, blocking the icy winds of depression. Right now, though, he felt like saying she'd have to lie in the bed she'd made.

Not the best metaphor, maybe.

He pulled his coat collar up around his ears. "Yeah. It hasn't exactly worked out like I thought it would, either. Hard to believe, isn't it, that we used to be engaged back in the day?"

"Chris—"

"So, how do you expect me to feel now, Maddie? Now, when I can't—I mean, I would have—" His head went back, and he blew a steamy burst of breath at the darkening sky.

"I just thought... you ought to... you know, hear—"

He didn't want to hear. Wished he didn't know.

"It didn't seem like something I could just... text to you."

Maddie's teeth were audibly chattering. Before all this, he would have wrapped his arms around her. Now he had no warmth to spare. He took off down the sidewalk. It was better than puking right here in the snow. Once this passed, he was going to circle back to 348

East Oak Street, leave Maddie and her kid there, and drive away. Done. Finished. Over. No more cleaning up other people's messes.

The sidewalk stopped where the street ended at a creek, now trickling beneath a frozen crust of clotted snow and ice. A snow-fleck-ed barricade marked the end of the road. Chris stomped through the plowed-up snow at the barricade and clamped his hands on the top crosspiece. He looked at nothing but his boots, up to their tops in dirty snow, and his drenched jeans, already icing up. Maddie stomped her feet, trying to stay warm a couple of yards behind him.

Back near the car, her baby was seriously crying now.

Chris wanted to be alone, to think.

But Maddie spoke. "Chris, I'm so, so sorry. I failed you. You deserve so much more than what's left of me. I... I hope there is... someone special waiting for you, who will be—"

He was going to lose it, right here on this crusty snow. *Stop talking,* he wanted to say. *Just stop. No more.*

Her baby wailed down the empty street.

"I need to go feed him," she said.

Chris made no move to go with her. He let the silence build between them until she turned and walked to the car alone.

Tricia had never seen Reece kick a car before. She slid a step or two away from him, pretending to peer at something under the hood. As if she could tell a distributor from a radiator.

"Not now, you old beast!" Reece grumbled at the dead battery, his face half shadowed beneath the parking lot lamp post. This wasn't Reece's usual calm, ride-the-waves style. Something was bothering him. And it wasn't just the car.

Trying to see some bright side to their situation—usually Reece's approach—she said, "At least this didn't happen while I was out delivering diapers somewhere." She stopped at the look on his face.

"Diapers! For just one minute, can you think about something other than your work?!" He ran a greasy hand through his hair, leaving a black streak above his ear. "Ever since the earthquake, you've been 'Dos Almas this' and 'Dos Almas that.' You don't even know what's going on with your own family."

Tricia took a step back, her mouth open, but no objection rose to her defense. Even her own husband had things on his mind that she wasn't aware of. She hung her head. "I'm sorry, Reece. You're absolutely right." She waited, but he said nothing. "Is there something you need to tell me?"

Reece turned to her with eyes full of weariness. "Oh, sure. Right now, in the Walmart parking lot. Standing beside our old, broken-down jalopy."

A car door opened, and Drake unfolded his long legs out of their station wagon. He sauntered forward to look under the hood. "Battery, huh?"

Reece flared up again. "Yes, it's the battery! What did you think it was, Mr. Fix-It?"

Drake retreated with his hands up. "Just asking. I'll, uh, go entertain the troops." As he backed away toward his door, he caught Tricia's eye and pointed over her shoulder.

Tricia turned to see Mike Benson pulling into a parking space almost nose to nose with them. Leaving his engine running, Mike climbed out.

"Hi, there, Reece, Tricia. Saw your hood up. Trouble?"

Reece gave Mike a pained grin. "Battery."

Mike nodded toward his SUV. "I've got jumper cables."

Reece waved the offer away. "Nah, the old thing finally bit the dust." He pointed at something Tricia couldn't see but which made Mike grunt with some kind of secret male understanding.

"Sorry to hear that," Mike said. He shut off his motor and returned to stand by Reece at the grill.

Reece looked away, back toward the Walmart Super Store, out of which they had just carried three scrawny bags of groceries and an inordinately hefty receipt. He said, "I've been milking this battery longer than I should have. I just wasn't ready to replace it...right now."

Tricia glanced sideways at Reece. That "right now" was his budget-speak. But what was worrying him? They had been careful all through December, budgeting for each Christmas gift, for each bill coming due. Had she missed some new expense? How much could a battery cost that it would make Reece worry about covering it "right now"?

Mike followed his line of sight. "Well, better to break down here than miles from the store that sells everything, right?"

Tricia coughed. That was what she had tried to say, minus Mike's diplomacy.

Reece grunted. "Well, better get this over with." He patted his back pocket to check for his wallet.

Mike clamped a hand on Reece's shoulder. "My friend, you're in luck. Back when I was a skinny college freshman, stranded on the side of the highway, a total stranger stopped and bought me a new battery. He told me to pass the favor along someday. Finally, Reece, you have given me an opportunity to do so. Now, march me in there and show me which battery you prefer."

Reece shook his head. "Hey, that's kind of you, Mike, but—"

"But nothing. Let's go." He started for the store.

"Be with you in a minute." Reece reached for Tricia's hand and said quietly, "Trish, I'm sorry I blew up at you. Let's make time to talk later. Okay?" When she nodded, he turned to follow Mike toward the store. But first, he paused, opened Drake's door, and apologized for his second outburst. Drake shrugged and said, "Yeah, okay, Dad."

Tricia watched him go, still puzzled. Then, shivering, she crawled back into the car with the kids. Drake, a sullen pout on his face, had defaulted to playing a game on his phone, completely ignoring his siblings. So much for entertaining the troops. Joey was chanting a sing-song taunt in the direction of his sisters, and the girls at once launched into whining.

By the time the two men returned with the new battery, the girls sat up front with Tricia while Joey pestered Drake for another turn playing his game. Reece pulled his tools from the back of the station wagon, and soon he and Mike had the old battery out and the new one in. Tricia and the girls were singing "Yankee Doodle" for the hundredth time when Mike knocked on her window. She opened her door.

"Sorry, Mike, this window doesn't crank down anymore." Her face grew warm, even in the night air. She hurried to add, "Thank you very much for this. I—"

Mike shrugged it off. "No problem. Happy to help." While wiping his hands on one of Reece's rags, he said, "I actually wanted to tell you some news about the center."

"Oh?" With Alyssa bouncing on the seat to another round of "Yankee Doodle" while Lydia sang along and pretended to steer, Tricia had to stand up to hear Mike.

Mike chuckled. "The Banquet Committee met this afternoon. They phoned me later to confirm that they can indeed move the fundraising banquet up from fall to spring. To March 21, to be exact."

"March 21?" Tricia blinked. *Barely two months away?* "You mean, caterers? Speaker? Venue?"

"All willing and able to switch dates." Mike wiped the last of the grease from his fingers. "Paul assured me the committee did so much advance planning after last year's event that they are confident they can make this happen."

She hoped they were right. "That's amazing! Those three…"

"I agree. What a team, right?" Mike paused, looking down at his shoe scuffing side to side on the asphalt. He went on in a more subdued voice, "Now, with that enormous question answered, we've got another one ahead of us."

Tricia nodded. "The fundraising goal. And it all depends on whether we plan to rent or buy." She glanced at the kids inside the car, but her thoughts were far away. For years, Dos Almas people had dreamed of owning their own building. Having one place clients knew they could always find help, one permanent home tailored to their needs with no threat of skyrocketing rent. Tricia crossed her arms tightly as if that could keep her from deflating right along with their dreams.

Mike went on, "That's the question exactly. Glen offered to put together a financial projection for our next meeting once we hear back on what our insurance will cover. By then, too, Anne should have located some potential properties for us. Did I tell you she has offered to reduce her realtor fees?"

Behind her, Reece started the engine. Mike flashed him a thumbs-up.

"Hey, Mom said not to get into those!" Joey yelled, reaching for Lydia.

Lydia had already torn into their precious package of store-bought cookies. But before Tricia could snatch the package away, Lydia lifted one cookie toward Mike. "This is to say thank you, Mr. Mike."

Mike bowed and accepted the cookie. "You're very welcome, Miss Prescott." He lifted the cookie to his mouth, and Tricia gasped to see a bite already taken out of it. Mike just winked at her and bit into it himself. Chewing with exaggerated pleasure, he said, "Mmm. Previously enjoyed cookies. My favorite."

Tricia tried to tell herself Dos Almas, too, would be just fine renting another previously enjoyed office. But it was hard to swallow.

Avery slid into the back corner of the courtroom, furthest from the window. A bailiff directed Zachary Jarvis into the cage with a bunch of other suspects in matching orange jumpsuits, all awaiting arraignment. Seated just a few rows ahead of Avery, Officer Sherrill, uniformed up for his court appearance, glanced back and gave her a nod. She lifted her eyebrows in a question, which he answered with a shrug.

Jarvis was up on drug possession charges only. A baggie of Vicodin. Word on the street was Jarvis was moving up the drug dealing ladder. So what was he messing around with the small stuff for? This misdemeanor would only keep him locked up for a year, max. At least a conviction would let Maddie breathe easier for a year.

Avery frowned at Jarvis, sitting smugly in the cage. If only they could nail him for trafficking. That, plus the drugs, would have jacked up the charges to a whole new level. And kept women like Maddie safer. But neither Maddie nor any of the other women Jarvis victimized were willing to face him on a witness stand. Not yet, anyway.

Avery listened to Judge Andrea Greenfield step the accused through the preliminaries. Jarvis pled not guilty, of course, though Sherrill had caught him red-handed at the park with a bunch of juveniles in tow. When the public defender assigned to Jarvis stepped forward, she caught a quick look zipping between the two of them. What was that all about? Judge Greenfield eyeballed the PD over her reading glasses, her stern look firmly in place. But Avery was worried. Sherrill was, too, judging by the way he leaned forward in his chair.

The prosecutor lingered over the presence of minors at the scene and the amount of the controlled substance found on Jarvis. Was he pushing for possession with intent to sell? So far, so good.

But then the PD spoke up. Avery strained to follow his slick talking. Something about improperly processed evidence. *What?!*

Sherrill's hackles were up. Avery could see his shoulders tighten from two rows back.

The judge pulled her glasses up her nose and announced Jarvis was free to go.

Avery clenched her fists in her lap. No, no, no—they couldn't drop the charges! Who in the world would apply that phrase, "in the interest of justice" to this crap? Avery wanted to spit. She glared at Jarvis, but the perp was too busy grinning at Sherrill to notice.

Avery erupted from her chair and stalked out of the courthouse, fuming.

Sherrill caught up with her on the sidewalk. Avery tried to rein herself in and be civil. "What just happened, Pete?"

Sherrill hooked his thumbs on his belt. "Something I'm going to have to investigate. This is the third time this month where evidence—drug evidence—has been 'improperly processed.'" He started down the sidewalk, and Avery followed. "I *know* that evidence was processed correctly—from my hands to the locker."

He shook his head and kicked at the dead grass. "Much as I hate to say it, I'm smelling something rotten in the department. I just hate to think it's someone I know."

"I hear ya."

He pulled on his sunglasses and turned to look at the courthouse. "We've got to plug the hole, wherever it is. We can't keep letting guys like Jarvis just waltz in and outta there."

Avery jammed her phone into her back pocket. "I just want this guy to swing, Pete. It's like all the crap he's committing out here in the real world vanishes when he walks through those courtroom doors. In there, we have to act like we don't know it's happening. Meanwhile..." With a yank, she zipped her jacket against the chilling fog. But she had more to say. "That slimeball! Why doesn't his head just explode?"

Sherrill's mouth twitched.

A shiny black Ford pickup rolled slowly past them on the street.

"Jarvis," Sherrill muttered.

Avery couldn't see into the cab, but it didn't take much imagination to picture the driver's gesture in their direction.

Sherrill, his eyes locked on Avery's face and his lips pressed together in a flat white line, looked as if it took a supreme amount of self-control not to watch the crook slip by. After an impudently complete stop at the corner, the engine gunned, the tires squealed, and Jarvis fishtailed off down the city street.

Sherrill shook his head. "If that scum dog kills somebody..."

Avery's eyes followed the truck's smoking trail. "Exactly what I'm afraid of."

Tricia applauded and smiled at Reece, whose grin was as wide as the camera he held trained on the stage. Lydia and Alyssa, lined up beside their little dance classmates in matching sparkly tutus, took their final bows. Drake put two fingers in his mouth and whistled loudly.

Joey turned tortured eyes toward his mother. "Are we done yet?"

Tricia hugged him. "Yes, Joey. You've been such a good sport. Just like the girls are at your soccer games."

Joey sighed. "At least they can run around during my games." He scratched his neck beneath the collar of his sweater vest. "We *are* going out for ice cream, right?"

Somehow Reece heard him over the noises of families chattering and gathering their things to leave the auditorium. "Yes siree, Joey."

Joey's smile matched his dad's now. With renewed energy, he tromped out of their row behind his brother, flipping down each folded seat and watching it bounce back up.

Just then, Tricia spotted Bob Slayter a few yards away. In his sport coat and blue jeans, the stocky man looked every bit the proud owner of Slayter Construction from whom her center had borrowed hard hats. She waved and moved to speak with him. Reece put a hand on her elbow, which she took for reassurance of his presence, even though it dragged at her a bit.

"Hi, Bob," she said, loud enough to be heard over the buzz of the moving crowd. "I just wanted to thank you for the loan of your hard hats a couple of weeks ago."

Bob nodded and smiled, less jovial than she'd seen him before. He looked down at his large, callused hands. "Least I could do. Under the circumstances."

Tricia chatted on, "Oh, I assure you it was a big help." The men still hadn't said a word to each other. Now, strangely subdued, they greeted each other with a handshake.

Tricia looked back and forth between them. Something was different, and she was out of the loop.

"Great show, huh?" Reece said, sounding a little flat.

"Yep." Bob eyed the exit. "Oh, there's Darla. Time for pictures with our granddaughter. Better go." He hurried up the aisle and out the door.

Tricia stopped and turned to face Reece. The crowd and its noises no longer filled the room. She folded her arms and said, "Okay, Reece. You have been ultra-quiet all evening. Now you and Bob are as friendly as frozen fish. What's going on?"

Reece ran a hand through his thick hair. It seemed less brown, more gray, in this light.

He began, "We never did have that talk, did we? Then we raced off to this recital so soon after I got home tonight that I missed another chance," he said.

Tricia looked uneasily in the direction Bob had gone. "I've never seen Bob so ill at ease around you. He's always been one of your best clients."

"Until this week." Reece's shoulders slumped.

Tricia felt chilled. "What happened?"

"After the earthquake, Slayter Construction's workload reached what Bob called 'the tipping point.' They finally had enough work to justify bringing on Bob's youngest son Mick as a full-time draftsman." He shrugged. "They don't need a freelancer like me anymore."

Tricia reached for a nearby seat to steady herself. "But... Reece. They were our bread and butter. Their projects alone earned you four times my salary."

Reece sighed deeply and looked up at the ceiling. "I know. Everything else I have right now doesn't even equal your salary." His gaze slid back down to rest on her. "I was so busy with Slayter and those other smaller jobs that I hadn't done much prospecting for new clients lately. Bob told me last year that this was his ultimate goal after Mick finished college. But there had been nothing more said.

The night I borrowed the hard hats, Bob told me they wouldn't be renewing my retainer contract when it ran out. It ran out Monday."

A heavy ball of anxiety dropped into Tricia's stomach. She closed her eyes. "What are we going to do?"

Reece put his hands in his pockets. "Pray. Hard. There's gotta be new work. For the same reason I lost Slayter Construction. I've started hunting up new clients, checking in with old ones. But do I also raise my rates? Or do you—" His voice trailed away.

Tricia opened her eyes. "—find work that pays better."

Maddie's voice whispered in her head, *I don't know where I would be without you. I felt totally abandoned…* Leaving Dos Almas would feel like she was abandoning Maddie and the other women she'd come to know and care about.

Reece turned to watch the lights go out on the stage behind them. "We'll have to cut back on the kids' activities…"

Tricia blinked back tears. Giving up dance would crush the girls. Those lessons were the highlight of their week. Joey, the homebody, would probably be least affected. But what about Drake and his robotics team expenses? How would he react if he had to cover it all on his own? Reece had dubbed Drake a "mood field" they had to step gingerly around. The thing with Laci had only spotlighted the challenging stage he was going through.

Reece stepped toward her and took her hand. "I can see those contingency gears of yours turning. I've been doing the same thing for the last week and a half. But let's not get ahead of the Lord, Trish. He knew this was coming. And he knows the way through. Let's ask him what to do before we go jump off any bridges. Okay?"

Tricia tried to pause the scrolling list in her head. She took a deep breath and nodded to Reece. After studying him for a long moment, she said, "I owe you an apology, Reece. You've been carrying this burden all alone for a week and a half while I've been fixated on the center. I should have been more available for you, more sensitive to what you were going through. I'm so sorry."

Reece shook his head. "I forgive you, Trish. I needed some time to process it for myself anyway. Figure out what I could do next. Check the budget, make some calculations. We can look at what I worked out later this evening when everyone is in bed. But right now, tonight is about the girls."

"Agreed," Tricia said. The settled look Reece now wore lightened the weight in her stomach. He put an arm around her waist, and they finished their climb out of the auditorium.

At the exit doors, she turned to him. "Can we still go out for ice cream?"

Reece chuckled and gave her a gentle push toward their kids waiting in the lobby. "No question where Joey got his sweet tooth."

Maddie waited for Tricia to answer her call, almost hypnotized by the snowflakes falling past the Dahlgren's living room window. They were like tiny white leaves in a frozen fall. She had missed Minnesota autumns. There had been no fall in southern California. Hardly any winter, either. It was just one long season. One long, sad season that spiraled downward from crushed dreams into a horrifying nightmare.

Lucas squirmed restlessly against her chest. He couldn't be hungry already. And his diaper was still fine. She stood and walked to the window, jiggling him gently in her arms.

"What's bugging you, Lucas? Are you teething? When do babies do that? Are you sick?" Worry made her eyes water. She had so much to learn. She would never be a good mother.

The phone still rang without answer. When Tricia did pick up, Maddie would ask her about the teething thing.

There was more she wanted to ask, though. Like, about God.

The Dahlgrens had invited her along to church yesterday, even though she wanted nothing to do with church people. Or, more accurately, she knew church people would want nothing to do with her. So, sure, she had gone along, but only to prove once and for all that God and His crowd didn't want her around. Just like Chris didn't.

But things didn't go as planned. Again.

When those red-cheeked church ladies came over to fuss over Lucas, she made no secret of being a single mom. Not married. Never was. Never would be. She'd thrown it in their faces. Couldn't have been more blunt if she'd written Prostitute across her forehead with a red Sharpie. It's like the women didn't get what she was saying. It creeped her out. She shut up after that. Just watched the parade of smiles go by, searching for the one disgusted face that would prove the others were lying.

And that pastor. Where did he learn to tell stories like that? He just opened up his big, floppy Bible and started reading. She expected a lecture on how to make yourself holy. Then, of course, every single person in the pews would turn and look at her: the one person who didn't have her act together. But what that pastor read wasn't a lecture. The words sounded more like a song she'd forgotten. Something about knocking, and seeking, and finding.

The phone stopped ringing. "Hi, Maddie. It's Paloma. Tricia is in a meeting right now. Can I help you?"

Maddie hesitated. She wasn't ready to talk about the deep stuff with anyone but Tricia. Well, Paloma was good with the baby facts, anyway. Maybe the God part could wait. She said, "Oh. Well… So, Lucas is really fussy. Could he be teething?"

"Most babies don't start teething until they're three months old or later. Does he do anything else that seems unusual?"

"Not really." But then, how would she know what was unusual? He could be dying, and she wouldn't know it. She didn't know anything. Her own mother had barely talked with her about marriage, let alone sex or pregnancy or parenting. Mama must have assumed she'd marry Chris, and there would be time to explain it all then. All those things she promised to explain later… And then she got cancer. And died.

"Maddie, it is good to hear from you," Paloma said. "Is there anything else I can do for you today?"

Eyes burning, she rubbed hard at them. There was a ton of stuff she needed. She needed a mother. She wanted Tricia. But she answered, "No, I'm good. Thanks."

"We pray for you every day. Call anytime. And give Lucas a squeeze from me and Tricia."

As Maddie hung up, Lucas whimpered and squirmed some more. She shifted him into the football hold Emily had taught her. That didn't help. She tried cradling him on his back, facing her. Tried cooing to him, like she had seen Flora do. Nope. He fussed even more, scrunching up his eyes and pressing out baby tears, his tiny fists trembling in baby rage. Nothing Maddie did seemed to help. She was useless. Zach had been right. What was she doing here? She could have just ended her pregnancy, and then this poor child wouldn't have had such a wreck for a mom.

"I'm so sorry, Lucas," she whispered.

She drew him up until they were cheek to cheek, sealed together by their tears. She just wanted him to be okay. But what should she do?

Flora entered quietly and laid the day's newspaper on the coffee table in front of her husband's dark leather recliner. With that full head of strawberry blonde hair and her plump pale blue sweater, she reminded Maddie of her favorite quilt from childhood. Flora's eyebrows dipped when she saw Maddie. "Tough day today?"

Maddie assumed she meant Lucas, but Flora only looked at her.

"Yeah..." Maddie said. Next thing she knew, she was bawling. Crying like a baby herself. She had to stop. But she couldn't. Behind her flooding eyes, a tornado was whipping up, and thoughts and fears about Mama and Lucas and Chris and Zach were flying around in her head. She had to let them out.

Tender arms circled her and guided her until the backs of her legs touched the sofa. She sat, leaning sideways, wrapped up in Flora, the quilt lady who whispered words she couldn't hear and who kept on holding her close.

Flora pressed a tissue into her hand. Then when that was soaked, another. Maddie must have cried for days and days, big hiccupping sobs, until the tornado lifted and she sat in the eerie silence. Her own words sounded small and far away. "Don't know where that came from. Sorry."

Flora patted her shoulder. "That must have been bottled up for a long time. I'm glad you could let it go a little. Crying lets some steam off, you know."

Maddie wiped her eyes. What a visual those words dredged up: Mama in the kitchen, preserving her garden produce, letting off a fountain of steam from her enormous pressure canner. She would always smile and sigh, "There's good work all done." *Oh, Mama...* Was it hard for her to be a mother, too?

Maddie remembered Lucas suddenly. He was quiet now, almost too quiet. "Flora, do you think Lucas is sick?"

Flora tipped her head to study him. She laid her soft, rounded hand alongside his face. "He doesn't have a fever. You think he's extra fussy?"

Maddie nodded again.

"Well, a mother's instincts can be pretty accurate." Flora took her arm from Maddie's shoulder and looked into her eyes. "Tell you what, let's schedule him for a check-up with my favorite pediatrician. I bet you haven't had time for one of those yet, right? That should help put your mind at ease. And if there is something going on, the doctor will know exactly what to do. How does that sound?"

"Good." She sniffed, too embarrassed at her outburst to say more.

Flora's blue eyes sparkled like a lake in sunshine. "Maddie, being a mother is a big job. Sometimes it feels impossible. All moms feel that way, on and off. But hang in there. Things should start settling down for you now. You and Lucas will develop a routine, and you'll begin to feel more confident." She smiled. "You've just started getting to know each other. Give yourself time to grow into this."

Maddie pushed her lips into a weak smile. "Thanks." *Things should start settling down.* But not if there were more tornados where that one came from.

CHAPTER 8

Tricia waited inside the back door as her groaning garage door wobbled its way down. Then she turned and tossed those three property descriptions straight into the recycling bin. She felt like tossing her cell phone in after them. Instead, she breathed deeply, shuffled to the kitchen, and placed the phone gently on the counter. Two pieces of bad news in the same evening were a bit much.

Lydia and Alyssa squealed, "Mommy!" from the living room and came racing around the corner to crash into her legs. Tricia crouched to hug them both at once, savoring the scent of their wet hair and clean nighties. Reece watched from the doorway, one finger between the pages of the storybook in his hand.

"Oh, girls, I'm so glad I made it home before you went to bed!" Tricia said, drinking in the sight of them. Had she truly only been gone a couple of hours? "May I come sit in on the story Daddy's reading?"

"Yes, yes, Mommy!" They each took one of her hands and pulled her toward the living room. She leaned back to catch a kiss from Reece on her way by. The four of them cuddled together on the sofa, one girl on each parent's lap. Reece resumed reading about the baby llama who had a hard time sleeping. Tricia was so busy soaking up the nearness of her girls that at first, she didn't know why Reece stopped and held the book out to her. Then she took it and nearly choked up as she read,

Little Llama, don't you know Mama Llama loves you so?
Mama Llama's always near, even when she's not right here.

The girls giggled and snuggled deeper. When the book was finished, Reece said, "There you go, girls. Time for bed now. Who do you want to come pray with you?"

"Mommy!'

"Daddy!"

"Mommy *and* Daddy!"

So, it was settled. Soon the girls were snug in their beds and all prayed off to sleep. Tricia followed Reece out the bedroom door, giving one final glance to the wavy blond heads on their matching Minnie Mouse pillows, bathed in the soft glow of their nightlight.

Reece took her hand and pulled her close for a longer kiss. "Come on into the living room and tell me how your meeting went. Want anything to drink?"

"Cup of tea? Thanks." Tricia kicked her shoes off under the coffee table and sank back onto the slipcovered sofa, massaging her temples.

When Reece brought two full mugs and sat beside her, she watched him with a smile. The tension from her meeting started to melt. It melted more with her first sips of Earl Grey.

"Okay, so, the meeting." Tricia placed her mug on a coaster and turned toward Reece, pulling her legs up tailor-style. "There's bad news, and there's… more bad news."

"Uh-oh," Reece said.

"Just before we met with the realtor, I got a call from one of our major donors. They have decided to terminate their regular giving. They felt bad, but something changed in their asset portfolio, they said. I don't know any more than that. No matter what I said…" She reached for her mug again to bolster her waning energy.

Reece sympathized in his mild way and sipped along beside her. Just having him there, waiting to hear the rest of the bad news, made the whole mess easier to swallow. Tricia took another sip, then went on.

"The other bad news is about the property search. Anne found four possible options for us—all with good access for our clients, locations close to our previous offices, and somewhat reasonable rents.

However, one of the properties has a landlord who is so strongly pro-abortion that he has refused point blank to rent to us."

Drake lounged into the room from the kitchen, a half-eaten banana in his hand. "Hi, Mom. Got my homework done early. Me and Joey were playing video games." He flopped into the recliner across the coffee table from her and shoved the other half of the banana into his mouth.

Reece said, "Mom was just telling me about a landlord who won't rent to Dos Almas on ideological grounds."

Drake threw his banana peel like a football penalty flag. "Whoa, hang on! Can he do that?" he asked around his mouthful of banana.

"Well—"

"You gonna sue him?" Drake's eyebrows went high.

Tricia shook her head. "No, Drake. I'd be the last person to force someone to transact business in opposition to his values. The really aggravating part is that this landlord spoke to the property manager, who happens to manage all three of the other potential properties. The first man convinced the second man that we were some kind of 'fake clinic.' And he told him that public protest against other 'fake clinics' has resulted in property damage. So now that property manager thinks we're a bad risk as a tenant."

Drake swallowed, so his cheeks looked less chipmunk-y as he said, "So, because he believes some vandals somewhere defaced pregnancy centers, this landlord won't rent to a pregnancy center now?"

"Pretty much."

"Well, that stinks." Drake leaned back in the recliner, his hands interlaced behind his head. "Couldn't you, like, offer to pay an extra deposit or something?"

"Mr. Benson proposed that to him. He didn't go for it."

Reece raised his elbow onto the back of the sofa. "What about the dream of Dos Almas buying its own building? Is that even a possibility?"

Tricia pursed her lips, shaking her head. "Not likely. Replacing the things our insurance isn't covering will really sap our bank account. We won't have enough to make a significant down payment, even assuming our banquet income tracks with previous years. All our neighbors have just been through this earthquake, too, so asking them for even more than they can usually afford to give seems kind of… inconsiderate."

Reece rubbed her knee. "People can surprise you. God can, too."

Drake stood and stretched his long arms toward the ceiling. "Yeah, Mom. Weren't you the one who was always telling me, 'Ask, seek, knock'?"

Tricia peered up at him. She never knew what to expect out of her son's mouth.

Drake, meanwhile, sauntered toward the kitchen.

Reflexively, Tricia pointed a limp finger toward the floor. "Drake. Peel." Immediately, she wanted to snatch the words back. Couldn't she just enjoy something he did right and let the rest go?

Drake returned, picked up his banana peel, and waved it at his parents on his way past. In the voice of his younger self, the one who had always seemed wise beyond his years, he repeated, "Ask, seek, knock, Mom."

"Thanks, Drake. I needed that," she said.

In the kitchen, the pantry door opened, some kind of bag crackled, and the door banged shut. Tricia's eyes shot open, but this time she held her tongue.

Drake called, "'Night," and ambled down the hall, closing his bedroom door with a click.

Through a drowsy smile, Tricia murmured to Reece, "How'd your son get so smart?"

"He's a good kid, that Drake. I have high hopes he'll turn out okay."

"It'll be by the grace of God," Tricia sighed.

"Always is."

Tricia's neck muscles slowly relaxed. She unfolded her legs and turned to rest her head on her husband's lap. He stroked her hair and then placed his hand on her head as if in a blessing.

"We'll find our way through this, Trish. You may not have to give up the work you love, and that I'm so proud of you for doing. And meanwhile, you know your family loves you. Especially me."

Tricia sighed. "I love you, too, Reece Prescott." There was something else she wanted to tell him…but it was already slipping away from her. Maybe tomorrow she would remember it. Maybe tomorrow, there would be answers for her concerns about her family… about Dos Almas… about… that other thing…

The next morning, Tricia awoke under their plaid fleece blanket, curled up on the sofa, in the pale dawn of a new day.

Maddie liked this Dr. Sarah Balinga. With her musical voice and her long dark hands moving in graceful half-circles, it was like the pediatrician was dancing in the open air and not just reciting medical facts in a sterile examining room.

"Lucas is in good health today," Dr. Balinga said, smiling widely. But before Maddie could exhale her tension, Dr. Balinga went on. "However, there is an irregularity to his heart sounds that we will want to pay attention to, especially in light of your medical history. Such things are sometimes hereditary, though rarely. For now, the sounds I hear from his little heart indicate he will not need intervention until he is a bigger boy."

Flora leaned forward in her chair to look up into Maddie's eyes. "What a good mother you are, Maddie! You had a hunch there was something to keep an eye on."

Maddie wasn't sure she wanted to be right about Lucas having a heart defect. But Flora's words still felt good in her ears.

After the appointment, bundled up against the cold, Maddie followed Flora to the faded blue Dodge Dart. She squinted and turned her head away from the icy snow that drove into her eyes and nose. At the car door, she hesitated. Yes, Lucas needed to be inside this car, to be warm. She shuddered as her hand reached for the door handle, talking herself into yet another car ride. She was with Flora. Flora was taking her home. Her safe home. Holding her breath, she yanked on the door handle and climbed inside with her baby.

Once Flora settled into the driver's seat, her hard work began. She turned the key multiple times. Silence. She patted the dashboard. "Come on, Old Blue. I know it's cold, but you can do it," she said. The next time, the car seemed to groan with effort.

Maddie pinched her nose. "I had forgotten how your nose hairs freeze when it's below zero!"

Flora waited until the engine turned over to answer. "I hear this whole week is expected to stay below zero, night and day," she said over her shoulder. "Kind of a tough time to leave the warm west coast."

"I don't think so." Cold wasn't her biggest concern. Flora gave Maddie a glance in the rearview mirror that showed she fully understood the real reason Maddie ended up here. Maddie caught the look just before Flora turned her attention to backing out of their parking spot. How did a woman say so much with just her eyes?

In the window beside her, Maddie's own face reflected back, blank and expressionless. Surviving life with Zach taught her to mask every feeling, erase all emotion. Somehow, he still read every hint of body language, every bead of sweat. And everything he read, he used against her.

Her shoulders tightened, and her panting fogged the window. She had to get her mind off Zach. After a deep breath and a backward roll of her shoulders, she cleared the window with her coat sleeve.

The shoveled sidewalks and colorful shops of Sargent's downtown slipped by, giving way to tree-lined streets bordered with neat one- and two-story clapboard houses. None of it looked familiar yet. But then, she hadn't been out much in her first two weeks with the Dahlgrens. Only that one time she went to church. Maddie watched the houses move past. She took refuge in imagining the happy families who lived inside each one. The daydream warmed her heart and drowned out the sounds of the car.

"Say, Maddie," Flora said as she steered left onto Oak Street, "isn't tomorrow the day your friends said they would come visit?"

Maddie, startled, looked into Flora's eyes in the rearview mirror. "Already?"

Flora turned the Dart into her driveway. "They said two weeks. I'll check my calendar inside."

Maddie sighed and unlatched her seatbelt, then released Lucas' car seat from its base. He stirred slightly and peered up at her through the little round opening of the cover. She tried to muster a smile for those bright little eyes. "It's gonna be cold for a minute, Little Buddy," she said, hefting him out of the car.

She clutched the hood of her coat tight at her throat and hurried to the front door as the icy cold seeped into her. Cold, she thought, might just be the best way to let things stand between her and Chris.

Tricia came out of the bathroom, toweling off her hair and humming to herself. She opened the curtains to let in the weak morning sunlight. Then her phone on the nightstand gave off the "PC ding," as she called it. She bent to pick up the phone and pulled in a short breath. Maddie.

Tricia are you there?

With a last fluffing of her chin-length hair, she sat on the edge of the bed and texted back, *Hi, Maddie. What's up?* The reply came quickly.

Got a question and need your advice.

Want me to call you?

Maddie texted a thumbs-up emoji.

Tricia dialed, praying, "Okay, Lord. Give me the wisdom she needs."

Maddie answered immediately, sounding anxious. "Here's the situation. When Lena and Chris dropped me off here, they said they would come visit in two weeks. That's today. They're probably already on their way."

Tricia tapped her pursed lips. Two weeks ago, Maddie had told her Chris was so upset over hearing more of her story he could hardly speak to her. "How do you feel about that?"

"Um, nervous. Not about Lena. But Chris—" There was a long silence. "He's disgusted by what I've done. I—I just don't know if I can face him."

Tricia frowned, waiting for wisdom. "You said you had a question that you'd like advice on. What is that question, Maddie?"

"I guess it's…" Her voice grew smaller, tighter. "How do I act around someone who used to love me but now hates me?"

Tricia closed her eyes, speaking carefully, "Maddie, why do you think Chris hates you? Did he say so?"

"He didn't have to. He was so angry…"

"Many things make people angry. For instance, I get angry when I'm scared. I get angry when someone hurts my child. What makes you angry, Maddie?"

There was a long silence before the words started trickling out. "Same. Being scared, being hurt… Lies… failing, broken promises, feeling foolish, death—" Maddie paused, then said, "Sorry, I got on a roll."

"That's a lot of different reasons to be angry. Is it possible that Chris could have a lot of different reasons of his own?"

"Oh."

"Unless he told you, you would have to guess at the reason why Chris got angry. Right now, after a long time of believing the mean things Zach said about you, it would be easy to assume Chris believes those things, too. But do you *know* that's what he believes?"

"No…"

"Even more important is what you believe about yourself, Maddie. Can you name some true things you've learned about yourself since moving back to Minnesota?"

"Um…" Her voice brightened. "Well, like, yesterday, I learned that I'm a better mother than I thought. I thought something wasn't quite right with Lucas, and I was right. The doctor found he has a heart defect like mine."

The problems this girl has to deal with. Tricia shook her head. "So, the truth is, you're a better mother than you thought. That's one. I can think of something else that's true of you. You were brave enough to leave a very dangerous situation and smart enough to seek the help you needed. Not only that, remember when you went into labor? Over the phone, you learned how to breathe through your contractions. I was amazed how well you handled that."

Maddie gave a half-hearted laugh. "Well..."

"So, how do you act when your friends visit today?" Tricia stood to her feet, looking through her window, far into the distance. "You act like Maddie, the good mother who is brave and smart and able to do hard things. You act like these are the friends who crossed the country for you, the friends who are coming to see you again, even knowing the rest of your story."

Maddie didn't answer right away. At last, she murmured, "I'll try."

Flora, her eyes sparkling, studied Maddie from the kitchen doorway. "You look extra nice today, Maddie. I've never known anyone else to dress up just to cook us lunch."

Maddie giggled like a little girl and smoothed the hem of her sweater. "I just couldn't help it. I'm hoping things go really well today."

"Of course you are," Flora said. "Nick and I can be pretty sedate company, can't we?"

Maddie grinned. "Oh, no. I kind of like how quiet your home is. It's... peaceful."

The doorbell rang, and Maddie jumped. Flora gave her a quick "so much for that" look and went to answer it. Maddie put the last of the dishes into the dishwasher, rinsed and dried her hands, checked her appearance in the gleaming microwave, and straightened her sweater three or four times as she walked out to meet her visitors.

Trying to remember Tricia's advice, Maddie put on a smile and rounded the corner.

Only Lena stood in the entry, holding a pale blue knit hat in her gloved hand and slipping off her ankle boots beside the door. Hadn't Chris come?

Maddie swallowed and tried to recreate her smile. "Hi, Lena. Here, let me take your coat." Hanging the coat in the front closet gave Maddie a clear view out the side light window. Lena's car stood empty in the driveway. Chris was nowhere to be seen.

Flora said, "Lena, Maddie, may I bring you something warm to drink? Coffee, tea? Cocoa?"

Lena agreed to cocoa. Maddie mumbled, "Same, please."

As Flora headed for the kitchen, Lena gave Maddie a warm hug. "Hi, Maddie. What a lovely outfit you have on."

"Thank you." Maddie cleared her throat. Then her manners kicked in, and she gestured toward the living room. "Would you like to sit down?"

"Yes, thank you." Lena led the way toward the couch.

Maddie lowered herself into the recliner. She could think of nothing to say. At least, nothing that would sound like small talk. After the call to Tricia, she had psyched up for having a heart-to-heart with Chris. For giving him the benefit of the doubt. Apparently, he wanted none of it.

Lena said, "It's so nice to be inside and warm."

Maddie nodded and glanced toward the kitchen. How long did it take to make hot cocoa?

Lena spoke again, "You look as if being a mother agrees with you, Maddie. How is little Lucas doing?"

For some reason, all that question brought to Maddie's mind was the heart defect she had probably passed on to her son. But saying "his life is in danger" sounded extreme. Even though it felt totally true. Finally, she eased out a mumbled, "He's doing fine."

She looked out the front window at the glare off the snow. Not a single positive thing would come to her tongue. Her sweater felt itchy. The room was way too cold. Lena and Flora must have stood a long time with the door open. Not very considerate. Where was that hot cocoa?

Maddie stood up, then sat right back down as Flora came in with their cocoa.

Flora placed each mug on a napkin on the coffee table and said, "Is there anything else I can get for either of you?"

"I'm good," Maddie said, picking up the mug and instantly burning her tongue on the first sip. She put the cocoa back down on the table, sloshing some onto her napkin. She rolled her eyes and sat back in the recliner.

When Lena agreed, Flora said, "Then I'll just slip out and tackle something fun, like balancing my checkbook. You two enjoy your visit." Her expressive eyes nudged Maddie to be courteous to her guest.

Maddie wished she could make her own eyes say, "This isn't going the way I wanted." But Flora was gone. And there was only Lena in the room.

Lena rotated her napkin a half an inch, picked up her mug, and blew across the cocoa before putting it back down.

"Maddie," she said, looking at her directly, "Chris was sorry he couldn't come with me today."

Something bitter exploded inside Maddie. "Really? Or was he just sorry that there wasn't a good reason to come?"

Lena didn't answer right away. She blew on her hot cocoa again and tried a sip. Then another. Finally, she set down the mug and clasped her hands in front of her. Her gaze rose to hold Maddie's. "Maddie, Chris took the story of your experiences very hard."

"It wasn't much fun having those experiences, either."

Lena nodded, her gaze dropping momentarily. "I'm sure it wasn't."

Maddie had never spoken to anyone this way except her mother. Lena was here as a friend when she could have stayed home. Could have spared herself the two-hour drive. She could have been as judgmental as Chris.

Maddie ran her finger around the inside of her sweater collar. "I didn't want to end up…the way I did, you know."

"Yes, I know."

"I just couldn't stand it after Mama died. You and Chris thought I could just… go on, and… do everything we'd planned as if nothing had happened."

Lena remained silent.

"I just couldn't take it anymore!" Her hands tightened into fists.

Suddenly Maddie stood and whirled behind the recliner, grabbing its upper corners. "Everything had changed! All my hopes and dreams were gone; I had no family—" She swung her hand out toward space, "—except for my father, who may or may not still be alive, somewhere. But honestly, I hope he's dead. I do. 'Cause he ruined Mama's life, and he ruined mine, too."

Lena's face was pale, but she hadn't moved. Her hands were still clasped. Her knuckles were white.

Maddie felt a new tornado building inside her chest. In Chris's absence, Tricia's words about truth blew away. The rising whirlwind whipped up all the pain she had firmly packed down inside her heart. Voices roared in her ears: Chris, her father, Zach, her mother, Dr. Balinga. Danger was mounting. Danger to her, danger to Lucas. She dug her fingers into the corners of the recliner, trying to keep this tornado from touching down and destroying everything. But the voices were driving thoughts toward her mouth with a force she could no longer control. And Lena stood there alone in the tornado's path.

Lena said softly, "Some very terrible things have happened to you."

Maddie stared at her. Couldn't she hear the roar of the tornado? Why didn't she run away? Maddie tried to push back against the storm of words, but it overpowered her.

"Yes! Terrible things happened to me! You have no idea how terrible! As bad as what my father did to my mother. And worse. But could I walk away? No! I was trapped!" She clutched the recliner in a death grip.

"But you're here now, aren't you?"

Maddie laughed. "Sure, I moved to a different state, but it hasn't all vanished. That man is still out there somewhere. I can't just wash it all out of my head, Lena." She grabbed her long hair, where it hung beside her ears. "Because he's in here, too. Sometimes I still hear his evil voice in my head, telling me how stupid I am, telling me my whole life is just one stupid mistake after another."

Maddie circled the recliner, came to stand one foot from Lena, leaned toward her face. She whispered hoarsely, "And you know what? He's right."

Lena shook her head. Were those tears in her eyes?

The tornado carried Maddie along. "It's true. And I'm not only stupid—I'm dirty. Too dirty for God and too dirty for Chris. That's why he's not here today, isn't it? He's disgusted by me. Of course he is. He's a good Christian man, and I'm a—" Maddie couldn't say the word, she hated it so much. Before Lena could interrupt her, Maddie continued. "I'm stupid, dirty, and defective. Did you know I've probably passed my heart defect on to Lucas? We just found out yesterday. And my brain must be defective too. I'm twice the nut case my mother was. I should have aborted Lucas and spared him all this!"

Maddie stumbled back suddenly and clapped a hand over her mouth.

Lena's eyes grew wide. She drew her lips in.

A tremor started across Maddie's shoulders, spreading upward to her forehead and downward to her knees. Lena, now pale and open-mouthed, rose slowly from her seat and opened her arms as Maddie toppled into them.

Big ugly sobs came rolling out of her. They were two-syllable sobs that gurgled into noises like "ugly" and "stupid" and "dirty" and "broken." They disappeared into Lena's neck and shoulder, places that smelled like home and better days, places that hadn't changed after all. For a moment, Maddie was in the arms of her mother. And the sound of her sobs changed into "Mama, Mama, I miss you. I'm so sorry. So, so sorry."

Then it was Lena again, holding her, easing her to a seat on the sofa. Maddie was aware of tissues in her hands, and Flora's voice, and Lena's saying, "It's okay." When she had wiped her eyes, Flora was gone, and only Lena's face looked back at her.

She whispered, "What's wrong with me, Lena? How could I say such a terrible thing?"

Lena placed Maddie's hand in her own. "You've needed to say a lot of things for a long time, I think. Whether you truly believe any of them—well, that will settle out when you're calmer."

Maddie's eyes filled again as she watched Lena. "I—I'm sorry. I—You—"

Lena squeezed her hand. "Maddie, I'll always be your friend. The kind of friend who loves you enough to stand with you in the storm until it passes by."

Maddie nodded. "Thank you," she whispered. They sat in silence for several minutes. After a steadying breath, she ventured, "Lena, can I ask you a question?"

"Please do."

"Mama—She wasn't always... um, unbalanced... was she?"

Lena shook her head. Her lips formed a small, sad curve. "Maddie, your sweet mother was a lovely, whole person when we were friends in high school. Your father's drinking and... abuse... made her fearful. And—as you know—fear can make a person act in ways they wouldn't otherwise. Some of her decisions, such as how to raise you and how much to tell you about adult life, were based on her desire to protect you from the experiences she'd had."

Maddie looked down at her lap. "'Adult life'—like sex."

"Yes." Lena paused before continuing, "By the time your mother began re-thinking that decision, she learned she had cancer. And soon, her disease and its treatment altered her thinking completely."

Though silent on the outside, internally, Maddie's mental gears were clanking into place. Her mother hadn't had a mental illness that could be passed on. Not the way her father had passed on his heart defect. Maddie sat up straighter. It felt like someone had just lifted a piano off her back so she could breathe. But that meant—

Suddenly, she needed another of Flora's tissues. She pressed one against the tears flooding her eyes as she choked out, "All these years—All these years, I acted like I loved Mama. Everyone always told me what a wonderful person she was. But inside, I thought she was a horrible mother. She did things that made no sense. She didn't act like other mothers. But now... Now I realize she was doing the best she could. She wasn't horrible. She was human."

Lena sat silently while Maddie mopped up her fresh tears. As she finished, she became aware of Lucas crying nearby. Footsteps approached, and Maddie looked up.

Flora, holding a very fussy Lucas, had an apologetic smile on her face. "He was crying, and it seems nobody will suit him but his mama."

Maddie stood quickly and took him in her arms. She cooed his name to him, gratitude surging in her chest. She drank in the feel of his soft, dark curls tickling her fingers, the look of his pudgy clenched fists, and the sturdiness of his warm body inside his blanket.

"Thank you, Flora." She glanced at Lena. "Do you mind if I feed him here?"

Lena's eyes crinkled. "Not at all. I can only stay a few more minutes anyway."

Maddie reached one hand out from under Lucas' blanket. "Lena, thank you so much. You have—You have helped me more than I can say."

Lena took her hand in both of her own. "I'm so glad, my dear. I'll stay in touch, and we'll set up another visit soon. Maybe I could go to church with you and the Dahlgrens?"

Facing all those strangers again might be easier with Lena beside her. "Yes, please!"

Lena smiled long and warmly into Maddie's face and then let her hand go. "I'll check my calendar and confirm that with you later."

Flora walked with Lena to the door. "Let me get your coat," she said.

Maddie settled herself and Lucas into the recliner but then turned suddenly toward the door.

"Oh, Lena, about Chris…and the stuff I said about him hating me…"

Lena pulled her pale blue knit cap over her graying blonde hair. "Maddie," she said, "if he hated you, he wouldn't have cared what happened to you." She walked back to the recliner and bent to give Maddie a soft kiss on the top of her head. "Give him time. He's not horrible. He's human."

CHAPTER 9

Tricia parked at the curb in front of Paloma's house, a ranch-style rambler with a red Spanish tile roof over creamy stucco walls. That description might fit any house in the neighborhood, but there the similarity ended. As she climbed out of the car with her laptop case, Tricia let her eyes play over the front yard. Her friend called this tumbling collection of succulents and rocks and art "God's Garden," she said, because there were always surprises here.

Like Paloma's poppies. She had once dropped a tiny California poppy seed right over there by the bird feeder. Just one. But seeds from that one little plant were the reason lacy gray-green leaves were spreading into the gaps between Paloma's plantings all along the stone walkway Tricia now followed. This spring, Paloma's yard would feature a bright orange river of bloom. Surprising abundance, from just one seed.

Tricia stepped up to knock on the royal blue front door, but paused, looking back at the poppies. Just one seed… She rapped on the door.

"Come on in!" came Paloma's voice from somewhere inside.

Tricia opened the door to the sweet aroma of freshly-baked corn bread mingled with the spiciness of her friend's famous enchiladas. Paloma rose from reaching into the oven, her well-worn oven mitts holding a glazed stoneware baking dish brimming with a rich red sauce and cheese. She placed the enchiladas on the stovetop, tossed her mitts aside, and came to give Tricia a hug.

"Your kitchen smells wonderful!" Tricia said. "I'm so glad we decided to work here today. If you had come to my house, we'd be having tuna sandwiches and pickles."

Paloma waved the compliment aside. "Everyone has their favorites." She gestured to the little tile-topped kitchen table. "Make yourself at home. These need to sit a few minutes, and then we can eat."

Paloma pulled a salad from the refrigerator and set it on the counter next to a steaming stack of cornbread squares. After she had prayed over their meal, they dished food onto their plates—the only white items in the entire kitchen—and carried them to the table. From the first forkful, Tricia felt warmed.

Between bites, the two women caught up with each other's news from the last few days of working separately. Tricia saved her best news for later, for just the right time.

After setting their dishes in the sink, Paloma sat down across from Tricia with a sigh. "Trying to do parenting lessons with our clients is difficult now. Sometimes a woman can come here. Usually, I go to their home or school or a study room at the library. But our portable DVD player is getting so unreliable. Sometimes a client will be looking forward to discussing a particular topic, and the DVD won't play. So, I have to switch topics. Or try to cover the material using only the worksheet." She leaned her cheek on her hand for support. "Not having our own office is getting old."

Tricia nodded. "I agree. But—" she leaned forward with an eager smile, "—I have some good news for you. The budget committee approved subscribing to the streaming curriculum. Now, as long as you have internet, you'll be able to teach any lesson anywhere."

Paloma leaned back with closed eyes and hands raised to heaven. "This is wonderful news! *¡Gloria a Dios!*" Then she opened her eyes and leaned forward on her elbows, frowning. "But can we afford it? I know how expensive it is."

Tricia shrugged. "The board agreed it was necessary to continuing our work. Even before the earthquake, you met with an increasing number of women off-site. This will equip us to serve women right where they are. And with automatic updates—" She stopped, interrupted by Paloma's raised eyebrow.

"That did not answer my question."

Tricia looked at her friend squarely. After a pause, she answered, "This decision will impact what we can spend on a future building. But we don't see any other option. We have to keep serving women somehow."

Paloma's hands landed on the table with a slap. "Yes. *Dios sabe lo que necesitamos.*"

A smile tugged at the corner of Tricia's mouth. "I must believe God knows. Or I could not go on. With my atrocious lack of success finding new supporters lately, I sometimes think…" She swallowed before continuing. "I sometimes think this would be a good time for Dos Almas to have a new executive director."

Paloma tipped her head to study Tricia. "My friend, such thoughts do not come out of nowhere. Tell me the rest of the story."

Tricia pinched the bridge of her nose and breathed out a long sigh. "Paloma, I suspect God may be writing on the wall for me. On the one hand, Dos Almas needs a tremendous amount of money. And I'm failing to raise it. On the other, our family's income was recently slashed to about one-quarter of what it's been. That may compel me to… look elsewhere for a job."

Paloma frowned and shook her head as Tricia explained Reece's present shortage of work. Her deep brown eyes looked ready to overflow. "Why have you been carrying this all alone?"

Tricia simply shrugged. "I just learned of it recently. At first, Reece was confident he would quickly find more clients to replace that one. But… well, it hasn't happened."

"Yet," Paloma corrected her. "It hasn't happened *yet.*"

Tricia made herself smile. "Meanwhile, we are trimming expenses—the kids' activities, date nights, new clothes, things like that. The girls are so disappointed to miss dance classes. Everyone will be moving up except Lydia and Alyssa Prescott."

"And the boys?"

"Drake went ballistic when we told him we could no longer help with robotics expenses. But then he went out and found three more lawns to mow. He's hoping that will help make up the difference." Tricia pulled her hands back to her lap. "On the flip side, Joey is absolutely delighted. Dad is home more, we're running around less—It's exactly what he would wish for."

Paloma nodded, interlacing her fingers on the table. "So maybe this season of scarcity will bring abundance to Joey's heart."

"Surprising abundance," Tricia murmured to herself. She sat up straighter. "Well, thanks for listening, Paloma. I would appreciate your prayers for us. And in the meantime, you and I still have work to do."

"Just a minute." Paloma rose to start the coffee maker for Tricia and pull her own diet soda out of the refrigerator before returning to the table. She lifted her laptop from its case beside her chair. "There. Now we can begin."

As Paloma detailed her visits with clients in the last week and what types of network referrals or material aid she had offered, Tricia once again marveled at how Paloma kept track of clients' needs and Dos Almas' resources. In her own home, Paloma had only a sampling of their print materials, diapers and formula, and some baby and maternity clothes. Everything else was scattered among the board members' houses and Tricia's garage. It was a record-keeping nightmare.

"It was about time I learned to use a spreadsheet." Paloma laughed. "Now I no longer zigzag across town for the supplies I forgot."

"Had to happen sometime, didn't it? Meanwhile, I hope you're keeping track of your mileage."

Paloma looked away. "Now and then."

"Paloma…" Tricia scolded.

"We all contribute something when things are tight." Paloma gave her a grin.

Tricia shook her head. "Paloma, Paloma… What would I do without you?"

Paloma stood and fetched a cup of freshly brewed coffee for Tricia. "You'd be thirstier."

Tricia warmed her hands on the cup and smiled. "On many levels, my friend. Many levels."

A thin shaft of winter-white light lay across Maddie's lap as she nursed Lucas on a Sunday morning. Looking at him now, she marveled at this moment. It wasn't just that the two of them were nestled up on this cozy bed, feeling welcome in the home of people who had been strangers only a couple of weeks ago. It was this: this strange satisfaction she had discovered in feeding a baby from her own body. For so long, her body hadn't been anything but someone else's plaything. Now it was hers. Hers to dress as she pleased. Hers to live in, to move around in wherever she wanted to be. Hers to share as a gift to her little baby. Crazy how that could be sort of healing.

At first, the whole thought of breastfeeding felt creepy. Repulsive. She remembered sitting in the hospital, on the phone with Tricia, who had listened to all her feelings about it, good and bad, without judging her. She could still remember the moment when she looked down at her own breasts and didn't despise them as tainted or dirty. It was when, with Tricia's voice talking her through it, she had let Lucas latch on. Her eyes had gone wide, and she almost yanked him away until it hit her: her mother had probably done this for her. She was being a mother. A good mother. The mother Lucas needed.

Now Lucas opened his eyes and turned them in her direction, still sucking. She smiled down at him and gently stroked his back with her free hand. "Hi, Lucas," she said softly. "Mommy loves you." He closed his eyes and went on nursing.

The sound of her words brought a prick of sadness. Lucas had a mommy who loved him but no one else. There was no daddy for him. No grandparents. The Dahlgrens were sweet and protective, but someday she wouldn't live here anymore, and they would welcome a new mom and baby into their home. In a way, she supposed, Lucas would always have Lena. In her latest texts, Lena had said she loved her "best friend's grandson."

Maddie reached for her phone on the bedside table and did a quick check. No, still no new text from Lena about whether she would be driving over to come to church with her today—and whether Chris might ride along. Seemed like they would have left already if they wanted to get here in time. Maybe the silence was her answer.

Just before Maddie put the phone down, it buzzed in her hand. She glanced at the name.

Not Lena. Chris. Her heart sped up. The message was a long one.

I got called in for another EMT who is sick today. Sorry I will have to miss going to church with you. But Mom is already on her way. She will meet you at the house and ride with you. If that's ok.

Maddie re-read the text. He had actually considered coming? She tapped out, *Sorry to miss you.* She added a crying emoji, then deleted the whole message. Too sappy. Instead, she added, *Glad Lena is coming. Yes she can ride with us.*

Chris had more to say. *Maddie, I really want to talk with you. Soon. Can I call you tonight? About 5?*

She stared at the words. Why would he want to call? What would he say? Was he still mad?

There was only one way to find out. She typed, *Ok. 5 is good.* She sent the text, then added, *Hope all goes well on the ambulance today. Thanks.*

And that ended it. Lucas was finished, too. She turned her attention to burping her baby and getting the two of them ready for church. She would simply try not to think about Chris and his message. She would go to church, enjoy Lena's visit, try not to think about Chris. Rest, play with Lucas, try not to think about Chris. Until five o'clock…

Lena slid into the back seat beside Maddie. Lucas cooed from his car seat on her other side.

"Everybody buckled in?" Nick asked from the front.

The last seatbelts clicked into place. "I think we're good back here," Lena said. She sounded almost excited as if they were heading to an amusement park, not church.

Nick checked the dashboard before he backed out of the driveway. "Looks like we've got some engine heat now. We'll have a nice, warm ride to church."

Lena turned to Maddie, and her smile lost a bit of its shine. "Is something wrong?"

Maddie shook her head. Then she forced herself to smile. "Sorry. I'm looking forward to this day with you." *Not sure about the call to come later. And not sure about facing all these church people.*

Lena nodded, but her smile stayed dim. God was probably like Lena. He could see right through her.

Lena squeezed her hand. "It's good to be together."

An hour later, they had greeted the church people, taken Lucas to the nursery, sung the songs, and settled in for the pastor's message. As she bent to make sure her phone was silenced, Maddie stole a glance at the people in the row behind her. Those people knew Nick and Flora had her with them because it was their job. But what did they think of Lena? Did anyone think Lena was her mother? Perhaps she should make it clear Lena wasn't too closely associated with her. Better not to tarnish Lena's reputation. Maddie scooched a few inches to the right.

The pastor dove in where he had left off the previous week. "Today, we'll look at the next time Jesus was challenged, in Luke 7, starting in verse 36." Lena found the passage in her Bible and held it up so Maddie could read along with her. But after the first few verses, Maddie's face started burning and her ears filled with a loud hum. She wanted to leave. She scratched at her jaw, then at her forehead. Out of the corner of her eye, she counted three people between her and the aisle to the right. Lena plus Flora and

Nick made three blocking her way out on the left. Oh, why had she come? This was horrible.

The pastor looked up from his reading. What a young, kind face to be pouring such burning words down on her head. It was as if he didn't know that the wicked woman from the story was sitting six rows back.

"So, picture the scene," he said.

Oh, great. He was going to elaborate. She had to get out of here, away from this story. Should she vault over the strangers? Or stumble over her friends? Sweat trickled at the edge of her hairline.

The pastor pushed on. "Here's Jesus, reclining at the table of Simon, one of the religious leaders. It's a dinner party, with several of Simon's friends seated around the table as well. And while they pretend to be jovial and friendly, their eyes shrewdly watch Jesus, the radical rabbi they don't quite trust. The air is tense.

"And then someone sneaks into the room. Luke calls her 'a sinner.' The Pharisee's reaction to her in verse 39 has led some scholars to believe she was a harlot. A prostitute."

Nausea roiled in Maddie's stomach. Her hand went to her mouth. She was going to lose it right here in church.

Lena whispered near her ear. "Are you okay?"

"I feel sick," she whispered back. But which way to escape? What a scene she'd make, standing up just as the pastor described how Jesus would condemn a woman like her.

In that split second of hesitation, a strange calm took hold of her. In slow motion, she relaxed back against the wooden pew, and everything in the room moved to the edge of her vision. The hum in her ears stopped. She could only hear the pastor, only see the story unfolding as if she was in the room with Jesus. He was looking at her. And she was that woman. The sinner.

"Look what this woman does," the pastor went on. "She slips in and kneels at Jesus' feet. She weeps so profusely that her tears wash his feet. Then she wipes them with her hair and anoints them with the perfume she carries."

The pastor's eyebrows rose as he continued, "Simon the Pharisee is appalled. Jesus has let that woman—that sinner—touch him. 'Aha,' Simon says to himself, 'this proves the man is a fraud. A real prophet would know this woman was wicked and refuse to let her touch him.'"

Maddie leaned forward. Why *did* Jesus let her touch him? Didn't he know what she was?

From beneath the podium, the pastor pulled out two huge pieces of poster board made to look like giant IOUs. "Knowing Simon's thoughts," he said, "the Lord tells him a little story. The story of two men who both owed money. One owed a little," at which he waved the IOU for 100 dollars, "and the other owed a lot." The other IOU read 1,000,000 dollars.

Wait, I've heard this before, Maddie thought.

"When the creditor saw that neither person could repay him—" The pastor ripped the two giant IOUs in half and threw them on the floor. "Done. Debts forgiven. 'Nothing more is owed,' he told the men."

A woman behind Maddie said, "Amen."

The pastor nodded at the woman. Then his gaze roamed the crowd. "Now I ask you, Sargent Christian Church, just as Jesus asked Simon: which of the men will love that creditor more?" He scanned the audience, waiting.

A man in the third row said out loud, "The one who was forgiven the most."

The pastor nodded. "Exactly. And that's when Jesus draws attention to the woman."

Maddie edged forward to listen. What was Jesus going to do?

The pastor's voice softened, almost broke.

"He says what the woman has done with her tears and her hair and her perfume is a lavish act of worship, born of a love so deep that those self-righteous Pharisees can't even comprehend it. Listen again to what he says next—" The pastor read directly from the floppy Bible in his hand: "'Her sins, which are many, have been forgiven, for she loved much…' And he said to her, 'Your sins have been forgiven… Your faith has saved you; go in peace.'"

Maddie sank back against the pew, her mouth falling open. Lena laid her open Bible on her lap and reached over to hold Maddie's hand.

The pastor concluded gently, "That woman—like you and me—is welcome to touch Jesus because he is willing to forgive the debt we all owe but cannot pay. He bought our forgiveness when he died in our place on the cross. If we want that forgiveness, all we have to do is trust what he did on that cross and receive his awesome gift. And once forgiven, we are free to go forward in peace."

Maddie closed her eyes. *Forgiven. Go forward in peace.* Was it really possible? *Jesus, you didn't just die for good people? You even died for people like me? You'd forgive…me?* Her chest swelled, throbbing, as surprising gratitude broke open the hard, protective shell around her heart. She gave Lena a wavering smile and then sobbed into her hands.

Drake leaned over Tricia's shoulder to peer at the image of the banquet invitation on her computer screen. "So, that's your theme, huh? 'Unshaken'? I see what you did there: earthquake can't stop you, right?"

Tricia twisted to smile up at him. Her son was fresh from a pick-up game of basketball. Fresh smelling, however, he was not.

Tricia wrinkled her nose but still looped her arm over Drake's shoulders and pulled him down for a quick kiss on the cheek. He barely resisted. "Heading for the shower?" she asked.

Drake rolled his eyes. "Subtle, Mom. Real subtle." He played a drum beat on the top of her recliner and loped toward the bathroom.

Tricia turned back to her screen as her phone rang.

She set her laptop aside and rose from her chair. It was Maddie's number. After a quick stretch, she answered, "Hello, Dos Almas. This is Tricia."

"Hey, Tricia."

It wasn't hard to tell the girl was smiling. "Maddie, you sound happy this evening."

"I am! Some wonderful things have happened. And I wanted to call to tell you because you and Paloma are some of my best friends."

Near-strangers as best friends? Tricia allowed herself to smile at the bittersweet compliment. "I'm honored, Maddie. What's your news?"

"So, you know I've gone to church with the Dahlgrens, right?"

"Yes… I think you have mentioned that."

"Yeah. Here in Sargent. And their church is super friendly—"

Maddie went on, raving about the church family: people who had played with Lucas in the nursery, who had welcomed her without reservations.

As Maddie continued, Tricia relaxed. Maddie was finding a place for herself in a new life. And she was far enough from her hometown that even if Zach ever acted on his threat to track her down, he would have a harder time of it. Maybe this girl really was finally free of him. Tricia tuned back into Maddie's story to hear something about her "crying her eyes out."

"—So, when the pastor asked if anyone wanted to come pray with him after the service, I did. He was so chill, Tricia. Here I thought he'd be all judgmental about my past, but he just listened to my story. Then he asked me if I believed that God loved me so much that Jesus, His Son, died in my place. That He wanted to forgive me and give me a fresh start and life forever with Him. I said, 'After that story today, yes, I do believe it!' Then we prayed together right there. Now I know, Tricia, God *has* forgiven me! He loves me."

Sudden warm tears spilled down Tricia's cheeks. "Oh, Maddie—" Her living room disappeared in a blur, and her throat tightened. This was what she and Paloma had been praying for: true, lasting freedom for Maddie.

Maddie's voice wavered. "It's like you told me, Tricia: God doesn't hate me. He loves me." Sniffles muffled her words. "And he wants to be my Father. I've never had a father like that before who loves me this much. It's going to take me some time to get used to it."

A rich silence followed. Then, in a hushed voice, Tricia said, "I've been his child for years, and I've never gotten used to it. He never takes his love away, either. He says, 'I have loved you with an everlasting love.' You now have the God of the universe for your very best friend. Forever."

Maddie either hiccupped or laughed, or both. "Crazy, huh?" she said at last.

"Oh, Maddie. There are so many wonderful things you will discover about God as you walk with him. His love is bigger than you can imagine."

"And Tricia, there's more." Maddie cleared her throat. "Remember how upset I was after Chris didn't come with his mother to see me? Well, this morning, he texted me and asked if he could call me tonight. He said he had something to talk to me about."

"Oh?" Tricia sipped her tea, wanting to moderate the girl's exuberance. It sounded like Maddie's recent spiritual experience had her hoping she and her ex-fiancé were moving toward reconciliation. But what if Chris had something else in mind? A final, definitive breakup, for example. Could Maddie's new faith withstand that kind of heartbreak?

On the other hand, if Maddie and Chris did reconcile, and this repaired relationship eventually led to marriage, what would that mean for Maddie? Didn't Chris live and work in Jefferson? If Zach actually came to track her down, could Chris protect Maddie from an angry drug dealer and sex trafficker?

Tricia took a deep breath. She was borrowing trouble from tomorrow; that's what Reece would say. She smiled into the phone. "Well, Maddie, you sound very happy about these developments."

"Yeah," Maddie breathed the word out slowly, dreamily.

Tricia searched her mind for a good coaching question. "It sounds like you're starting to gain confidence and feel stronger. Apart from speaking with Chris, are there other things you hope to do in the days ahead?"

"Yes. The Dahlgrens are helping me prep for getting a job in town as soon as I can leave Lucas for a while. I'd like to keep living here with the Dahlgrens right now. They're so good with Lucas, and I learn a lot from them. It's like I'm part of an intact family for the first time in my life. Someday, I want to have a relationship like Nick and Flora's."

"Listen to you! You're setting career goals, relationship goals… You've come a very long way in a short time."

"I guess I have." She laughed. After a brief pause, she spoke again in a more somber tone. "Another reason I like it here is that Sargent is far away from Jefferson. I doubt even Zach would come this far out in the country if he ever decided to come looking for me."

Relieved to hear Maddie still considered her own safety, Tricia asked, "Have you heard anything about him?"

"Only one thing from Avery. She said the police are keeping an eye on Zach because of his drug dealing. But right now, there's nothing to stop him from driving to Minnesota any time he wants to. She said to 'stay watchful'."

"Good advice." Tricia was glad Maddie couldn't see her frown. She, too, had talked with Avery. Her friend had shot down her naïve hope that Zach would leave Maddie alone if only he figured out she didn't steal his cocaine. Avery's reply had been chilling: *Drugs can only be sold once; women and children over and over. Guess which one Jarvis wants back most?*

Tricia heard a baby fussing in the background. She should probably end this call on a positive note. "Maddie, you have implemented a good safety plan. Now you can leave the unknowns in God's hands. Remember how much he loves you."

"Yeah. That's right." The brightness came back into Maddie's voice. "I just wish God would tell me Lucas and I were safe. Once and for all."

Tricia opened her mouth and then closed it. Only God could teach Maddie about true safety.

Maddie spoke again, "Well, Lucas is ready for both a change and a feeding. I'd better go. But please don't tell my news to Paloma. I want to call her myself."

"Of course. Thanks so much for telling me your happy news."

"You bet, Tricia. God bless you!"

She'd taken the words right out of Tricia's mouth. "You too, Maddie."

Tricia laid her phone down gently on the table and sat perfectly still. *Oh, Lord my God. The things you can do...*

Finishing off the last of her lukewarm Earl Grey, she closed her eyes and savored the comfort. Around her, ordinary family sounds ebbed and flowed like waves on the shore.

Joey emerged from his bedroom, padding toward Tricia in his blue flannel pajamas, his math book under his arm. "Mom, can you help me with my homework?"

She patted the cushion beside her with a smile. "I'd be delighted, Joey."

He plopped down on the sofa and gave her a sideways glance. Then he slowly leaned over until his damp, tawny head rested against her upper arm. "I'm glad you're here, Mom."

"Me too, Joe-Joe. Wouldn't miss this for the world."

He twisted to look up at her, his face quizzical. "What, math?"

She circled him with both arms and hugged him tightly. "No, silly. You."

True to his word, Chris called at five o'clock. Maddie grabbed her phone and the baby monitor and snuck a quick look at Lucas in his crib. He slept soundly with his head turned toward his raised fist. She slipped out and down the stairs, past the living room, where Flora read the paper and Nick dozed in his recliner. She hurried into the kitchen. Breathless, she answered the phone on the third ring.

"Hello?"

"Hi, Maddie. It's Chris."

Old, familiar words. "Hi, Chris." He didn't say anything for a moment, so she asked, "How was work?"

"Quiet, mostly. We were called out to a fender-bender. A car slid on ice, right past a stop sign and into another car. Fortunately, it was a low-speed impact, so there wasn't much for us to do."

"Oh. Good."

"Yeah." Another silence passed between them. Chris cleared his throat. "Say, Maddie, could I come see you?"

She put a hand to her cheek, suddenly warm. "Um, okay… When?"

"I could come right now. I'm, uh, parked out front of the Dahlgrens.'"

CHAPTER 10

Chris sat in his red Jeep Renegade, watching the Dahlgrens' front window. There she appeared, phone in hand, sunlight catching in her gorgeous red hair.

He waved tentatively.

Maddie laughed in his ear. "Oh my gosh! What are you doing out there?"

"Requesting permission to enter," he said. When she beckoned him in, Chris tapped the End Call button and clambered out his door. He fumbled his phone into the icy slush at his feet. When he straightened up, wiping it on his sleeve, Maddie had disappeared from the window. He stuck his phone in his pocket and zipped his coat, bracing himself for the conversation ahead.

Then, there she was, in the doorway, with her arms wrapped around herself.

Two hours of rehearsing his speech, gone, just like that.

He had to stop staring and get himself up the driveway. Maybe the words would all come back once he settled down. Or maybe he should just shoot from the hip. When he asked the Dahlgrens' permission to visit, that's what Nick told him. Be yourself, he said, be honest. Maddie hadn't had much honesty for a long time. Chris squared his shoulders and started up the driveway.

He stomped slush off his shoes on the welcome mat. "Hey, Maddie," he said.

"Hey yourself. It's freezing out there. Come on in." She turned and led the way inside.

He pulled off his black knit cap and stuffed it into a coat pocket. He reached up to smooth his cowlick down at the same moment Maddie reached for it, too, just like she used to. She pulled her hand back with an awkward little laugh.

Slipping his shoes off gave him a reason to pretend he hadn't noticed her embarrassment. Nor the sweet, familiar, half-teasing look that had flashed across her face, then disappeared in an instant. Fast enough for him to doubt he had truly seen it. He started shrugging off his coat and then hesitated. "I hope it's not a problem, me just showing up like this."

"Not at all," she said. "A surprise, maybe, but not a problem."

The Dahlgrens, both a little disheveled and drowsy, rose from their recliners and came over to greet him. Chris wondered how much, if anything, they had told Maddie about his coming.

He got his answer when Maddie launched into a rapid-fire introduction. "Nick and Flora, this is Chris, my friend from Jefferson. He's the one who drove me here. With his mother. Lena. Oh, but... you probably... remember that..." Her mouth closed abruptly, and a faint blush colored her cheeks. She clasped her hands in front of her.

Flora smiled as if all this was the most natural thing in the world. "Hello, Chris. It's nice to see you again. May I hang up your coat for you?"

"Sure, thanks." Chris handed it over.

Nick shook his hand. "Hi, Chris. Welcome. Come on in where it's warmer." He walked ahead of them to the living room and then turned and said, "Day like today, we ought to have something hot to drink. I can offer either coffee or cocoa. What'll it be for you ladies?"

In unison, Flora and Maddie said, "Cocoa!"

Nick turned to Chris, who asked for black coffee. "Got it. Coming up."

Flora followed him from the room, saying over her shoulder, "We'll have those ready in no time. You two just get comfortable."

Comfortable wasn't even on Chris's radar at the moment. He took a seat near the far end of the sofa. At the other end, Maddie sat down. Perched, really, on the edge of the cushion. Like she would fly if she had to.

Maddie's eyes watched the Dahlgrens go. When she glanced back at him, there was something cloaked about her. Was she nervous? Scared? Suspicious?

He licked his lips, letting his gaze roam the room. Trying to see this encounter as Maddie would. After all, last time they spoke, he was furious. Couldn't wait to leave her and go home. She was probably gearing up for him to attack her again. Wondering what more he could possibly want to say to her now.

She was studying him. Holding her face completely still. Only her hands moved, fidgeting in her lap. So, then, she was scared.

He'd better explain. "It was sure nice of Nick and Flora to let me come visit you."

Her head lifted slightly.

He went on, aiming for casual. "They have quite the screening process, you know. Not just anybody can walk through that door."

Still, she said nothing.

"Yeah, Nick gave me quite the grilling when I asked permission to come talk to you."

Maddie's face softened for a split second. A smile flitted across her mouth, then disappeared. "I see," she said quietly.

This was where his practiced speech was supposed to go. If only he could remember it. He finally turned to face her directly and just dove in. "Maddie, there's something I've been needing to say to you."

Maddie looked down at her fingers, intertwining one way and then another. "Okay…"

Chris shifted position again and cleared his throat. "Maddie, I want to tell you I'm sorry for the way I reacted when you told me what you'd been through. I was totally wrong to act that way."

Maddie shook her head in short, tight motions, eyes still on her hands. "No, it was all my fault. I made the stupid decision to run away and mess up my life. And then… to tell you everything like that. All at once, without any warning or anything—No wonder you freaked out. It's all so ugly."

Chris shook his head. "Ugly or not, my response was wrong. I was angry and judgmental, and I hurt you." He sighed. "Maddie, can you ever forgive me for how badly I acted?"

She stared at him, unmoving, for the longest time. He wished he could read her mind. It was like she was trying hard to understand what he had said.

When Maddie spoke, she almost coughed out her words as if she were clearing them of dust and cobwebs. "Me?" she said. "Forgive you?"

With sudden and profound clarity, Chris realized he was offering Maddie a chance to regain a sense of power she had long lived without. He leaned toward her earnestly. "Yes. Please, forgive me, Maddie."

Her hand darted toward his, then pulled back. "Oh. I—I do. I do forgive you, Chris. Completely."

Chris inhaled deeply. "Thank you, Maddie." He relaxed, feeling a load lift from his shoulders. More remarkable, however, was the new light in Maddie's eyes and the way she sat taller now.

Flora and Nick entered just then, a steaming mug in each of their hands. Chris turned to take the mug Nick offered him.

"There you go," Flora said, placing Maddie's cocoa on the coffee table before her. "I hope you'll excuse us, but our son just texted. This is our chance to have a video call with our granddaughter for her birthday. If you don't mind, Maddie, we'll be around the corner in the kitchen."

Maddie answered, "Sure. I mean, no, I don't mind. We're… just fine…here."

Chris found her awkwardness strangely encouraging.

Maddie caught him watching her. She ducked her head and reached for her cocoa. He did the same, hoping to put her at ease. A little.

After blowing the steam from her mug several times while sneaking glances at him, she lowered it to the coffee table. She spoke in a voice so quiet he had to crane forward to catch each word. "To be perfectly honest, Chris, what you said wasn't any worse than I expected. I mean, from anybody. For so long I've felt just …dirty. Disgusting. So, your reaction didn't surprise me. I thought that was exactly what I deserved."

"No. That's not true. You are a precious human being. What you deserve is to be treated right, to be protected. Not betrayed or abused. And certainly not judged by me."

Maddie cocked her head like a curious little bird. He would have given anything to know what she was thinking. Had he messed up somehow, said the wrong thing? He was trying to speak the truth carefully while reining in the feelings rushing around inside of him. Even though Maddie said she forgave him, knowing he'd hurt her still ripped up his heart. If only he could take back his earlier words, reverse his actions. Yet the feelings that drove him to react that way were real. And he needed to be up front about that part, too.

He took another swig of his coffee but barely tasted it. Maddie no longer looked puzzled, but she remained silent. Could he really say what he wanted to? It was time to try. He wrapped both hands around his warm cup. "You know, Maddie, after the day I brought you here, I had to think long and hard about why I was so angry. Finally, I figured it out. Most of it boiled down to being angry that all those terrible things had happened to *you*. To you, my… my friend Maddie. And I was angry that… I wasn't there to protect you from it all."

Maddie's lips parted. But instead of speaking, she stood and walked over to the front window.

Crud. He must have said too much. Maybe she wasn't ready to hear that he still cared about her. But surely she had to know. Driving clear across the country wasn't something he'd do for just anyone. She did realize that, right?

She didn't move, didn't speak. Just looked out the window. Chris was suddenly warm. Too warm. He put the coffee down but never took his eyes off Maddie's back. What if she didn't care about him the way she once did? What if, now that he thought he might stand a chance of winning her back, she wanted to go forward without him? All his life, she had been the only one for him. Only Maddie. Could he let her go—again?

Chris stood slowly, wishing he knew what to do next.

After an eternity, she turned to face him with misery in her eyes. Then words came pouring from her mouth. "Chris, I'm the one who needs to apologize," she said. "For years and years, you were nothing but good to me. Then I broke off our engagement and ran away, chasing some crazy dream of a new life in California."

She turned her face to the farthest corner of the ceiling. "Ugh, I was such an idiot. What was I thinking?" Maddie's hands squeezed each other, and she dropped her gaze to the floor. "I wasn't thinking. I was just angry. Angry at God, angry at life, at my mother—and I took it all out on you. I hurt you so much, and you didn't deserve that at all. I am truly, truly sorry. So…I guess it's my turn." As her chin trembled, she hurried to ask, "Can you ever forgive me for the way I treated you?"

Chris came around the coffee table. He'd had four long, painful years to wrestle with this question. And only in the last few days had he finally been able to answer it. "Yes, Maddie. I already have. Completely," he said and opened his arms to her. She covered her face with her hands. He stepped forward, touched her arms, but she winced and stepped back.

"Please…" she whispered, sniffling. "I'm glad you're close. But I can't… yet."

He frowned. *She "can't" what?* Then Nick's cautionary words clicked into place. He had warned Chris not to expect Maddie to flip a switch. For four traumatic years, every male touch she had experienced was connected to sexual abuse. Unlearning that connection would be a long, slow process. Nick had urged him to be patient and earn her trust all over again.

To Maddie, he said only, "Of course." But every inch of him was clamoring for her. After all these years without her, she was right here. In this room. He wanted to sweep her up in his arms, hold her tight, feel the familiar fit of her against him.

God, help me.

He had to keep his head on straight here. The last thing Chris wanted was to be just like all those animals she had been thrown to in the last four years. He needed to give her some space. Give himself some space.

Maddie drew a long, ragged breath. The day might come when he could catch all her tears on his shoulder. But today was not that day.

She used her sleeve to wipe her eyes, then lifted them to meet his.

She was so lovely, even with puffy eyes and smeared mascara. After all they had been through together, this was vintage Maddie. He gave her a gentle smile and stilled his hands by pushing them into his pockets.

She had forgiven him; he had forgiven her. The slate was clean now. But was that all he wanted?

He had come all this way. He had to ask. Especially when she looked at him like that.

His voice came out husky, "What do you think, Maddie? Think we can start over? Can we get to know each other again and see where we go from there?"

Maddie nodded and dabbed at her eyes with her cuff. She sniffed once more and added, "I would like that. A lot."

Chris sighed, relieved. "Ah, Maddie. Me too."

Tricia woke with a start, her heart jumping around in her chest. She stared into the darkness of her bedroom. What had awakened her? Reece snored softly at her side. It wasn't him. No sounds from the kids' rooms—

Her phone flashed once, with a soft buzz on the nightstand. A text. Rarely a good thing at this hour. One hand flew across to pick up the cell phone as the other unplugged it from the charger, and her feet met the floor almost before she finished her mental question. Only then did she check the incoming text.

Tricia? the message read. From Tanisha's number.

Barefoot, Tricia tiptoed across the soft shag carpet and out to the living room. *What can I do for you Tanisha?*

zach got me into his truck. taking me to MN to help him find Maddie and his coke. Im screwed.

Where are you now?

gas station bathroom riverside

Can I call you?

no cant talk

Has he hurt you?

yes

Do you need help?

gotta go hes banging on door

Keep in touch.

The messages ended. But Tricia's mind, now fully awake, flooded with all the things she could have and probably should have said to Tanisha. Plus all the danger this implied for Maddie and Lucas. She stood and paced the living room, wishing the phone would buzz again.

Zach was making his move. But Tanisha was with him. She was in danger but also in a position to keep Tricia apprised of Zach's whereabouts. That is, *if* she kept possession of her phone. If she was under the power of this drug-dealing sex trafficker... Tricia shuddered. She ran through Maddie's safety plan in her mind, trying to detect any weaknesses that Zach might exploit. Why did Zach think he needed Tanisha? A hostage?

Tricia craned her neck to see around the corner into the kitchen. The blue digital clock on the microwave read 5:30. That would be 7:30 Minnesota time. She drummed her fingers on her leg.

It would take Zach and Tanisha days to get to Minnesota. Two days? Three? Had Maddie ever filed a restraining order? What else could Maddie do to protect herself? Avery would probably know.

She would have to call Avery when morning came. In the meantime, though, Zach would get that much closer to Maddie.

Tricia drew a deep breath. It was time to tell Maddie. She texted, *Maddie, I need to talk with you as soon as possible. Please call me.*

She waited.

Outside, the streetlights dimmed as dawn tried to break. The clock said Zach was two minutes closer to Maddie. Tricia pressed her fingertips against her clenched brows. *God, stop that man. Free Tanisha. And please, oh please, keep Maddie safe.*

Maddie parted the lined blue curtains, letting morning sunlight flood her second-story room. Where a dull grayness had so long smudged the boundary between snowy land and dreary sky, now a brilliant blue silhouetted all the rooftops she could see from her window. Beautiful.

She sighed, half hoping the sound would wake Lucas, so she could see his happy little smile on this bright morning. But no, he slept on. Maybe that meant he was getting over the flu, or whatever had made him spit up more and act so fussy lately.

Maddie couldn't sleep in, though. She felt a surge of joy flowing in with the sunlight and blue skies. Apparently, so did the neighbors. There were people stirring up and down the street.

She pulled on the hoodie she wore yesterday, right over her flannel PJs. It might be sunny, but this was still the coldest winter she could remember. This morning, the radio announcer had listed all the Minnesota cities where the temperatures broke records. Snow was piling up everywhere, hardening in place.

A neighbor's snow blower started up across the street. Maddie returned to the window to watch. Snow was already piled five feet high on either side of his driveway. Still, the man pushed the blower forward into the fresh drifts in the driveway. Maddie admired his determination. But the machine couldn't fling the new snow high enough to top the snowbanks. It just hit the piles and fell in a heap beside them. The man finally stopped, rolled the blower back into the garage, cut the engine. He came back out with a shovel.

Just the thought of shoveling snow made Maddie's neck and shoulders ache. Each crunching scrape of the man's shovel took her back to that Christmas break that now seemed so long ago. She could feel, all over again, the cold pressing against her face and numbing her fingers through her gloves. The sweat trickling inside her parka. The fear and anger tightening her chest. She'd come home from college and needed to do something—anything—outside the house. Mama watched her from her chair by the front window where Chris had placed it. He had said he wanted her to see something other than her bedroom walls.

Sometimes Mama lifted a hand to wave. But Maddie tried not to look. That hand Mama waved was a knobby claw. She was wasting away. Her skin had gone thin and papery, her whole body older than her years. When she slept, her lips were always parted, drawing back from her teeth in a skeleton's grimace.

Maddie had shoveled with a vengeance, scooping and tossing that heavy snow while her cheeks glazed with frozen tears. When she finished, she hung her shovel on the garage wall and stomped the snow off her boots. After one last deep breath of lung-burning air, she opened the squeaky back door as quietly as she could. Hoping Mama would be asleep. Hoping she wouldn't have to see Mama's watery eyes and wan smile. Hoping that strange, raspy voice wouldn't thank her yet again for all her help.

Oh, Mama. Maddie wished she had handled it all so much better.

She had never gone back to school after that Christmas. Couldn't bear to be away from Mama. Couldn't bear to be with her, either. But she had stayed at home. Lena and Chris came so often, they practically lived there. They carted in huge warm meals to share, cleaned the house when Maddie forgot, sat with Mama and talked quietly, or just held Maddie's hand.

They were trying, Maddie knew, to keep her from caving into the darkness that had plagued her since the dark days of her childhood, since the first time she'd encountered someone who had been, well, like Zach. She squeezed her eyes shut, pressing the memories back down. She'd trusted that neighbor. But he made her feel vulnerable and dirty. The shame had kept her from ever telling Mama. Mama had her own battles to fight. In the end, she fought cancer and lost.

During that last battle, Maddie's troubled heart had shriveled tighter and tighter. It formed a hard, protective casing around the fear that was gnawing away at her like a parasite: she would be all alone. Mama was leaving her. Chris, home from the military, would soon be busy with his EMT training. That sharp loneliness she saw approaching on the horizon shadowed the last few days she had with her mother.

Then when Chris proposed to her in the middle of it all, some tiny un-hardened remnant of her heart had cried out for his love. So she said yes. After all, they had planned this from the time they were kids. While spinning themselves dizzy on the tire swing under his tree fort, they had mapped out all the steps. Go to college, marry Chris. It was just the next thing to do. It was easier than trying to come up with anything else.

But two weeks later, Mama had died. Her frail and ancient-looking body was placed in the satin-lined casket. And when the lid closed, Maddie closed her heart, to anything and anyone that reminded her of her past.

She wanted something new then, something entirely different. And she got Zach.

Lifting her face to the blue sky beyond her frosty window, Maddie scrubbed at her eyes with the cuff of her hoodie, wishing to erase the memory of Zach. The movement brought traces of a familiar aftershave fragrance drifting around her face. She closed her eyes again and this time breathed in Chris's aroma like fresh air. Now, she was getting a second chance at life, at happiness. And this time, she knew she wasn't alone. Not just because of Chris. God would never leave her. She was convinced of that now, deep down inside.

She had a future. And if Chris wanted to give their relationship another try, then things were looking up for both her and Lucas. Warmth from her heart poured out in a smile.

She spun from the window with a giddy desire to whisk Lucas up from his crib and dance around the room with him. Little noises told her he must have awakened.

Maddie bent over his crib and froze in terror. Why was he twitching and jerking like that?

"Lucas, baby?" She grabbed his spastic left hand, but his fingers stayed tightly curled upon themselves. His eyes stared through her. She put her face directly over his, but it was like he couldn't see her. She cried out, inches from his face, "Lucas! Lucas! What's wrong?"

Her baby continued to twitch as if invisible strings jerked his left arm and leg. His mouth made strange chewing motions below eerily vacant eyes.

"Flora!" she screamed toward the door. "Flora! Help me!"

Dr. Balinga's graceful hand caressed Lucas's dark hair, where he lay quietly in Maddie's arms. As Maddie watched the doctor's long fingers, she fought the urge to pull her baby away from the woman. She told herself, "The doctor is here to help. It's not her fault something's wrong. She's here to help."

"Lucas did very well during the MRI scan," Dr. Balinga said. Her hand drew back to rest on the folder on her lap. "We were able to get a good look at what is going on in his sweet head." Dr. Balinga went gently to the point. "Based on your description of his seizure and the information from the scan, it appears Lucas has a tumor at the base of his brain. The seizures and the amount of fluid we saw in the scan would indicate that it has probably been growing there for some time."

Maddie gulped for air and leaned away from the doctor and her horrible words, clutching Lucas to her chest.

Flora put an arm around Maddie's shoulders.

Dr. Balinga reached for the plastic model of a skull that she had carried into the room. When she lifted the top off it, Maddie felt dizzy. She tried to focus on the doctor's words more than her gestures.

"This is where his tumor is located," the doctor said. "It may be exerting some pressure on his brain stem and cerebellum and blocking the flow of cerebrospinal fluid that keeps his nervous system healthy. So, you were wise to bring him in right away. Have you seen him have a seizure before today?"

Maddie shook her head, over and over, as if she could make this nightmare go away.

"Any vomiting? Unusual fussiness?"

Maddie cringed, remembering. "Yes," she whispered.

"Those symptoms often accompany tumors like this."

"I thought he just had the flu or something," she said to Flora. *I knew it. I'm a terrible mother. I should have realized*—She folded her lips back into her mouth and bit down to keep from crying out.

A brain tumor. Cancer. Lucas was going to leave her, too. How could God do this to her? Just when she'd been sure he loved her. Liquid heat burned lines down her face.

Flora squeezed her shoulders and waited. When Maddie said nothing, she spoke up. "What can be done for Lucas, Doctor?"

Dr. Balinga carefully put her model aside. In her velvety voice, she answered Flora's question while looking directly at Maddie. "Your little boy needs to be seen by a specialist who can help you decide on the best treatment. There are specialists who care for infants like Lucas—they are called neonatal oncologists. Do not give up. Lucas still has a chance."

Flora's voice stepped into the tide of Maddie's rushing fears. "Did you hear that, Maddie? Don't give up. We will do everything we can for Lucas. And we will pray. Because God can do more."

Maddie could only stare at Flora through wide eyes that kept blurring with tears.

Dr. Balinga opened her folder and pulled out a half-sheet of paper. She handed it to Flora. "This is the one specialist I highly recommend: Dr. Jackson Murphy. He has had remarkable success and is highly esteemed in this field. I understand he has been perfecting a new surgical technique for infants. If anyone can help Lucas, it is most likely to be Dr. Murphy."

Flora scanned the referral sheet. Maddie closed her eyes until Flora spoke. "How soon should we see the specialist?"

Dr. Balinga pursed her lips. "As soon as you can get there. This tumor has been growing for some time, as I said. Until now, his unfused skull bones have flexed to make room. But the seizure signals that the growth is now creating serious problems. Time is of the essence."

Maddie rocked forward and back in her chair. Questions ping-ponged in her head. How would she get Lucas to this doctor? What if he said it was too late to save Lucas? How could she ever pay for a specialist? Was Lucas going to die? Did God hate her after all?

Dr. Balinga placed a gentle hand on Maddie's. "Are you all right? May I get you some water? Or something warm to drink?"

Maddie felt wooden. Her heart hammered and her arms stayed locked around Lucas. She couldn't stop shivering. Then some faint hint of the doctor's words finally reached her.

"Cocoa," she whispered. "I want cocoa."

"Of course." Dr. Balinga rose and opened the door, signaling a nurse and passing on Maddie's request. When she faced them again, she said, "If you decide to see Dr. Murphy, I can call his office today and reserve his earliest appointment for you."

Maddie could only stare at Flora. Her mouth wouldn't move.

The doctor's slim hands made a graceful figure eight between them. "While you talk it over, I will see about the cocoa."

As the door closed behind Dr. Balinga, Flora offered to take Maddie into a hug. But Maddie had gone rigid. This was no time to be soft, to let the tears flow. They might never stop. Maddie closed her eyes hard and waited until her voice would come out steady. Then she said, "I want Lucas to have the best chance possible. I think I should take him to Dr. Murphy."

Flora patted the hand that cradled Lucas' head. "That sounds like a wise choice."

Maddie stifled a shuddering breath. Flora's approval thawed her clenched jaw, threatening to melt her altogether. When she dared to turn her eyes toward Flora's, Maddie asked, "Can you possibly take us there?"

The corners of Flora's mouth rose slightly. "I would gladly take you and this little boy anywhere in the world. Maybe you would like to call Chris and Lena, too, and have them meet us there?"

Maddie nodded, then stopped. "I can't call them. My phone isn't charging. Can you call?"

"Certainly. We'll pick up a new charger for you on our way." She went on, "Maybe Nick will even come along for moral support. Let's see… We'll be heading to—"

Flora frowned as she read the referral sheet. Her expression made Maddie's eyes go wide. Flora glanced up, then back at the paper. She seemed to be smoothing the concern from her face.

"Where?" Maddie asked. "Where is this doctor's office?"

Flora held out the paper toward Maddie. "St. Olaf Children's Hospital. In Jefferson."

Avery's phone buzzed in her back pocket yet again. As soon as the police were done interviewing this runaway sitting beside her, she would be free to find out what everybody was texting her about so early in the morning. Meanwhile, she had to stay focused on the girl slumped in the chair. The kid was clearly scared about speaking up for herself against the abuser who had called in the missing person report. The same man who was now waiting out front planning to take her home with him.

Eventually, Officer Wong had heard enough to get the picture. He agreed to bring her abuser into a separate room for questioning, allowing Avery to get the girl out and away. Keeping the two from catching sight of each other at this small station was tricky but critical. But this officer knew the drill well. Avery had to admit it: she got a rush from all this cloak-and-dagger stuff. And she never forgot that the slumped girl in the chair had once been her.

Slipping into the hallway, she closed the door and leaned back against the wall. She made a visual sweep of the station and reviewed their exit plan. The abuser was at the front desk area, separated from them by some windows of frosted bullet-proof glass. So far, so good. Subtly, beside her leg, she gave a quick rap on the door. Officer Wong then stepped out, giving Avery just a moment to send a reassuring nod to the runaway inside before he closed the door.

"Five minutes," Wong said, then went up front.

Avery's moving eyes stopped at a newly cleared desk, the one where she used to see Officer Steven Cobb at work. She hadn't really liked the guy—a little too slick for her taste—but she hated to think he might have been killed in the line of duty. Maybe he just moved on to another precinct. She ought to read the paper more. *Yeah, in all my free time…* She pulled out her phone but hadn't even opened to the texts when Officer Sherrill stopped beside her.

"Hey, Avery. There's been a breakthrough you might want to hear about. Stop at my desk later?" His eyes sparked like he'd won the lottery.

"Can't. Gotta escort a client," she said. "Tell me here?"

He opened the file he held, just far enough that she could see the name inside.

Zachary Jarvis. Avery stepped away from the wall. He had her attention.

"Okay," he said, "the quick version. We have at least one witness that has agreed to testify to being trafficked for a reduced drug possession charge."

"Whoa." This was good.

"Yeah," Sherrill said. "Only one problem. Jarvis has skipped town. We know he's gone, but not where."

"Figures." Avery blew out her frustration. Finally, someone he had hurt comes forward willing to risk testifying, and the guy runs. Would the woman be intimidated into recanting by the time law enforcement caught up with him?

"Oh, and by the way..." Sherrill lowered his voice and slid his eyes toward Cobb's desk and back. "The department plugged that hole you and I were worried about. When we catch Jarvis this time, the evidence will be properly processed."

Cobb was crooked? Antipathy aside, Avery wouldn't have guessed that one. She studied Sherrill, who said no more. There must have been a long, convincing trail of evidence for them to move so fast against one of their own. Now, if only they could catch that slippery fish, Jarvis. She tapped Sherrill's file folder with a knuckle. "Well, a creep like this is bound to cause trouble wherever he goes. He'll be back on the radar before long."

Lots of developments. But she had to stay focused on the girl behind her. She checked her phone clock. Three minutes left. When yet another text came in, she gave it a quick glance. *Tricia.* Then something else caught her eye. She opened the text.

"Okay, I'll let you get back to work—" Sherrill said, turning away.

She waved him back. "No, wait, hold on. This may be our guy."

"He texts you?"

"No, but something's going down." She showed him the phone.

Avery, a woman I know has been taken by Zach Jarvis to MN to help him find Maddie. I haven't been able to get through to Maddie. I need to talk with you soon about this. Please call when you can.

He inhaled, and the sparks reignited in his eyes. "This could bring him down," he said. "But we'll have to play it just right."

"No kidding, Pete," she said. She fixed his gaze with her most laser-like look. "There's now a woman trapped in the middle."

Avery's phone registered one minute to go. She tipped her head toward the door at her side. "Let me get this one settled safely, and I'll get back with you."

"Good. I'll call his plates in to the Minnesota troopers and see what they can do for us."

Avery gave him a thumbs-up. Just then, Wong's shape moved past the frosted window. Pretending to scroll through her Facebook feed, Avery leaned back against the wall. Wong walked the girl's abuser past her into an interrogation room two doors down and shut the door. Avery clicked off her phone, counted to ten, then led her client out to freedom.

Tricia silenced her cell phone with a sigh. She still hadn't reached Maddie. She would just have to try again after this board meeting. Meanwhile, she hoped Maddie was right, and Zach would never think to look for her as far away as Sargent.

Dr. Joe Walker opened his front door to her. "There you are, Tricia. Everyone's in the dining room." He thrust a printed property description into her hand. "Look what Anne found."

Tricia scanned the sheet as they walked. Dr. Joe said, "I had a friend who used to practice in this building, so I know it well. The floor plan would be ideal."

Tricia's ears perked up. "Did your friend retire recently?"

Dr. Joe laughed. "No, he moved away. He's a young guy, just getting started. Keith Bair, a fine Christian pediatric specialist." He pulled out a chair for Tricia.

Anne stood at the head of the dining room table, surveying the board members whose excitement was almost palpable. "It seems you can tell why I thought this property deserved your attention."

Mike's voice cut through the buzz of discussion, "This place has great potential. I can see where we'd have ready-made educational rooms, staff offices, a boutique for material aid, and probably storage space for donations. Even room to grow into those medical services we've been hoping to add."

Tricia knew from the way his face turned somber what Mike was about to say.

"But the price is currently beyond our reach."

A muted hum of voices gave disappointed assent. Tricia dropped her gaze back to the sheet. 480 Main Street—an ideal downtown location. Near the bus line—easy access for moms without cars. Up to date, with little or no remodeling needed. Tricia's words slipped out almost before she realized she had spoken. "I think we should see it. Take a tour."

Mike's eyebrows rose above a hint of a frown.

Tricia went on, looking at each of the board members in turn, "Mike just said it's *currently* beyond our reach. I suggest we pray about it and tour it before we decide it's also out of God's reach."

"We do have our banquet coming up," another board member added. "What if God's about to do something big and surprising? We shouldn't tell him he can't!"

Mike, still looking mildly dubious, nodded along with the others around the table. "You're right. Sounds like a wise plan. Anne, will you schedule a showing for us?"

Tricia sat back in her chair. Dr. Joe leaned closer and said quietly, "I think I'll give my friend Keith Bair a call. See what he knows that could be of help to us."

"Couldn't hurt," Tricia said, trying to keep smiling even while her momentary enthusiasm trickled away. What was she thinking? This place was almost three times what they were hoping to spend. The thought of campaigning for that much money made her nauseated. Staring at the sheet now, she had no idea why Anne had even brought up this property. Except that it was perfect—in every way but price.

What if...? Tricia thought. *What if...?*

CHAPTER 11

Tanisha screamed, "We're gonna hit that semi!" She braced herself against the dashboard and her door as the dark highway spun past her window in a terrifying blur.

Zach jerked the steering wheel right, but the pickup kept spinning left.

Headlights rushed toward Tanisha's window.

Cursing, Zach jerked the wheel to the left. Now the semi's headlights bore down on them from behind. Suddenly, the pickup found traction, and Zach gunned the engine. The semi roared up beside them on the left, sucking them toward its churning wheels. For a wild second, the semi's front fender hooked the pickup's bumper but then tore loose and hurtled on ahead. In a spray of slush, their pickup slowed.

Zach's eyes were wide open. So was his mouth.

"Oh. God." To Tanisha it felt like a thank-you prayer thrown into the dark night.

Zach looked like a zombie clinging to the steering wheel. She smacked his arm. "Hey! Aren't you going to stop? Like to catch your breath?"

He shut his mouth and looked at her. He was coming off his last high. Dopey, red-eyed. This boy should not be driving. But tell him that. At least he hadn't smacked her back this time.

He turned his eyes to the road. "Shut up," he grumbled. Muttering as if to himself, he said, "Better turn around. Heading the wrong way."

Tanisha pointed to lights off the road less than a mile ahead. "Look. I gotta eat and I gotta pee. Let's pull off there and take care of business."

"You gotta, you gotta… Like it's about you." Zach peered through the streaked windshield. In the flickering light that reached them from the lonely truck stop, his face tightened, his eyes narrowed. Slowly he nodded and relaxed. "Sure. I know this place. This'll work. Yeah. This'll work."

Tanisha turned away to the window and sighed. Another place he knew. This routine was getting way too familiar. He'd find one of his old contacts and make him a deal, so he'd keep an eye on her while they both used the john. The dude almost never needed money at these places. Little baggies changed hands, and soon he'd have whatever he wanted. Well, at least for a few minutes, she could unwind in the ladies' room, alone.

There was plenty of parking to choose from. Of course. Who in their right mind would be out driving through the dark in this weather? As she climbed out and trudged through the frigid Colorado night with Zach at her elbow, heavy snowflakes blurred Tanisha's view. Zach glanced back and cursed the trucker who had scraped his paint job and folded up his fender. She cursed her stupidity in wearing a chic coat that wouldn't keep a flea warm in the sunshine.

Just before they reached the convenience store entrance, Zach locked his arm around her shoulders. She had learned not to flinch. It was all part of the show he made her put on for the public.

"Here, babe, let me get that door for you," he said, all slimy-sweet. Two-faced creep. He smiled at a mom and her little girl as they came out of the c-store. *Watch your daughter, Mama*, Tanisha thought, hoping the lady could read minds.

Once inside, Tanisha spotted the restroom sign and muttered to Zach, "I'll be out in a minute." *Or as long as I can hide in there.*

The last time she stretched out her bathroom break, he had barged in after his "poor, sick girlfriend." Whatever. At least for now, they'd stopped moving. For this moment, there was no icy road, no heavy and hypnotizing snow pelting the windshield. Maybe she could spend a few extra minutes indoors by taking her time deciding what to eat.

Sitting in the stall, she rubbed the sides of her head. This had to be the worst mess she'd ever gotten herself into. Not only had she screwed up her own life, but she was about to drag Maddie down with her. Zach was a lunatic. She'd swear he was possessed. He was powering through this trip on less than four hours of sleep and a diet of Adderall. He said nothing was going to stop him. Not snow, not ice. She just hoped there wasn't more where that last slippery patch came from. Going over the Rockies had been something else. But that near-miss with the semi—

She exhaled hard and slow as the memory replayed in her mind like a horror flick. That was way too close. A shiver rocked her from head to toe.

Tanisha stared at the graffiti carved into the back of the blue metal door. If only she could get hold of her phone. But whatever Zach gave her zoned her out, and she never saw what he did with it after she texted Tricia. Probably tossed it in a dumpster. She pressed her fingers against her forehead and rubbed. That boy might be a loser, but he had no trouble outsmarting her.

"I quit." They were words scratched into the door, but they sounded like something Tanisha had already said to herself. She never thought of herself as a quitter before. Not her. She had never let a man get the best of her. But this time was different. Zach was not only mean, he was sly. That was the word. Sly like a fox. He spotted her weaknesses and preyed on them. When another round of homelessness loomed over her, he offered to take her in. And he wasn't bad looking, so… She thought she had him pegged; he wouldn't be a problem. But after that, Zach and his ready supply of happy pills got harder and harder to turn down. By the time she realized he was just using her to get at Maddie, she was too far in to climb out.

Sometimes it just felt easier to do the drugs and let the disaster play out. She couldn't remember anything between Riverside, California, and Las Vegas, Nevada. Besides, what could she do? Zach only stopped to use the bushes when they were out in the boonies or at the occasional c-store like this one where he "knew somebody." He watched her like a hawk. A dopey hawk at times, but she could never assume his guard was down. She'd tried to run off once. Thought he was too wasted to notice. Wrong. Zach had caught her and nearly taken her arm off. *Not gonna try that again.*

Better not try anything at all.

She closed her gritty eyes and rubbed them. But that just made her see the trusting face of Maddie, the only friend she had. And she was about to deliver her gift-wrapped to Zach the psycho.

Her eyes popped open. That's right: Zach must have kept her phone. How else could he make her call and sweet talk Maddie into letting her "drop by for a visit?"

Tanisha groaned aloud. Someone flushed in the stall next to her. She wanted to cry. She wanted to beg whoever was out there washing their hands to help her. She had to stop this. She couldn't do this to Maddie. Somehow, she had to ditch Zach. Messing up her own life was one thing. But Maddie's? No way.

If only she could convince someone at this c-store to call 911. Would anyone believe her? Could she make Zach stick around long enough for the cops to get here? If not, and the cops came chasing after him, he'd be a wild man at the wheel. Better not chance it at night.

Tanisha tapped her forehead. *Get free of Zach.* Where she'd go, she didn't know. But one thing was certain: hanging with Zach was sure to get her killed. Almost happened just ten minutes ago. She could see it now: herself on one of those gurney things.

She sat up straight. That was genius, if only it would work. She would laugh out loud at the look on that boy's face when she got carried away by ambulance...

But could she pull it off? She had seen a friend OD once. She could put on a scene like that. *It just might work.*

When the person in the other stall left, Tanisha walked to the sink. That scrawny Black girl in the mirror—was that really her, with ice crystals melting in her short 'fro and three-inch hoops dangling from her stretched ear lobes? She looked like a drowned rat in that worthless faux-down coat. She was really letting herself go. Never mind the bruises from the beating Zach gave her when she fought getting into his truck. And the gash—

She felt the thick bandage near her waist. Still hurt. That one put the fear of Zach's blade into her, for sure. She was lucky to be alive.

Or not.

Tanisha washed her trembling hands slowly in the lukewarm water, then dried them even more slowly, sliding them in and out under the noisy automatic dryer. In and out, in and out. Deep breath. This little act had to work. Another glance in the mirror told her she looked as good as dead already. She might not have to fake a scene too much after all.

But the minute she opened the restroom door, she knew her scheme was a fail. A huge boulder of a dude stood watching her with his fat arms crossed. He tipped his chin up once. "Evening. Right this way."

Zach had it wired. Her bodyguard escorted her to the checkout, where Zach was buying a couple of sandwiches, a pair of waters, and one dinky bag of chips. When he looked up, she knew he'd crushed and snorted those pills of his in the men's room. He was already getting what she called his Twilight look. Like any minute now, his eyes would glow red. He would look at her from under those dark vampire brows, and he would somehow know what she was planning.

He rapidly counted out some cash to the skinny kid at the register and threw her a smirk over his shoulder. "Feeling better?"

"Nope." She was trapped, and Maddie was doomed.

Sniffing, he rubbed at his nose, then turned serious. "Well, here's good news: We can do the rest of this drive in a day. One good, long day. Then things'll get a whole lot better."

Tanisha didn't reply. She couldn't do a thing now with Bodyguard Boy standing way too close, breathing down her neck. She couldn't move until Zach was ready for her to move.

Now Zach was staring at her with that creepy look. Was he reading her mind? She couldn't risk making him mad.

"Here, take these," Zach said, sliding her the sandwiches and chips. She zipped her coat up to her chin, grabbed the food, and followed Zach out the door.

Dr. Jackson Murphy glanced up when the nurse knocked and entered his office. "Yes?" he said, bestowing a raised eyebrow upon the nurse by way of acknowledgment.

"The digital files have finally come through for your next patient, Doctor. Lucas Clouse."

He gestured toward his screen. "Yes, I can see that." Some nurses—like his ex—thought they had to lead specialists by the hand, it seemed. He scanned the images before him, his chin between his left thumb and forefinger. The nurse laid the patient's intake paperwork on his desk, and he grunted his thanks just as he heard the door click shut behind her.

He shook his head at the screen. The analysis by this country doctor was sparse. Wisely, she was deferring to his judgment on what he could plainly see in this MRI. Amazing, he thought, that they had the equipment to run such high-quality scans out in the hinterlands.

Then he leaned forward to study the vital stats. Age of infant: four weeks, one day. *Good. Still classified as a neonate.* Slowly, his pursed lips inched up at the outer edges as pieces clicked into place for him.

Medulloblastoma in posterior fossa of a newborn. The perfect opportunity to run with his new technique. Saving this tiny patient would make him a hero. And including this case in the paper he was writing would guarantee his promotion to Chief of Neonatology. Bing, bang, boom.

And if the baby died, well, everyone already knew that was the most likely outcome. He would simply find another tricky case and conquer that one.

He crossed his arms, feeling a deep satisfaction sweep through him. *Dr. Jackson Murphy, MD, Chief of Neonatology at the foremost children's hospital in the state.* He pictured Cherie's face as the medical world honored him, the man she thought she could live without. Yes, Dr. Jackson Murphy now has great expectations. Meanwhile, all she and her scrawny anesthesiologist husband Gil were expecting was a baby to sidetrack their careers. Good luck with that.

He lifted the intake file and flipped it open with one hand. Only one parent listed: Madeline Clouse, 24. Single mother. At least, then, if the surgery were unsuccessful, she would be relieved of one burden in her life. Ms. Clouse probably had no insurance, lived in poverty. Well, that was the business office's problem. This posterior fossa tumor was his golden ticket to everything he had been working for.

His eyes skimmed the forms until he hit a snag. *Complications: potential pulmonary valve stenosis, congenital, unconfirmed.* He rolled his eyes to the ceiling. He could hear the team now: "We might have to bring Bair in on this case." That could get awkward. He did not want Bair anywhere near this one. Even if he was the best cardiologist on board. No, Bair would just have to find a case of his own if he wanted to steal the Chief spot. *The Clouse tumor is mine.*

The rest was perfunctory reading. Murphy began rehearsing his speech to the mother even as he skimmed. "A tumor in the posterior fossa, clear from the scan… quite evident… The potential for brain damage is, of course, significant. In fact, I'm surprised the seizures haven't been worse… You must understand that the chances of survival are slim—it's a very sensitive surgery. But you've come to the right place. I will put all my expertise to work for your baby…"

Murphy bent to his computer screen and pulled up the scheduling tab. He squinted at the available time slots. Bair had Theater One tentatively reserved for tomorrow morning, pending weather-related travel problems for the patient's family—Ah, excellent. That was just a routine procedure. But Theater Two was wide open. He slated himself in there. Tomorrow at eight a.m., he'd make medical history. And Bair would be occupied, so there would be no resistance to pulling in a different cardiologist. After all, no one would fault him for tending to this time-sensitive Clouse case immediately.

Murphy drew his sleek monogrammed stylus pen from his shirt pocket and jotted down a list of names on a pad. He tore off the sheet and clipped it to the front of the Clouse file. Humming something tuneless to himself, he walked to the door where his navy blue wool blazer hung on its wooden hanger. He slipped it on, adjusted his silk tie, slid the pen into his chest pocket, and exited the office.

"Nurse," he said, "here's the team I want assembled for surgery tomorrow at eight." He handed her the list of names.

She started in about the storm outside, but he paid no attention.

"Tell them there will be a briefing this evening at five. Send each one of them the digital files on Clouse, Lucas. It's pressing. Must be done right away if we're going to save this little boy's life."

Icy gusts made a wind tunnel of the sheltered entryway to St. Olaf Children's Hospital. Maddie could feel snow spraying up underneath her parka as she rushed Lucas from the Dahlgrens' car to the glass doors. Flora, head down against the storm, scurried along beside her as Nick drove off to find a spot in the parking garage.

Once inside, Maddie shook the snow from her hood, brushed Lucas' blanket dry, and stamped her feet on the snow-caked entry mat. At least it didn't smell like a hospital in this lobby, nearly empty in the uncertain afternoon light. It didn't look like one, either. The glossy brown marble pillars that rose clear to the ceiling of the second floor made it look like a hotel, in fact. Not the kind Zach took her to. A fancy hotel, like she had seen in pictures.

Lucas fussed and stirred in his blankets. Reflexively, her arms stiffened around him. Halfway here, he had gone into another seizure.

She wanted to scream to make it stop. Flora calmly reached back from the front passenger seat, laid her hand on Lucas' head, and prayed aloud for him until he lay still. In a few moments, Lucas was back to normal: no arm twitching, no pointless chewing motions. For the rest of the trip, Lucas slept while Maddie found herself praying like she had never prayed before. Not even for her mother. Something was different now. Now praying felt more... real.

"Whew!" Nick blew out a breath as he dashed inside, along with a blast of cold air. Swatting snow off his coat, he added, "We made it! That drive added a whole new meaning to the term 'white-knuckle ride.'"

"I really appreciate this, Nick," Maddie said.

"You bet." Nick grinned, still puffing after his jog from the parking structure. He pulled off his stocking cap and gloves and clapped them together to knock the snow off.

"That's what we're here for, Maddie," Flora told her. "Now, shall we figure out where to go next?"

Maddie nodded and led the way across the deserted lobby to the receptionist. One heaping pile of paperwork later, Maddie finally received a map of the building with key locations circled in red, along with three printed wrist bands identifying them as Lucas Clouse's "Support Team."

Maddie read the instructions she had been given. "We're off to see Dr. Murphy in Neonatology, in the wing to our right," she said. It came out all professional sounding, just like when she had taken her mother to appointments, as if having a life-threatening disease was normal. She took a deep breath and put on a smile for Lucas. "Here we go, Little Man," she said.

Side by side, the three adults marched down the gleaming hallway. Maddie thought that from behind, they probably looked like the friends from the Wizard of Oz, trying to be brave as they went to ask the mysterious wizard to solve their problems. She, of course, must be the Cowardly Lion. Still, she hoped against hope that the Great and Powerful Dr. Murphy didn't turn out to be just an ordinary man behind a curtain.

"Hey, look who I found," Nick said, standing aside at the examining room doorway. In came Lena, red-cheeked from the cold but smiling. Maddie's chin quivered.

"Oh, Sweetie," Lena said, cupping Maddie's face with her hands. "We're here for you."

"Thank you," she whispered. Then she saw Chris in the doorway. She couldn't breathe. The next thing she knew, Chris was down on one knee beside her chair, talking quietly. She couldn't make out a word he said over the effort it took to dam up her tears, but the sound of his voice gave her strength.

After a few minutes, Nick cleared his throat and said, "Looks like a good time for me to duck out for the chapel, give you all some more room." The door closed itself behind him with a soft click.

Chris tipped his head to meet Lucas' gaze. "How's he doing?"

"I guess that's what Dr. Murphy is supposed to tell me," Maddie said.

Lena said, "I've read about this doctor in the paper. They said Dr. Jackson Murphy is the best neonatal oncologist around."

Maddie suddenly felt a shiver snake up her spine. Some distant memory of a dinner table, green beans, and… "Megamind!" she whispered.

Flora leaned down. "What's that, Maddie?"

Maddie took Lucas' hand in hers. "Megamind Murphy. It's what one of the other moms at The Harbor called her doctor. She said he had a big head and was—"

After a brisk rap at the door, a tall man in a dark blue sport coat entered. He gave the whole group a tight smile, a mix of surprise and disapproval. He squeezed himself in amid the crowd and eased the door closed at his back. "Hello, I'm Dr. Murphy."

Maddie swallowed and held Lucas closer.

He cleared his throat. "Are all of you the family of little—" he glanced at the tablet in his hand "Lucas?"

An awkward moment of silence.

"Yes," Maddie said, "they're my family."

"I see. So, you must be Ms. Clouse." His eyes scouted the room, probably looking for a spare chair.

Dr. Megamind took the little black rolling chair at the desk by Maddie's elbow. She leaned away from him, pretending she was just getting closer to Chris and Lena.

"Now then," he began, "let's talk about what can be done to help Lucas get well." He folded his hands together on the desk and looked straight at Maddie. "It's important to understand that while surgery can be done, it is very risky."

Maddie sucked in her breath. "Surgery? But you haven't even looked at him. Don't you want to, like, run tests or something? Get a second opinion?"

The doctor's lips stretched in what was probably supposed to be a smile, the kind he might give a child who wasn't very quick on the uptake.

"I have reviewed your pediatrician's findings and studied the MRI she sent," he said. "The tumor's size and location, coupled with the seizures you described, make it extremely clear that we need to remove the growth right away. As one of the few doctors who is experienced in procedures of this nature, I can assure you that your son will be in good hands. But, as I said, surgery near such a tiny brain is quite tricky. There is some risk that we may encounter adverse outcomes."

"'Adverse outcomes'?" she asked, feeling a chill steal into her core. "What do you mean?"

"I mean, he could be left with some brain damage," Dr. Murphy replied. He almost sounded compassionate as he added, "Or, to be frank, he might not survive the operation."

Maddie rubbed her forehead as if she could smooth away the frightening words. Somehow, despite all she knew and all she feared, she had hoped this expert would tell her that for him, surgery like this was a breeze. Some doctors removed tonsils; he removed babies' brain tumors, with the same rate of success.

Instead, he sat here, confirming her fears. She would probably lose Lucas, no matter what this doctor did. How could she survive that? How could she lose one more person she loved? The sounds around her disappeared behind the pulsing of blood in her ears. *No, no, no...*

A touch on her arm. "Maddie," Chris was saying. "The doctor wants to examine Lucas."

Dr. Megamind stood by a soft-topped counter like a changing table, laying a sheet of something absorbent on the surface. "Place your baby right here, if you would."

She stood and woodenly moved toward him. Why did it feel like she was laying Lucas on a pagan altar? And why was it so cold in here?

"Please undress him down to his diaper, Ms. Clouse."

"He'll be so cold," she said, even while her hands mechanically obeyed.

Dr. Murphy said nothing but reached for the thermostat and made an adjustment.

Then it happened again. Lucas's left arm and leg twitched repeatedly. His eyes glazed over, and his little mouth made crazy slow-motion chewing movements.

Maddie gave a muted cry. Chris stepped up beside her. She reached for Lucas, but Dr. Murphy placed his hands on either side of Lucas like barriers, leaning over him with eyes intent on his frightening, jerky movements.

"Ah, a seizure. Let's see here." He watched until it had passed, then examined Lucas' eyes, moved his arms and legs a little, and looked inside his mouth. He rested his stethoscope on several spots on his body. Especially over his heart. "Was that rather typical of the seizures you've seen?"

Maddie nodded, her hand caressing Lucas's belly. "Can I pick him up again?"

Dr. Murphy pulled out his stylus and turned to the desk. "Yes, go ahead. And you may put his clothes back on." He wrote on his tablet, his back to her.

Maddie held Lucas close, drinking in the warm, milky smell of him. He nuzzled into her chest, then started fussing. She thought Dr. Murphy might excuse himself so she could nurse him in privacy then, but he just sat there writing. She pulled Lucas' clothes on with Lena's help.

"I think he's hungry," she said, hoping the doctor would get the hint. Maybe he would go away and come back with better news. But he didn't seem to hear her.

Suddenly, Dr. Megamind swiveled to face them. "All right. All symptoms line up with what I see in the MRI scan run by your doctor. This tumor needs to be removed as soon as possible. Each seizure carries a degree of risk, and an aggressive tumor like this one grows rapidly, increasing that risk. I have surgery scheduled for tomorrow at 8 a.m." He slid his stylus back into his pocket.

Maddie gasped. "Tomorrow?" She looked down at Lucas, nudging her sweater with his nose and making insistent little sounds. How could she send him off to surgery tomorrow? What if he didn't survive? Then this would be their last night together. In mere hours, she would have to say good-bye to him without knowing if she would ever see him alive again.

Flora said, "Doctor, this is rather sudden. What if Maddie would like a second opinion? Our doctor thought you would want to do your own MRI."

Dr. Murphy sat up straight. He looked them all over as if he thought maybe they hadn't heard him right. "I don't think there is time for a second opinion. If you want to save Lucas' life, he needs that surgery right away. I can order a pre-op MRI if you like, though the other one is quite clear and recent enough to render that uncomfortable procedure unnecessary. However, the surgery must go ahead immediately. There is no other hope for him."

No other hope? Maddie stared at him, clenching her teeth. She could feel her whole body trembling. But this time, she wasn't afraid. She was angry. Hoping he felt the full force of her glare, she said, "Who are you to tell me there is no other hope?"

Never taking her eyes off him, she yanked up her sweater, unfastened her nursing bra, and practically forced Lucas to latch on. As she let the sweater drape her son's face, she said, "You are just a doctor. I have hope you don't even know about."

Dr. Murphy stared at her. She could even feel Chris staring at her. Flora, standing just behind the doctor, closed her open mouth.

Maddie continued, "We *are* going to get a second opinion."

"What? From whom?" Dr. Murphy sputtered.

"From God," Maddie answered. "We're going down the hall to the chapel, and we're going to ask him what he wants us to do."

Flora bent to gather their purses and the diaper bag, her secretive smile as broad as her face now.

Dr. Murphy stood, toppling his little wheeled chair over backward with a clank that startled Lucas. His tiny arm flew away from his mother, then settled back on her sweater while he resumed nursing. Dr. Murphy said, "You do that. Whatever makes you feel better. But if your God knows what's good for Lucas, he will see things my way." He stormed out of the examining room. Behind him, in the momentary silence, the wheels of his chair swung from side to side, the bearings rattling.

Chris jumped to his feet. "That was awesome!" He looked like he might hug her but then stepped back and held up his palm. Maddie gave him a limp high five.

Lena agreed, "You are absolutely right, Maddie. We do have hope." Her smile warmed Maddie clear through.

Maddie gathered Lucas tighter to her chest. "I want to get out of this room."

Chris helped her stand while Lucas kept nursing. Lena pulled a light blanket from the diaper bag and draped it over Maddie and her baby. Maddie's confidence deflated as her anger dissipated, and she could almost feel the eyes of Dr. Megamind Murphy boring into her as they walked past him at the nurses' station. But the company of her friends buoyed her along the thirty-foot journey to the chapel. They entered a peaceful, softly lit space filled with warmth and quiet.

The six modest wooden pews were empty except for Nick. He lifted his head as they entered. "What did you find out?"

Flora filled him in while Maddie sank onto the pew in front of him. Chris slid in after her. On the wall ahead was a crucifix. Jesus' compassionate face could almost have been watching Lucas, who was still nursing away as if all this fuss had nothing to do with him.

"There's a lot to pray about," Nick said, "if Dr. Murphy knows his stuff. And I'm sure he does. But let me read you all something I came across while I was sitting here." He opened a Gideon Bible and read: "'He who did not spare his own Son, but gave him up for us all—how will he not also, along with him, graciously give us all things?'"

Maddie listened, studying the crucifix. "So does that mean…that even when things don't go the way we want, we know God would never hold back anything good from us since he has already given us the hardest thing there was to give?"

Nick answered, "I think you're right, Maddie."

"Then," she said, "we should ask God for the very best thing for Lucas."

CHAPTER 12

"Are you sure you're okay with this?" Chris watched Maddie's face, hoping her calm countenance wasn't just a mask. He would never have guessed their prayers here in the chapel would lead to this conclusion.

Maddie's eyes stayed locked on her son, who slept peacefully on her lap. "Yes, I'm sure," she said quietly. "But that doesn't make it easy."

Chris could guess what she meant. She had trusted God back when her mother had cancer. Then Patricia died. How hard must it be to try trusting him again with her own child?

Maddie lifted her gaze to meet his. "I don't understand it, but I can't ignore this… answer. I am supposed to wait for one day. Twenty-four hours. We all—I mean, that is what you all… kind of… heard, right?" Her voice wavered as she looked at the group in the pews. One by one, each person nodded. She took a deep breath and let it go, shaking her head. "Then that's what I need to do."

She looked so frail sitting there, his slim friend Maddie with her tiny baby boy. Where was she finding this courage? As far as he knew, she hadn't prayed in years. And now, in this life-or-death moment, she was convinced she had to obey this counter-intuitive answer from God.

This wouldn't be how he would have answered their prayers if he were God. Maddie's faith was so fragile—or so it seemed. Maybe God knew something he didn't.

Chris wanted to wrap his arms around her, but he resigned himself to a reassuring nod. "Okay, then. We're all with you on this."

Flora spoke from the next pew back. "Maddie," she said slowly, "who will announce your decision to Dr. Murphy?"

Maddie shook her head. "It should be me, but I don't know if I can do it." She closed her eyes for a moment. Everyone waited silently. When her eyes opened, they were fixed on Chris. "Why do you think God is asking me to do this? Is there something he needs a whole day to do? Or is He just giving me one more day with my little boy before—?"

Chris's heart hurt like it had the day Maddie's mother died. What could he say? Only the truth. "I don't know, Maddie. I wish I did, but I don't."

She inhaled sharply. "I guess this is called trusting."

Chris looked down at his hands, lying useless in his lap. She was still studying him when he lifted his head. "Maddie," he said, "would you like me to face that doctor for you?"

Her tight lips softened, and her eyes shone their deepest green. "Would you?"

"You got it." He stood and moved out of the pew.

She sniffled and said, "Wait. I'm coming with you."

Flora reached for Lucas. Maddie hesitated but eventually passed him to her. On an impulse, Chris offered Maddie his hand to hold. When she took it after only a moment's pause, warmth shot up his arm. He led her out of the chapel.

At the far end of the hallway rose huge windows, flecked with snow one minute and scoured bare the next. The blizzard conditions had worsened since he and his mom had arrived. Even then, their short trip from one side of Jefferson to the other had been nerve-racking. This howling storm would keep them all stranded here for the duration.

But Maddie wasn't paying attention to the blizzard. She pointed out Dr. Murphy, standing at the nurses' station with two nurses and another doctor. Maddie tightened her grip on Chris's hand as their winter boots squeaked along the shiny floor. Every head at the nurses' station swiveled toward them.

Chris leaned closer to whisper to Maddie, "Just like walking the halls back in grade school."

Maddie gave him a quick look. "And you're helping me face the principal. Again."

"We can do this," Chris assured her.

"I don't like how empty my arms feel," Maddie said, glancing back toward the chapel doorway. "And I don't like having to face Dr. Megamind in front of all those people. They probably think he's a genius. I'm going to look like an idiot."

For his part, Chris didn't like the smug way Dr. Murphy watched them approach.

"So, will I see you tomorrow at eight?" the doctor said, his shiny stylus hovering over the tablet on the counter.

Chris cleared his throat. "Actually, sir, after praying about it, Maddie has decided the wisest thing to do is to wait one day."

Dr. Megamind laid down his stylus with slow, exaggerated precision. In an ominously steady voice, he asked, "Wait? For what?"

Chris stepped a few inches in front of Maddie, between her and Dr. Murphy. "For whatever God has in mind," he said. "We'll keep praying, and after one day, we'll know what to do next."

Dr. Murphy leaned his elbow on the counter and glared at Chris. "Are you the father?"

That was a gut punch, and the doctor didn't even know it. "No, sir."

"Then you have no place coercing this vulnerable young woman into some purely religious decision contrary to sound medical advice." His face had gone hard and pale.

A surge of anger straightened Chris's back. He braced his feet wide, hands clenched behind his back, for the extreme effort it would take to keep his voice under control. "Sir, with all due respect, this was the mother's decision. The rest of us are simply standing by to support her. And Lucas."

Dr. Murphy's mouth cinched tight. He inhaled, puffing his chest forward.

Before he could speak again, Maddie blurted, "No one coerced me. I decided this, after my friends and I prayed hard about it."

Dr. Murphy crossed his arms, drawing himself up to his full height. He said, "I am shocked by your decision. If you loved your child—"

Chris took a step forward. "Hey, now—"

"I do love him!" Maddie cried. "This is the hardest thing I have ever had to do. But I know in my heart it is right!"

"Your heart, your heart." Dr. Murphy moved a step closer. He sneered, "Perhaps your son would be better served if you used your head!"

The other doctor nearby, a balding younger man with light blue eyes, interjected, "Dr. Murphy, I believe we will need to respect the family's decision for the time being."

Dr. Murphy barely looked at him. But his pallor began to redden. "Of course, you would think so, Bair." He continued to glare at Chris and Maddie. He kept his voice low and even. "The nurse will schedule a follow-up appointment for this time tomorrow. I hope you can *all* make it. Especially your poor baby."

With that, he stormed off.

In the uneasy silence that followed, the younger doctor stepped around the nurses' station toward them. "I must apologize for my colleague. He is an excellent neonatal oncologist who is…still working on his bedside manner." Extending his hand to Chris, he said, "I'm Keith Bair, in cardiology."

Chris shook his hand. "Chris Nelson. And this is Maddie Clouse. Her son Lucas is in the chapel with our friends."

"And I bet you'd like to get back to him," Dr. Bair said. "May I walk with you?"

Maddie looked like a wilting flower. Chris wanted to wrap an arm around her waist for support but offered her his elbow to hold instead. She took it readily enough. She nodded toward the doctor, and they started for the chapel.

Dr. Bair said little, but enough to convince Chris the doctor was a man of faith. Before they parted at the chapel door, Maddie's chin rose, and she stood straighter.

She turned to the young doctor. "Thank you. I really needed to hear that."

With a gentle smile, Dr. Bair bowed his head slightly.

Reluctantly, Chris let Maddie release his arm and slip into the chapel.

As he was about to follow her, Dr. Bair pulled a business card from his wallet and scribbled on the back of it. He handed it to Chris with a quick tip of his head toward the wind-battered window. "Since it looks like we'll all be spending the night here, please take this. It's my cell number. If your group needs anything tonight, please let me know. I'll be camped out in my office upstairs."

Chris accepted the card, struck wordless by his kindness. He shook the doctor's hand again and joined the group in the quiet chapel. All eyes were on Lucas lying in Flora's arms.

Flora looked up. She said quietly, "He just had another seizure."

It was going to be one very long night.

Chris found his skimpy supper from the hospital cafeteria to be far from satisfying. But Maddie had eaten even less. Flora, bless her, had purchased extra snacks from the vending machine and laid them on the coffee table in the lobby. Nick had talked someone into loaning Maddie a charger for her phone and located an outlet to plug it into.

Chris and his mom moved sofas and chairs into more comfortable positions and stood back to look at their arrangements. Not ideal, but the best they could do in a hospital lobby. Nobody was going anywhere in this storm. Snow pelted the windows; the wind howled as it circled the walls. Twice already, the power had gone out, leaving them nervously watching one another in dim generator-run lights. He looked toward the hallway, wondering if St. Olaf's had any children on life support tonight.

"I'll go see about getting us some blankets," Chris said, taking a count of the group.

His mom nodded. "Good idea. And maybe some pillows?"

"Will do." The sound of the wailing wind faded as he walked toward the center of the building. Waiting out a blizzard in a children's hospital wasn't his idea of fun. Probably wasn't a thrill ride for Maddie, either.

It was a whole different experience, being in the hospital as a patient's family—or, well, support team. As an EMT, he always got the quick adrenaline rush of the emergency without any of the soul-sucking, dragged-out waiting periods. He hadn't even had much of that during Patricia Clouse's battle with cancer. Hospice at home was how her story had ended. Seemed like a whole lifetime ago. What Maddie must be feeling now, he could hardly guess.

Up ahead, he saw a tall, lanky guy in green housekeeping scrubs in conversation with the nurse they'd met earlier. Nurse Jenny shook a finger at him the way she might scold a naughty child. "No, I won't," she said. "You know that's not legal."

As Chris walked closer, he got the impression he'd seen the housekeeping guy before.

In a harsh stage whisper, the man said, "C'mon, Jenn. Just this once." He swung his arm toward the window at the end of the hall. "Where am I supposed to get any on a night like this?"

"Not from me. If you have a prescription, you can always—"

The guy winced and pressed a hand to his back. "It's just this back pain is so bad. Ever since the accident..."

The nurse held up a hand and turned away. "Oh, stop. My answer is no. Period. Just quit asking, or I will have to report this conversation."

After she picked up her tablet and moved off down the hall, Chris cleared his throat.

With wide, startled eyes, the man turned to face him. Now Chris recognized him. It was Kyle, the OD case he and Brent had pulled back from the brink on New Year's Day.

After Kyle's eyes quit darting along the hallway beyond Chris, he said, "Uh, can I help you?"

"I hope so," Chris said, watching Kyle's hands fidget with the stacks of folded sheets on the cart at his side. "My friends and I will be sleeping in the lobby tonight. Any chance you could find us some spare blankets?"

"Spare blankets." Kyle nodded. He started to move away.

"Six or seven. Oh, and that many pillows, too?"

"Six or seven. You bet."

"Thanks, man." Chris hoped the message registered with Kyle. The guy seemed more intent on his back pain than Chris's request.

"Here you go," a man's voice said behind Maddie.

She glanced back, away from the snow swirling past the lobby windows. A tall man in green hospital scrubs was loading Flora's arms with blankets. Looking at the man, for just a moment, Maddie had one of those déjà vu feelings. She shivered and went back to watching the blizzard. The storm was so mesmerizing. Light and darkness, rushing past each other so wildly, it messed with her mind. Which one was actually advancing? The light or the darkness?

"Excuse me, Miss," the man in green said at her side.

She jumped and took a step away from him. His musky body spray instantly nauseated her. Red flags flew in the back of her mind, though she couldn't think why.

"Pillow?" He held one out to her. Then his head tipped, and he seemed to be studying her. A strange expression crossed his face, hinting at a smirk.

Maddie shook her head and walked away from him, past Nick, to the far window. The last thing she wanted was a pillow with that musky smell on it. Maddie couldn't shake the uneasy feeling that she had seen that man before. Her neck hairs crawled until the man's footsteps, squeaking their way out of the lobby, could no longer be heard. Then she let herself be hypnotized by the snow once again, let the numbness seep into her. She wasn't cold, but she felt no warmth, either. In her mind, three thoughts echoed: "God, help me. Save Lucas. Show me the way."

Occasionally, she'd hear Nick's verse threading through it all. God had already given her the hardest thing ever. How could he withhold anything good now? But what would God see as "good"? The same "good" as when her Mama died?

Chris came to stand beside her. "Doing okay?"

Maddie shrugged.

"Sure didn't plan on getting stuck here, did we?" He was trying to sound light-hearted, she knew. It wasn't working.

She hugged herself, her hands clutching the elbows of her sweater. "I quit making plans a long time ago. Just riding out one storm after another."

"It's a season, Madd. This isn't how it will always be." His hand gently touched her arm.

Her muscles jerked away from him. She sighed and made herself relax just the tiniest bit.

"I hope you're right," she said. Then she looked at him, gray in the dim and fluctuating light reflecting off the blowing snow. Why was he here, by her side, after everything?

Flora walked toward them with blankets. "Sounds like employees that hadn't already left by noon are spending the night here, just like us. Doctors, nurses, and a skeleton crew of janitors, maintenance workers, cooks, and a receptionist are all hanging out in the hospital. Along with a small number of young patients and their parents." Her voice dropped like a conspirator's, "Nurse Jenny brought us these games, too, in case we were interested."

Chris took a Scrabble set and a worn green Mille Bornes box from under Flora's arm. "Here we go. This could help pass the time, don't you think?"

Maddie gave him a half-smile. "Scrabble. We used to play Scrabble all the time."

"I bet you can still beat the socks off me. But I'll give you a run for your money if you're up for it," Chris replied. "Wanna try?"

Maddie looked off down the hallway. "Maybe later. I think I'd like to go pray again."

Chris laid the boxes down on a coffee table. "Want some company?"

"Sure. Thanks." She accepted the arm Chris offered, and they headed toward the chapel, detouring to sneak one more peek at Lucas, who slept all snuggled up in Lena's arms. Maddie felt torn. Half of her wanted to pick up her baby and hold him through every single second they had left together. But the other half of her wanted to build a wall around her heart again, to walk away and not look back, ever. It might be the only way to survive losing someone all over again… She pressed her lips together and turned toward the chapel and its crucifix. Maybe looking into that compassionate face would help her find her way forward.

Scratching noises dragged Tanisha from a patchy sleep. Those crummy wiper blades were scraping uselessly across the icy windshield again. She rubbed her eyes, which just made them burn more. Whatever Zach had given her was wearing off. Beside her, Zach looked frozen in place, hunched over, his hands locked on the steering wheel. He squinted to peer through the windshield's wrinkled skin of ice. Ice coated every inch of glass except for two small circles over the tired defroster.

"Zach, honey," she said, putting a whole helping of sugar in her voice.

He didn't respond.

She placed a hand on his arm and tried again. "Zach, baby, don't you think—"

He flapped his elbow. "Don't touch me. Look through your side. Can you see anything?"

He couldn't see? Geez. This guy was gonna get her killed. Craning her neck and leaning toward the dashboard, she could see something, all right. Snow. Lots of it. Snow on the hood, snow blowing every which way. Then she spotted a huge dark shape—something with colored lights, like signs. "Hey, there's some kind of building over there."

"Where?" the dude's voice cracked, like a scared kid's.

"Ahead, on the right. Big ol' truck stop. Take this exit." If Zach was as anxious as he sounded, maybe he'd agree to a real rest.

"Yeah. Yeah. I got it now." He turned on his signal and eased toward where the exit lane ought to be. A car horn blared as a reddish shape pushed past on the right, flinging icy snow across the hood. Zach swore, overcorrected, then recovered. "Idiot! Where'd he come from? I'm going over," he announced like any other drivers had better move aside. This time he made the lane change safely, and they curved away from the freeway.

The truck stop, a blurry black thing, got bigger by the minute. When at last they crunched to a stop somewhere in what was probably the parking lot, Tanisha leaned her head back on the headrest. "I can't believe we're still alive."

Zach turned his pasty face toward her. Whatever he'd been jacked up on was fading. "Get out. I'm going inside, and you're coming with me."

"On one condition," she said over crossed arms, "and that's us stopping to sleep. I ain't riding with you when you're like this anymore. You gotta sleep, dude."

"Shut up and get out." Zach yanked his phone from the charger cord and opened his door. The wind almost tore it off. Cold shards of ice swirled through the cab.

"Close that door!" Tanisha squealed.

"No!" he yelled against the howling wind. "Not til you get out."

She groaned, zipped up her coat, and opened her door with two hands. Even so, it almost blew off its hinges before she could get around it and push it closed. She screamed into the wind, "This is wack! You hear me? Totally wack!"

But she followed him anyway, with the wind whipping her from behind. Her hand clutched the back of his coat to keep from losing sight of him. Typical. She had to block the wind for *him*. Icy wind bit her neck, attacked her ears and cheeks, pasted ice onto the backs of her legs before she'd gone ten feet. Where were they, Antarctica?

Squinting, she could make out only three cars in the parking lot. Out on the edge, a shadowy line of big rigs looked like they'd been parked there for days. A mountain of snow had piled up against the first one, and the gaps between them swelled with mounds of their own. Those truck drivers were probably hunkered down in the motel off this convenience store, all warm and toasty. Well, that's where she was going to be, too. And she knew exactly how to talk Zach into it.

Zach had to pull three times to get the door open, and they had hardly squeezed past it before it slammed on Tanisha's heels. They brushed snow out of their hair and clothes onto the slushy floor.

A fat old guy whose uniform shirt barely covered his paunch sat on a stool behind the cash register. He gave them a nod. "Some storm there."

Zach scowled up at him from under thawing eyebrows. He snorted, a sound Tanisha knew to be wary of. But the old man kept talking.

"I'm surprised you got through. Roads are closing all over the place." The clerk cocked his thumb at a television screen in the corner above the coffee dispensers. "News is full of it."

"No, no, no!" Zach groaned, pushing Tanisha aside to move closer to the screen. He held up his phone, checking his planned route against the newsman's map, crisscrossed with red lines. Across the bottom of the screen, a long list of closed roadways scrolled past.

The numbers meant nothing to Tanisha. Nothing but a better chance at a good night's sleep in this motel.

Zach swore at his phone, not quite under his breath.

Tanisha took that as promising. But she knew not to strike too soon. Let him stew over the roads a bit more.

Snow flew in at the entry door as another person pushed his way in from the blizzard. This guy hadn't walked far. Not enough snow on his dreadlocks. Probably holed up in the motel and just stopping in for a greasy meal from the roller grill.

Zach rubbed at the stubble on his chin. A good sign: obviously frustrated, but not yet angry. Tanisha moved toward him, dropping the zipper of her coat just enough for a guy to see what he wanted to. She leaned her curves against his arm and took her time speaking. "So, Zach, baby, maybe we'd better stay the night here, huh? Wait 'til this blows over?" She stroked his arm, looking as sweet as she knew how.

Zach gave her a look that would have withered a tree. "You got cash for a room?"

"Aw, come on, baby," she purred. "Just work your magic on the dread-head over there, and we'll have plenty. You got more o' them baggies, right?"

The dreadlocks guy was watching her. More like licking her with his eyes. Bad news. Zach's chin came up, and a creepy grin crossed his lips.

"'Work my magic,' huh?" He nodded slowly. Then he sauntered away from her, pretending to check out the candy bars as he made his way toward the dread-head. Next thing she knew, they were talking—Zach in a casual over-his-shoulder way, the other guy with his eyes burning up and down Tanisha's legs. The guy smirked, pulled a roll of bills from his front pocket, and peeled some off for Zach.

A shudder wormed its way down Tanisha's back. This was not the kind of night she had in mind. She spotted the exit door two yards away. One chance. She took it. She dashed to the door and shoved with all her might. But with the wind against her and her shoes sliding on the slushy floor, she had hardly shoved it open and squeezed out before Rastafarian Man came around from the entrance and wrapped his big hand around her arm.

He grinned, his big yellow teeth collecting snowflakes like bugs on a radiator grill. He shouted, "My room's this way," and towed her toward the motel entrance.

Shielding her eyes from the blizzard, she glanced back to see the fat old clerk with his mouth hanging open, watching through a window splotched with ice and snow. And Zach inside the entrance door, pocketing his haul.

Jackson Murphy shoved the heel of his hand against the vending machine's coin return. Nothing. Naturally. Not only were they out of granola bars, but the machine had eaten his money. It didn't matter that he was wearing a Hart Schaffner Marx label and leading the line for the Chief spot. Standing alone in this vacant doctors' lounge, he felt once more like a sleepy young resident in a threadbare clinic jacket on his thirteenth night shift in a row. As if he had no Ferrari parked out there in a reserved space, no spacious home on the east end of town, no gorgeous wife to show off—Well, all right, that last one was actually true. But by most estimations, he was a highly successful physician. Why, suddenly, did he feel so empty?

He strode rapidly away from the humming wall of vending machines and their glare of silver light to plow through the double doors into the hallway. He would go crazy if he didn't walk somewhere. A different floor. The lobby, perhaps. Somewhere with more windows. He loosened his tie.

Murphy punched the elevator button. With an obliging bell tone, the doors slid open immediately. He walked in and almost—but not quite—wished someone else would enter with him. It felt spooky to ride an elevator alone.

Just before the door slid closed, someone did dash inside. Dr. Keith Bair. *Delightful.* Murphy gave him a curt nod and watched to see which floor he chose. Ground floor. *Oh, joy.* If Murphy changed his own destination now, it would be too obvious. So he lifted his eyes to the lighted floor indicator over the door and counted down silently. Six, five, four—

"Some storm, huh?" Bair said.

"Indeed." Murphy did not roll his eyes, which he felt was quite an accomplishment. To outdo himself further, he even added a civil comment. "I've heard it's not stopping any time soon, either."

Bair nodded, also watching the numbers count down. "That's what I heard too. We may be working with this light staff for a day or two. At least until it slows enough to clear the roads."

Murphy shook his head. "Good thing our caseloads were light. I'd hate to think—"

All at once, the elevator jerked to a stop, smothered in complete blackness.

"Not again!" Murphy found the handrail just as dim emergency lighting kicked in.

"Another power outage," Bair said. "How long will this one—"

Then as suddenly as they had gone out, the regular lights came back on. With the push of a button, the elevator resumed its steady descent to the lobby.

"I think I'll take the stairs next time," Bair said.

Murphy grunted. "Good idea. Part of our heart health program and all, you know."

"Heart health. Right." Bair chuckled and tipped his head to study him, as though it might never have occurred to him that Murphy's skill set could include a sense of humor.

The elevator eased to a more natural stop, dinged, and opened onto the lobby.

"Where are you headed, Bair?" Murphy had no idea why he even asked.

"Front reception desk. A friend's mother was working there tonight but hasn't answered her son's texts. He wanted me to check on her. You?"

"Just needed to walk. I'm hoping the visitors' cafeteria is better stocked than the lounge upstairs."

Bair pointed forward with a tip of his head. "Looks like your patient's support team is spending the night in the lobby."

Though the lights were low, Murphy could see several forms curled up on chairs and sofas, a bluish glow from the outside spilling over them. No sign of the mother and her boyfriend. Well, he had no interest in encountering those religious fanatics just now. So he bid Bair good night and took an indirect route toward the cafeteria.

With his eyes on the snow whipping past the floor-to-ceiling windows at the far end of the hall, Murphy wouldn't have even noticed that he passed the chapel if the sound of weeping hadn't caught his attention. Trying not to be seen, he peered through the open door. Inside, the Clouse woman sat beside that boyfriend of hers. But she wasn't talking to him. Murphy could just make out the words.

"I know you love him, Jesus. And you love me. So please, please don't take him from me. I just don't know if I can lose someone else..."

Murphy looked away, pretending to study a painting on the opposite wall as he continued walking. The girl might be off her rocker, but the pain in her voice elbowed his heart. He wondered, momentarily, who she had already lost. He hated to think that he and this misguided girl shared so personal a thing as loss.

Loss? Hardly. Losing Cherie had actually freed him, hadn't it? Like an albatross around his neck, their marriage had been his punishment for associating with someone less ambitious than himself. Now she was Gil's problem, and he, Jackson Murphy, was free to pursue his goals unhindered.

Once clear of the chapel, he stopped trying to muffle his steps. Cherie had been hungry—practically starving—for attention. But personal, not professional, attention. She wanted him to do everything with her. As if he never sent her flowers or bought her things. No, she said, that wasn't good enough. He had to be *with* her, talking to her, listening to her. Acting like he *cared*. And then all the talk about having children would start in again. He grimaced. She didn't seem to realize what children would do to her career. And to his.

Well, now she was about to find out. Soon he'd be basking in his promotion while she chased rug rats around a house she and Gil could no longer afford. Then she'd see. Good ol' Murphy was right. Too late, she'd realize what she had lost.

Footsteps behind him made him glance back. The couple had left the chapel. They were walking away from him, toward the lobby.

When the young man offered his arm, and his girlfriend took it, a twinge of something like pain cramped Murphy's abdomen. Hard as it was to admit, at times he wished he had someone to take his arm affectionately. Someone who would look at him like that girl looked at her young man: trusting, fond, grateful.

Cherie stopped looking at him like that long ago, after… *After what?* Murphy's footsteps slowed. It was after he made her terminate that pregnancy. Strange, he'd never connected those dots before. From that time on, if she did look at him, her gaze was searching. Searching for something within him. But not finding it.

Murphy looked away, back down the lonely hallway to the cafeteria. He shook off the mood and resumed his hunt for a granola bar. Perhaps he'd also settle for—his lip curled—a cup of vending machine decaf.

When he emerged from the visitors' cafeteria victorious—if you could call finding two stale cookies and an off-brand sparkling water victorious—he had no intention of going anywhere near the lobby. Somehow he ended up there, on the back side of the decorative partition that visually separated the vaulted room into roughly equal halves. Things were so dead around this deserted place that those live bodies on the other side were almost magnetic. There was something about them that made him want to hover nearby. Near enough to eavesdrop. Yes, he told himself, he wanted to hear what religious nut cases said when they thought there was no one else around.

Silently he lowered himself into a large club chair and proceeded to unwrap his cookies with one hand. It was a trick he'd mastered during his residency. A way to flex his skilled surgeon's hands—hands he would put to use when that mother came to her senses. A long night of fretting about her son's future would surely drive her to the realization that Dr. Jackson Murphy, MD, knew what he was talking about.

The voices beyond the partition became clearer as he finished his first cookie.

"But, Chris, after the way I treated you—" the girl said.

"Maddie, I've forgiven you. We're going to move forward now, together."

There was a long pause. Finally, the girl said, "You say that like it's so easy. Like what I did didn't hurt you. You can just forgive me?"

"I didn't 'just' forgive you," he said. "You know how I was when you first came back. Mad. Resentful. Heck, I was furious."

Furious. Murphy shifted in his chair. His ex once told him furious was his baseline condition. A painful diagnosis. How was a man supposed to cure that?

The boyfriend, Chris, went on, "But there's this guy named Brent, an EMT I work with. He and his wife were on the brink of divorce a while back. Then recently, something changed. When I asked him what turned things around, he told me it was the way Jesus forgave the woman caught in adultery."

Murphy's eyes went wide.

"Brent said he and his wife decided they had to forgive each other. That's when it hit me. We're all like that woman. We've all sinned. None of us is good enough to please God. We all need Jesus to save us, to forgive us. You and me both."

Murphy caught himself leaning over the arm of his chair, waiting for the guy to go on.

At last, he said, "And if Jesus could go so far as to *die* to forgive me, then how in the world could I not forgive you?"

Murphy no longer saw the second cookie in his hand, though he felt it break in two within his tightening grip. Forgiveness had always been a foreign concept to him. He held others to rather high standards; people rarely measured up. And when they failed him, he let them know. *It's like you think you're a god,* Cherie had told him one night, her eyes flashing. *You're up there on your high and mighty throne, busy proving how great you are so you can make everyone else feel small.*

Perhaps—just perhaps—Cherie was partially right. Perhaps he did play god sometimes. The kind of god who drove everyone away.

Murphy rose to his feet, only half aware he carried his broken cookie and unopened sparkling water to the tall windows across the room. Outside, a floodlight perched on the wall of the building, shining down into the swirling fury of snow in the courtyard between the lobby and the west wing. White crystalline drifts lay heaped across what he knew were picnic tables. Now, though, they resembled small cars sinking into quicksand.

So much snow. Things buried so deep. How could they ever be dug out? It was all simply buried too deep for too long. Too late.

Murphy shook his head. *Get a grip, man.* Suddenly disgusted with himself, he left the cheap cookie and the generic sparkling water on a table and stalked out of the lobby. He needed sleep.

"'Vanquish,'" Maddie said aloud, placing her last tile on the Scrabble board. "That's 23 points!" She clamped her hand over her mouth and whispered, "Sorry."

None of the nearby sleepers stirred. Chris groaned and tapped the score into his phone's notepad as if he were angry, but his smile said otherwise. "Well, I should have known you'd whip me again."

Maddie grinned back at him. It felt good to be good at something again. In this spacious lobby, with soft blue light lying across everything, this moment felt peaceful. Calm. Maddie stretched her arms over her head, realizing all at once that she was tired enough to sleep now.

But, of course, Lucas woke up sounding hungry. Chris shook his head and gave her his "sorry 'bout that" look. She stepped past him to fetch the diaper bag. Leaving her phone charging in an outlet near their Scrabble board, she carefully picked her way toward the sofa, trying not to disturb anyone. Her head came up at the sound of someone else's cell phone buzzing. Could have been Flora's. But Flora slept on in her chair, her head lolling back on her rolled-up winter coat. A moment later, Nick's phone buzzed, too. But Nick was dead to the world, sacked out on the floor beneath his coat with a couple of pillows under his head.

Maddie lifted Lucas from beside Lena, who stretched, smiled up at her, and then rolled over on the sofa. Lena—what a dear friend. Maddie changed Lucas' diaper, then settled into a chair that had temporarily become her favorite for his feedings.

Precious little boy, she thought. *And I almost didn't let you live.*

Maddie's heart cramped at the memory. How would she have lived if not for this little guy? Because of Lucas, she had dared to escape from Zach and start over. Because of Lucas, she had been offered a safe home—at the Radners' and then at the Dahlgrens'. If not for Lucas, she and Chris would still be worlds apart. Out of the darkest time of her life had come this bright light, this little child named Lucas. Maddie felt suddenly that Lucas must be a gift from God. A sign he had not abandoned her—just as Tricia had once told her.

As Lucas nursed in the blue dimness, she savored their moment of closeness. She admired his soft, dark hair—the way it curled at the nape of his neck and also in the center of his forehead. She stroked his hair. What would brain surgery do to that perfect little head? Ironic—she had always feared he'd need surgery, only on his heart. But unless God stepped in and worked some kind of miracle, the abominable Megamind Murphy would soon be manhandling his tiny brain. She cupped her hand around the back of his little head and closed her eyes to pray.

But instead, in the darkness behind her eyelids, she could hear a whispered battle raging between her old fears and her new faith.

You're such a beggar, always asking for things you need but can't earn. Things someone like you doesn't deserve.

God loves you. So much that he sent his Son to die to rescue you. He is glad to be the one you ask for what you need.

God doesn't care about you. If he did, he would never have let your Mama die. You're on your own here, babe. Miracles ain't happening for you.

Maddie shivered, looking over her shoulder for Zach.

Yes, Zach will come looking for you sometime soon. And you know what he's like when he's angry. Remember the stairs?

Maddie clenched her teeth. How she survived tumbling down the flight of concrete stairs outside that dingy motel, she'd never know. She had gotten by with only one scar on her scalp, and lots of the nurse's questions to deflect. But the memory of that endlessly long moment when the shock of Zach's push gave way to the horrifying sensation of falling—that nightmare might never go away.

You were held. Now you're here. And God is with you. And you still have Lucas. Hold on. Trust God.

"Yes," Maddie breathed the words to herself. "Trust God."

A gentle touch on her shoulder made her open her eyes. Chris stood beside her, holding out her phone. "It was buzzing. I think you may have missed a call."

She studied the screen. "Oh, thanks. Yep, it was Tricia."

"Seems kind of late for a call, even by California standards."

"Well, it's only ten there." She tapped through to voice mail and put the phone to her ear. "Hmm. Sounds like I should call her."

She changed Lucas's position to the other side, settled him in, and hit the call button.

Tricia answered after only one ring. "Maddie! I'm so glad I finally got a hold of you."

"Sorry. My phone went dead, and my charger wasn't working. Somebody here at the hospital loaned me one tonight."

"The hospital? Are you okay?"

"Yes. I'm fine." She sighed, letting her drowsiness numb the pain of telling the story again. "Lucas has started having seizures, and his doctor did an MRI that showed a brain tumor. Now a specialist says he needs surgery."

"Poor little guy. Can they operate at this early age?"

"The doctor says so." Maddie's mind ran through a quick replay of their meeting with Dr. Murphy. "But we prayed about it, and I believe God wants us to wait twenty-four hours. Not sure why…"

"So, someone is with you?"

"Yes. Chris and his mom, and the Dahlgrens." She yawned and stretched her legs out in front of her. "We're all camped out at the hospital because there's this massive blizzard outside. Even some of the doctors and nurses are stranded here."

Lucas stirred, finishing his feeding. She struggled to hold the phone to her ear with her shoulder while she arranged her clothing and raised him to the other shoulder to burp him. "Sorry," she said. "Can you repeat that, Tricia?"

"I asked, 'Which hospital are you at in Sargent?'"

"We're in Jefferson. The specialist we needed is here, at St. Olaf Children's Hospital." She patted Lucas until he gave a satisfying baby-sized belch.

"You're… in Jefferson?" Something had changed in Tricia's voice.

Maddie went cold. "What's the matter, Tricia?"

A long pause. "Well, Maddie. I… I heard from Tanisha again. She's with Zach. And she's in trouble."

Maddie closed her eyes. "Oh, Tanisha. She never knew how bad it was for me with Zach. I should have told her, warned her. This is all my fault. If she had known what he was like, she would never gotten mixed up with—" Suddenly, Maddie realized she was doing all the talking. "Um, Tricia, what kind of trouble is Tanisha in?"

Tricia said quietly, "Zach has taken Tanisha with him in order to... He wants her to help him find you. She texted me early yesterday. They were leaving California then. They were on their way to Minnesota. To Jefferson."

Maddie's eyes darted to the big glass doors, the broad windows. Suddenly, the lobby felt far too wide, far too open. Nowhere to hide. Zach was getting closer. And she couldn't run away from him. She could only hunker down here and hope he would never think to look for her in a children's hospital.

Tricia's voice interrupted her thoughts. "Maddie? Are you there?"

"Yes."

Chris looked up from the chair by the window, where he had been checking his phone. He frowned as if he saw something on her face he didn't like. He came and sat near her.

He mouthed, "Are you okay?"

She couldn't even shake her head. She felt she ought to ask Tricia more questions, find out things. But she was shutting down, going into self-protection mode. She couldn't think anymore. She didn't want to think. Because thinking meant seeing Zach driving like a demon, hunting her down, demanding the cocaine she hadn't taken. He would never give up. And he would probably find her because he knew people everywhere. He could always find out what he wanted to know.

Again, Tricia interrupted her thoughts. "Maddie, are you all right? Who is there with you?"

Lost in her dark thoughts, she said only, "Chris," and then she handed him her phone.

Chris took the phone reluctantly, confusion in his eyes. "Tricia? It's Chris Nelson. Maddie wanted me to take the phone. What's going on?"

Maddie watched Chris's face change from concern to anger. His back straightened like it had when he had confronted Megamind

Murphy. Like he was heading into battle. "I see. Yes. I understand. We will be on our guard." Looking straight at Maddie, he said to Tricia, "The good news here is that in this blizzard, driving is impossible. Forecasts say that it will continue into tomorrow. Some major roadways and most minor ones have been completely shut down. That should give us time to strategize a new safety plan."

Maddie started shaking. Chilled to her core, she kept her eyes locked on Chris and tried to absorb strength from the confident way he talked to Tricia. A tiny voice from deep within her kept praying, *God help me. Show me what to do. I thought I was safe… but now I'm scared all over again.*

Chris gave Tricia his own cell number, just in case she needed it. When Chris hung up and handed her phone back, Maddie still felt frozen. Lucas was batting at her shoulder, but she couldn't think what to do about that.

Chris reached out for him. "Want me to hold Lucas for a while?"

She shook her head in tight little motions. "No. I need to hold him." She stared across the lobby to the windows streaked by flashing white snow. "Do you really think this blizzard will keep him away?"

"Only a crazy man would drive on a night like this."

She didn't look at him. "Zach is crazy. Especially when he's angry." Anxiety whipped her words up to high speed. "He's probably using as he drives, too. Popping more Addies before the last hit wears off. He'll be hell on wheels. Nothing can stop him when he gets like that—"

Chris seized the arm of her chair. "Maddie," he said. When she didn't look at him, he said, "Maddie, listen."

"No, Chris, you don't know what he's like. He's probably—" Her head was pounding, her heart beating its way out of her chest.

"Maddie, calm down." Chris swung his chair around in front of her. "Maddie, listen. Right now, you are safe. Zach is not here, and he can't get here anytime soon. No one can get through that storm. No one."

Maddie blinked several times, and Chris's face came into focus. The noise in her head subsided. Her heart's irregular drumbeat dropped to a steady knocking. She watched Chris's eyes, the way a drowning man watches for a life raft from shore.

"You're sure," she said, almost like an accusation.

"Yes. I'm sure." Chris nodded.

She clung to the look in his eyes. This was the old Chris, the one she had always trusted. If he had hugged her now, it would have been all right. Her first all-right hug in years.

But he simply held her gaze tenderly and reassured her, "You're safe."

Maddie closed her eyes. Lucas's hand patted her neck, and he murmured his funny little baby sounds like he was reassuring her too. For now, they were safe. And just maybe they would stay that way.

Maybe this time, Zach would be defeated.

Lucas belched again, a huge sound for such a little body.

"That's what I think too, buddy," she said.

CHAPTER 13

Maddie felt something drawing her out of sleep. A noise. Crying, far away. Someone shushing. Good, she could go back to sleep… A touch on her shoulder made her jump. She blinked into the dimness. "Wha—"

Lena's face came into focus. She whispered, "I'm sorry, Maddie. But little Lucas is hungry."

Maddie rubbed her neck as she rolled herself from slouching to standing. After yawning and stretching her shoulders toward her back, she reached for her baby.

Lena covered a yawn too. "I'm going to go freshen up. And maybe stop off at the chapel for a little while. Do you need anything?"

Maddie shook her head.

Lena motioned to the sofa. "Want to try a different spot this time?"

Maddie shrugged and settled down in the warm spot Lena had vacated.

Lena placed her pillow beneath Maddie's arm to help support Lucas' weight. "I see your water bottle is empty. I'll pick up another one," she said and quietly stepped away.

Lucas latched on and nursed enthusiastically. Maddie could see the giant clock over the reception desk from this angle. *Four a.m.* No wonder she was so groggy. She hoped Paloma was right and Lucas' feedings would eventually move farther apart. This was exhausting.

She yawned again, catching a whiff of that housekeeping guy's musky body spray from Lena's pillow. Maddie's back went rigid. That scent triggered the entire memory. She *had* met him before.

It was back when Zach was here in Jefferson to "court" her, as he called it. In hindsight, Zach's visit had been much too short for her to really get to know him. But her longing to escape from old, painful memories had blinded her to any warning signs she should have watched for. Little did she realize she was preparing to make a whole load of new, more excruciating memories.

This memory was of—what was his name? Caleb? Kirk? Kyle. Meeting up with Kyle had been part of almost every date she and Zach went on back then. She thought it strange that when Kyle wanted Zach to drop off an envelope of "parts," Zach would send Maddie to deliver it to him. Sometimes she and Kyle met up outdoors and swapped envelopes in the wintry air; sometimes, Zach parked around the corner from Kyle's house, and she was the one who walked the "parts" up to his door. Zach always had some reason why she had to make the delivery. He said he was glad he had a girlfriend he could trust to handle money for him. What a fool she'd been. How he must have laughed to himself at the moron he'd found.

Once she knew what she was really delivering, he had her trapped. She couldn't break free, or he would report her as a drug dealer.

No wonder Kyle looked at her the way he did last night. *Aren't you the dope who used to deliver my dope?* Yep, that was her. And it was her for a whole lot of other people over the last four years. One ruined life helping ruin others.

On Maddie's lap, Lucas stirred and grunted, then resumed contentedly nursing. Watching him, a silent growl rose within her. *Never again,* she promised herself. Never again would she give Zach or anyone else power over her. Mama Bear was going to fight for her baby and her life. And nobody, not Zach, not Megamind Murphy—

Ask for a new scan.

Maddie looked around the darkened lobby to see who had spoken out of the silence. Chris dozed in a nearby chair, head back, mouth open, lightly snoring. Nick and Flora now slept, leaning against each other on a loveseat. Lena had not returned yet.

Insist on a new scan.

Lucas came loose from her breast. For a brief moment, he looked up at her, then past her. She rearranged her clothes to move him to the other side, but even as she turned him and laid him down, his eyes stayed fixed on some point over her shoulder. She glanced back: nothing there. But Lucas' little hand rose in that direction, the fingers spread, then came back to rest on his head. He squeezed his eyes shut and patted the back of his head three or four times. Maddie watched his funny little movements, so unlike his last seizure hours ago in the chapel. Then his eyes came open, and his soft mouth sought her breast, latching on as before. She shook her head. Babies did the strangest things.

The thought of another scan chilled her. How could she subject this sweet little boy to another MRI? That whole process was at least as hard on him as it was for her as a helpless observer.

Get a new scan.

She shivered. Dr. Murphy had said he would probably do a pre-op scan, anyway. Did she really have to ask for one? She waited in silence, hoping for some kind of answer.

The only reply was a solid sense that she knew what she needed to do. Just as she had known the answer when they prayed in the chapel.

Lena returned as Maddie finished feeding Lucas. She handed a water bottle to Maddie.

"Lena," she whispered, "I think God wants me to ask for a new MRI for Lucas."

If Maddie hoped Lena would be surprised, maybe even talk her out of this idea, she was disappointed. Lena answered immediately, "Then that's what you should do."

Maddie watched Lena's face in the pre-dawn grayness. "Did you—?"

"What?"

"Never mind." She cradled Lucas close to her chest and breathed in deeply. Now Maddie faced walking the halls in search of a nurse, possibly meeting up with that creepy Kyle along the way. Maybe she should ask for help on this one. "Lena, would you be willing to talk to the nurse about scheduling the MRI for me? I've seen someone here I would rather not run into again."

Lena hesitated only a second. "Certainly. I will go now if you like. I saw Nurse Jenny working at the nurses' station just a few minutes ago."

Maddie nodded. "Thank you."

With a quick squeeze of Maddie's hand, Lena left on her errand.

With her clothes back in order, Maddie stood and walked to a shadowy corner near the window to finish burping Lucas. Outside, the wind still hurled snow through the black night. Snow seemed a fragile wall for keeping Zach away. And a new MRI seemed a pointless, difficult step on a road toward an inevitable surgery.

And your past once seemed a permanent future.

With a flourish, Murphy flipped the switch to start the pressure building in his personal espresso machine. At just the right time, he turned the knob that directed steam through the finely ground beans. Strong, dark coffee trickled into his white porcelain demitasse, a souvenir of his post-divorce trip to Paris. Knowing he would detect the precise sound when the cup was perfectly full, he turned to watch the snow blowing—more slowly now—past the expansive window in his spacious office. Another privilege of his position. A position that was about to improve. As soon as that Clouse girl came around.

With a tight gargling sound, the machine announced the completion of his double espresso. Murphy twisted the knob to the off position before the final drops could land in his cup. Perfect. Even the crema he had made on the surface was perfect. And the biscotti he had reserved in the bottom drawer of his desk would be the perfect accompaniment.

Murphy knew with certainty that this was going to be his day. After a sleepless night, worrying about her sick baby, listening to the wind howling all around her, the Clouse girl would give in and consent to surgery. She would soften like this biscotti in his espresso. By evening, he would stand squarely in the limelight of a press conference, propounding The Murphy Technique by which he had successfully treated a neonatal medulloblastoma impacting an infant's brain stem.

Espresso had never tasted so good.

A gentle knock on his door interrupted his thoughts.

"Come."

A nurse opened the door far enough to step halfway into the room. "Dr. Murphy, Lucas Clouse's mother has requested an MRI in advance of more discussion of her son's treatment."

Murphy's lips rose at one corner. "Excellent."

She came across the room to hand him a tablet. "I thought you'd agree. I have an order prepared."

"Thank you," he said. He could afford to be appreciative and conversational today, he thought, as he scanned the digital order and signed it. "This will make Ms. Clouse feel better. She'll find it difficult to deny what we'll see there."

He returned the tablet to the nurse. "I suppose Grainger is still on campus to perform and read the scan?"

"Yes, sir," she replied, "I'll have her paged right away."

He nodded and watched her leave. Then he dipped his biscotti into his espresso a second time. The caffeine would give him just the energy he needed. Not too much, not too little. Perfect.

Tricia set her empty coffee mug down on the morning newspaper. She had no energy to walk to the pot for more. Here she sat, feeling like a traitor, scouring the Help Wanted ads while her beloved pregnancy center struggled for its existence. Of course, she promised herself, she would never leave until Dos Almas was squared away. And, hopefully, Maddie as well. But her family's savings wouldn't last forever. And try as they might to trim only the expenses that had the least impact on their children, she and Reece both knew more cuts lay ahead.

This morning, after the younger kids had caught their school bus and Drake pulled out in the old station wagon, Reece left to meet with a potential client—one he had little optimism about engaging. Still, in classic Reece style, he had headed out the door with a smile and a kiss for her.

Her phone rang from somewhere over by the sink. She groaned. Tricia pushed herself up from the table and scuffed across the kitchen. When she tipped up the phone, she groaned again. Not Dr. Joe, not right now. "No more bad news," she begged the phone. With it ringing in her hand, she scuffed back to the table and sank into her chair.

After a steadying breath, she answered, "Good morning, Dr. Joe."

"Good morning, Tricia." He sounded perky. But he usually did. Long years of perfecting his kind bedside manner, she supposed. He went on, "I hope I'm not interrupting family time?"

"No. It's just me and my coffee." And the want ads. Tricia folded the paper to hide them. Then she rose again to fetch a much-needed refill. "What can I do for you?"

As the coffee gurgled into her mug, he told her, "I spoke yesterday with my friend, Keith Bair, the pediatric cardiologist. About his former office building."

She winced against the likelihood she wasn't going to like what he said next. "What did you find out?"

"He said he sold his share of the building when he moved to Minnesota. But he said he would speak to his former colleagues and see if he could negotiate a drop in asking price for us."

"That would have to be a pretty big drop." She sank back into her chair, sloshing coffee onto the front page.

"Yes, it would." Dr. Joe fell silent for a moment. "Well, I just wanted to follow up and let you know what I learned. Sorry it's not happier news."

"Thanks, Dr. Joe. I always appreciate your diligence. It was worth a try. You never know."

"That's right. You just never know."

He made a little small talk, asked about her family, mentioned Paloma had stopped by to get a highchair for a client who had earned it through lessons done via the new streaming curriculum on parenting. He seemed pleased. "Well, I hope you have a great day, Tricia."

"Thanks, Dr. Joe. You, too."

Tricia let him end the call while she surveyed her spill. She mopped it up with a paper napkin, only then noticing that the coffee stain ringed an article on a suspended police officer. She shivered. That name... Cobb. She scanned the article briefly, thankful for the trustworthy policeman who believed Drake's story. She hoped this change would serve the cause of justice.

Turning the wet pages, she found the weather forecast for the day: high of 45 today, overnight low of 39. At least there'd be no frost. What about Minnesota, though? The colored map looked nasty over the Midwest. How she hoped it was nasty enough to keep Zachary Jarvis stuck somewhere far away from Maddie and Lucas.

Maddie. Lucas. Something like an electric chill ran up the back of her neck. She stood up as if ejected from her chair.

The blue numbers on the microwave read 8:34. Ten thirty-four a.m. in Jefferson, Minnesota.

Tricia couldn't explain her sudden alertness. No coffee was that strong. She looked around the kitchen, focused on everything and nothing. There was something...something she needed to do. Right now. But what? She walked into the living room as if the answer might be there. Again, everything and nothing glowed dully in the bland winter sunlight.

Maddie and Lucas.

What was happening with Lucas?

Her phone rang. She rushed to grab it off the kitchen table. "Paloma?"

"Tricia. Are you praying for Maddie and Lucas?"

"Um, I just—"

"Pray. I don't know why, but I know we need to pray. Right now."

"I agree. You start, I'll join in." First, she shot off a quick text to their volunteer prayer team. It was vague, respecting confidentiality, but urgent. She hit send as she dropped to her knees before her kitchen chair, listening to her friend asking God to do what Lucas needed. Zach was forgotten. So was the storm. It wasn't safety they prayed for. This was something else, something about Maddie and Lucas…and God.

She prayed next, begging God to intervene for Maddie and to give her his very best gifts for her need at this moment. Then they continued, alternating as they felt prompted. When Tricia looked up, the microwave clock read 8:44.

Paloma said, "I think it's done."

"Yes, whatever *it* was." Shaking in her slippers, Tricia pushed herself to her feet. Something was finished. And they would probably never know what it was.

Maddie followed the nurse through a door marked Imaging and Radiology. As the automatic door swished shut behind her, doubts hit hard. Why in the world had she asked for a second MRI? The one back in Sargent had been stressful enough. Now she was going to put Lucas through it all over again. The IV tubes, the sedation, the enormous machine like a tubular coffin, making knocking noises she could hear even through the headphones. And her helpless little baby lying still as death inside it.

She started to reach out for the nurse, to tell her to call it off, when the nurse turned into a small room where a tall woman in a lab coat waited. "Ms. Clouse," the nurse said, "this is Dr. Grainger. She is the radiologist who will perform Lucas' scan today."

Too late to stop now.

Dr. Grainger gave her a friendly smile and said, "Hello, Ms. Clouse. Would you like to hold Lucas while we prepare him for the scan?" She gestured toward a chair nearby.

Maddie sank into the chair with her precious little boy. She opened her mouth, but no words would come. She wanted to tell them he was better, really. He hadn't even spit up this morning. He hadn't acted like his head hurt today. Really, it was all okay now. Couldn't she just take him and leave?

The two women's hands moved relentlessly, gently and professionally, over her baby. She wished she could make them stop. Just stop. Stop everything. Stop the needles from poking her baby's arm, stop Lucas from being sick, stop Zach from driving here to punish her for something she hadn't done...

Helplessness wrapped her up like a mummy. Once again, things were out of her control. She was alone, and all of this was happening whether she wanted it to or not.

"There we go," said the nurse, stroking Lucas' cheek with a gloved finger. She gently laid his blanket back over the arm where she had placed the port and injected the medicine. "You're a good little patient, Lucas."

The radiologist told Maddie, "We'll give the sedative a few minutes to work, and then Lucas can have his scan, okay?"

Maddie didn't bother nodding. It wasn't like they were asking her permission. She sighed, blinking back tears. Lucas' eyes focused on her, and his cute little lips formed a smile just for her. She talked to him softly, not really wanting the others to overhear their private conversation. Did he understand how much she loved him right now? How much she wanted him to get well, and why she was putting him through all this?

As Lucas' eyelids drooped, Maddie noticed the other women were enjoying their own conversation. All about the long night spent in the hospital, and what they would do when they could go home, and how they'd have to get certain rooms ready to receive emergency cases once the roads cleared in this area. Soon their lives would return to normal. But Maddie's life...? Where would hers go?

Dr. Grainger checked her watch. Then she came closer and studied Lucas. "How does he seem to you, Ms. Clouse? Is he relaxed?"

He looked so peaceful in her arms. Maddie hated to disturb him. But she answered, "Yes, he's pretty limp."

"Perfect," the radiologist said. "I think we can begin, then."

Into the next room they went, where the women led Maddie to a smaller version of the big white machine she was used to. They let Maddie lay Lucas on the child-sized pad that would slide into the machine. Miniature earplugs and scaled-down headphones were set in place for Lucas, and a pair of adult headphones placed into Maddie's hand. Then Maddie kissed her finger and pressed it to Lucas' cheek before retreating to the chair she had been assigned. The nurse slid him inside the giant white tube.

The radiologist handed Maddie a pink flag on a stick. "If you see him starting to stir, please wave this at us. We'll be just beyond that window," she said, pointing over her shoulder. "This will probably require only a few scans, each a few minutes long. You should be back in recovery with Lucas by 10:45."

Then both nurses left the room. Maddie put on her headphones. The MRI machine's faint knocking and pinging started up like a clock that didn't keep time very well.

Maddie leaned her elbows on her knees and stared at the ugly white machine. With the headphones on, she could hear herself breathing, feel her blood pulsing against her ears. Her long hair fell like a curtain around the sides of her face. Behind it, she had space to herself. Here it was just her.

And God.

Okay, she said to him. *This is when I find out what this one-day wait was all about. I'm trying to keep believing that it was your idea. But tumors, you know... They grow. And they called this an "aggressive" one. So now I doubt whether we heard you yesterday. Or was it just my fear, my anxiety about Megamind Murphy, feeding everyone else's?*

Maddie hugged herself tightly. And she waited like God might answer, but there was only silence and the irregular ticking of the MRI machine in the distance.

She pulled her hair back behind the headphones so she could watch the lightweight blanket that covered Lucas. Nothing moved. Her thoughts slipped back to the long afternoon in the chapel with her friends. Their murmured prayers, the decision to wait.

The others, she remembered, weren't afraid like her. They had all prayed. And they had all come to the same conclusion, strange as it had seemed. Twenty-four hours was what God "said," for some reason only he knew.

Maddie stared, unfocused, at the huge white machine under the subdued lights. Blank and white, it stood like a movie screen on which her mind projected what she had pictured that Sunday in church: the picture of Jesus forgiving her—her, Maddie, the sinful woman weeping at his feet. It was still so real. So personal. She could almost feel his hand touching her shoulder. He had forgiven her. He loved her. He loved her still, right here in this hospital. He would love her if all her friends turned away... He would love her if Zach found her...even if Lucas died. She would always have Jesus. No matter the storm, He would stand with her through it all. She was—in some way she had never realized before—safe.

Safe, at last. Maddie looked down at her hands, gripping the armrests of the chair. Breathing out, she unfolded her fingers one by one, relaxing. All her life, this was all she had wanted, to be safe. And now she was. Here in a hospital in the middle of a blizzard. Here, waiting to hear her son's brain scan results. Here, hiding from a violent drug dealer.

Yes, my child. Safe isn't about what you hold onto. It's about who holds you.

"Thank you," she whispered. She closed her eyes and listened to her heartbeat gradually slowing to a peaceful, regular rhythm. The MRI had stopped. Opening her eyes, she looked toward the window where the radiologist had said she would be. There she was, turned aside and pointing to something Maddie couldn't see. A computer screen, maybe. And beside her stood Dr. Megamind Murphy wearing his fancy suit and a big frown. He gestured at the MRI machine with a rolling motion. The radiologist nodded and moved back to her controls.

Through the window, Dr. Murphy's eyes locked on Maddie. He gave the slightest shake of his head and turned away, his frown even deeper than before. Was that his "I-told-you-so" look? What was wrong?

The radiologist gestured for Maddie to take off her headphones. Then her voice came over the speaker above the window. "Ms. Clouse, we're almost done. Dr. Murphy just requested a few additional scans. Are you and Lucas all right in there?" Maddie's voice wavered as she said, "Yes. Okay."

"Good. Just a few more minutes. It's 10:45 now. We should be all through shortly."

Maddie replaced her headphones. The mechanical knocking resumed, and Maddie leaned back in her chair.

Safe, Lord, keep us safe.

True to her word, the radiologist turned off the machine not too long afterward. Then the nurse entered the scan room. She beckoned to Maddie and pushed a button that slid the bed out of the machine. Lucas stirred, scrunching up his closed eyelids. Maddie giggled at the sight of him.

"What a cutie!" the nurse said. "You may pick Lucas up now, Ms. Clouse."

As Maddie scooped her sleepy baby into her arms, the nurse went on, "He did such a good job with his scan. And look, the sedative is already wearing off. Perfect timing. Let's go back to the recovery room and take out those tubes."

As the nurse worked, Lucas woke up further, cooing and curling his tiny fingers around one of Maddie's. "Hi, Buddy," she said, wiggling her pinky against the tug of his grip. "I love you so much."

His increased wiggling said he was getting hungry. Both the nurse and the radiologist stooped over him, making baby noises to him and saying what a sweet little boy he was. Maddie knew it was part of their training. She'd seen it with her Mama. They wanted to help her and Lucas feel special in this place where he would soon undergo a dangerous operation. If only feeling special could make the surgery a sure thing—not a slim-chance last resort.

When both women seemed satisfied with Lucas' recovery from the sedative, the nurse told her, "Ms. Clouse, you are free to take your little boy back to your friends now. Dr. Murphy will call you to an examining room when he has had time to… process the scan."

Maddie frowned at her hesitation. "Did the scan show anything new?"

The radiologist merely said, "Your doctor will go over all that with you."

The nurse walked with Maddie to the door, pressing the automatic opener for her. Just before Maddie passed through, almost as an afterthought, the nurse gave her a quick side hug.

Surprised, Maddie stepped into the hallway. When she looked back, the nurse smiled and wiggled her fingers at them just before the door eased itself shut.

Her friends stood waiting for her just inside the chapel.

"Ah, there you are!" Lena said. "How did it go?"

"Fine, I guess," she said, shrugging. "The radiologist wouldn't give me any information. We have to wait for Dr. Murphy to call for us. He had to 'process the scan,' or something."

Flora yawned. "I don't know about the rest of you, but I could use a bite to eat."

Chris stretched his arms, angling them behind his head. "Sounds good." He gave Maddie a questioning smile.

"Yeah," she said, "the cafeteria's as good a place to wait as any, I guess."

Nick said, "Tell you what, you all go ahead. I'll wait here in case they come looking for us in the last place they found us."

Flora gave him a peck on the cheek. "Good idea, sweetheart."

Maddie turned back, feeling a need to acknowledge that more than an MRI had happened. "Nick," she said, "thanks for praying. Whatever happens now, I know that Lucas and I are safe in God's hands."

A grin spread across Nick's face as he gave her a thumbs-up. He replied, "That's one of the things I was praying for."

Tanisha crossed her arms tight. Only the pickup's engine made a dent in the silence. Zach didn't seem to mind that she wasn't speaking to him. *Jerk.* Selling her so he could get a good night's sleep. He must have set it up with the dread-head to keep her locked in until he came back for her. At least Rastafarian Man let her shower in peace. If only she'd had a change of clothes. Whatever. Zach didn't smell so good either. Tanisha gave her scalp a good scratching.

"Bed bugs?" Zach smirked at her.

Now she itched all over. But she wouldn't give him the satisfaction of letting it show. She turned her face to the window. At least this morning, the snow was just falling, not flying. She could see between the flakes, and they dropped almost straight down. Slowly, like floating tears.

The roadside to the right was piled high with dirty snow. Zach steered along behind two other cars on the only open lane of the freeway.

Taillights flared ahead.

Zach's taunting mood vanished. "What now?" He slowed, skidding.

Tanisha squinted to see in the distance. Pairs of bright yellow lights shone above the other vehicles, and a spray of snow flew toward the roadside. "What's flinging all that snow around?"

Zach smacked the steering wheel and cursed. "One o' those, whaddyacallits. Snowplows." More cursing.

They crawled along, slow as a snail, behind the giant one-vehicle snowstorm. Tanisha chuckled to herself. Mr. Speed Demon had to drive like a grandpa. Then her laugher choked off. Fast or slow, every minute, they were getting closer to Maddie. Maddie, her friend, who would hate her for this. Her friend, who thought she had escaped the nightmare called Zach. There had to be a way out of this.

"Where are we?" she asked in her most innocent voice.

"That truck stop where we stayed was a couple miles into Minnesota. Only a few hours to go." He looked directly at her, smiling like a wolf. "Almost time for you to make that friendly call to your BFF."

A few hours. The clock said 10:38. In a few hours, Zach's Twilight eyes would be burning into her, making sure she followed the script: "Hi, Maddie. It's me, Tanisha. You'll never guess where I am… Can I come see you?"

And if she refused to call? He'd made that penalty more than clear. She shuddered.

"Cold?" Zach asked, frowning at her. He really creeped her out. It was like he could read her mind.

She lifted her chin. "Surrounded by snow? How could I be cold?"

Zach turned his face back to the road. "Just practice your lines. You can't afford to mess this up." A sadistic grin twisted the side of his face. "Don't wanna end up in the papers: 'Dead woman's naked body found along freeway. In pieces.' Not pretty."

"Shut up."

"Just refreshing your memory."

Silence emptied into the cab again. She spent the creeping minutes wishing that snowplow would break down. Or the pickup would. Other cars crowded into their lane from nearly invisible onramps. A long parade of snails. On a dirty white trail.

Zach's eyes flicked to the rearview mirror and down. Then to the side mirror. "Holy—"

"What?" Tanisha swung around to look out the pickup's back window. Some big dark brownish vehicle was following them.

She looked closer. The SUV, or whatever it was, had a light bar across the top. "Are those cops?" She tried to sound nervous, like Zach. But to her, C-O-P-S spelled H-O-P-E.

"State patrol." He checked the rearview mirror again. "No lights. Maybe they're just checking on all us good law-abiding citizens out here."

Now, Tanisha thought. *Jump out now while we're going so slow.*

But Zach thought faster yet. He veered right, taking an off-ramp she hadn't seen coming. Plowing through snowdrifts as tall as the wheel wells, the truck rocked from side to side, keeping her off-balance. She could only grab the armrest and hang on. With each drift he hit, snow covered them in white waves. Big enough to drown her. And him. Surely Crazy Man couldn't see any more than she could.

"What are you doing?" she yelled.

Zach pushed the pickup through mound after mound of powder. The wipers weren't keeping up with the load. Zach was driving blind.

Suddenly, the truck stopped. Tanisha's heart hammered in her ears. With slow scrapes, the wipers swept the windshield down to the ice layer. Tanisha couldn't release her death-grip on the armrest. Outside her window stood a white-flocked stop sign. An intersection. They were off the freeway.

Zach blew out a hard breath. He stretched his jaws, flexed his fingers off the steering wheel. Blew out a cloud of steam. Checked the side mirror again. Nodded. "That's better."

Tanisha let her breath out at last. "Do you think they were following us?" She peered through the back window, hoping they were.

Zach stretched his neck from side to side, apparently in no hurry. "Coulda been. The way that nosey old geezer at the c-store watched me—Looked like a 'see something say something' type." He muttered something about his California license plates.

Tanisha could only hope the old guy actually had reported Zach, the slime-dog pimp. She hoped the old guy was smart enough to know what was going down. If he had turned Zach in, though, then surely by now... The clock read 11:03. She massaged her forehead. How much more of this could she take?

CHAPTER 14

Murphy didn't know how long he'd been staring at his desk. He only remembered walking back from Imaging and dropping into his leather swivel chair. Then something like a river hit him. Thoughts, images, buried emotions flash-flooded him. And over the roaring flood sounded two simple words: It's gone.

It couldn't be.

Numb, he realized his computer screen had gone to sleep. He woke it up with a tap. Staring back at him was the original Clouse MRI, next to this morning's scan. There the tumor was. And now, in the new scan, there it wasn't.

He'd been over this already. Multiple times. This just couldn't be. It didn't make sense. But there it was on his screen.

The Clouse tumor—his perfect tumor—had vanished.

No tumor, no promotion.

No promotion, no fame. No vindication.

Twenty-four hours ago, he had assured himself another case would come along if Clouse failed him. Why didn't that make him feel better now?

Murphy lurched to his feet and crossed his office, a thirsty man staggering across a desert. All at once, he halted, his back to the wall of certificates, diplomas, awards.

Why didn't he feel better? Because this tiny baby and his insistent mother had shown him what he really was. Arrogant. Selfish. Uncaring.

Uncaring. He, Dr. Jackson Murphy, MD, simply didn't care about another human being. Somewhere along the line, he dropped all real compassion and resorted to looking out for only one person. Himself. It gave him a clear-cut modus operandi: erect walls, control his world, build a name for himself. Everyone else had better move aside. Jack Murphy was coming through.

He pressed the heels of his hands to his eyebrows. What had he become? Nausea rose from his gut.

Someone knocked at the door. He dropped his hands to his sides and swallowed. "Yes?"

A nurse, probably the one they called Jenny, opened the door a crack and peeked around. "Doctor, the Clouse family is waiting... in the cafeteria."

He sniffed in a quick breath. "Right. Yes."

She hesitated. "Shall I... call them to room 4?"

"No." He ignored her puzzled look. "Not yet. Is—is the whole group still here?"

"Yes, Doctor. Roads are only now getting plowed. No one has been able to leave. Everyone who spent the night in the hospital is still here."

Murphy knew he was acting scattered, but he couldn't seem to pull it together. "Of course. Yes. I just need a few more minutes. And Bair—Is Bair still here?"

"Yes, Doctor," she said slowly, "everyone is still here."

"Good. I'll need him shortly." Murphy's mind was already veering in another direction. If the Clouse party was in the cafeteria, then...

Still, the nurse hovered in the doorway.

Murphy wanted her to move. "I will let you know when I want to see them."

Still staring at him, she nodded and backed out the door, closing it softly. Murphy waited until she should be busy elsewhere, then he stepped out into the hallway.

The elevator seemed impossibly far away. He urged his feet to keep moving anyway. A tremendous quaking had begun, deep in his core. His inner life was crumbling, falling into ruins. He needed... help.

He pushed the elevator button and stumbled inside when the doors opened. Clinging to the hand rail, he stared at his reflection in the gleaming silver walls. Since when did Jack Murphy seek help?

Since a crazy woman and her religious fanatic friends prayed overnight and—Was he really thinking this? They had prayed, and a miracle occurred.

Murphy forced himself upright and swatted at the "G" button on the panel. The doors closed him in with his thoughts. Those scans had no medical explanation. Something had intervened.

He hoped no one saw him weave his way out of the elevator. He aimed his heavy feet toward the chapel down the hall. His surgeon's fingers shook when he reached out to steady himself in the chapel doorway.

The pale, yellow room was empty. Strike that. One man sat up front. Murphy tried to back out as quietly as he had come in, but his trembling got the best of him. He gripped a nearby seat back with both hands, breathing heavily. His gut clenched, forcing a groan from his mouth. He tried to stiffen his arms, but it was too late. In the next second, the great Jackson Murphy dropped to his knees.

Zach reached under his seat and pulled out Tanisha's phone. Without taking his gaze from the road, he dialed Maddie's number.

"It's time to 'work your magic.'" He shoved the phone at her, frowning when she hesitated. "Unless you want me to—"

She snatched it out of his hand and pressed it to her ear. For a half-hour, she'd racked her brain for some subtle hint she could give, some secret code that would put Maddie on her guard. No luck.

A bunch of tones went off in her ear, followed by a mechanical voice, "You have reached a number that is no longer in service." Tanisha almost laughed out loud. She pressed her hand to her mouth while the message played again and then hung up.

She looked at Zach. "Uh-oh. Sounds like she changed her number."

"Gimme that!" He tore the phone from her hand. He dialed again and listened, then threw the phone at the windshield. He roared a stream of curses and stomped on the accelerator. The truck swam sideways, their back end swinging toward the deep ditch on the opposite side of the country road. Zach brought it back under control, still swearing. "I shoulda known! That little—"

Tanisha gripped the dashboard. "Zach, slow down. Let's think about this."

Zach huffed and puffed. But he did slow down. A little. "She had someone helping her. She must have. But who? She had nobody. That's why I picked her."

Zach raved on, but the truck plowed more slowly through the snow. Tanisha's grip on the dashboard relaxed. Even though snow had quit falling, the roads out here in the boonies were deep with it. How did people tell where the edges of the road were? With the sun overhead, the glare smeared it all into one bright white blanket. No lines, no tire tracks, and no shadows. Hardly any trees except a clump around a house now and then. Neighbors were like miles apart. Who would live out here?

"Do you know where we are?" she asked him.

He jerked his chin toward the windshield. "'Course. Up ahead, about fifteen miles, is Jefferson. Little Miss Maddie's hometown."

Fifteen miles. Fifteen miles of driving through this stuff?

Zach eased to a stop at a little rise. To the right and left, triangular yield signs hinted at a crossroads. The snow lay a little less deep here. Zach's eyes narrowed to slits as the engine idled.

"Now what?" Tanisha said. Not like he was blocking traffic or anything. All the sane people were at home, eating lunch. Tanisha's stomach rumbled.

He turned his haggard face toward her. "Would ya let me think?"

She held up her hands and waited. No doubt he had a map of the town in his head. He'd told her once that he spent weeks here seducing Maddie into going to California with him. Tearing out any roots she had left in the place. Tanisha frowned. Maddie had nothing left to come back to.

Tanisha turned from the light to stare at her knees. Maddie had counted on Tanisha to keep her secret—and look where that had gotten her. And when Maddie found out...

Zach checked his map app, playing with the screen. "Bingo. A left up here gets us onto a highway in a mile or two." He narrowed his eyes in that direction. "They'll probably have that route cleared—goes right past some hospital. All right. I've got me a Plan B. Sneak in the back side of town and begin the hunt. First stop: her dead mother's house."

The words made Tanisha's skin crawl. As soon as they got into Jefferson, she'd make a break for it. Somehow. She just couldn't be there when Zach found Maddie.

Maybe she should just jump out now and take her chances in this God-forsaken—

"You hungry?" he asked her. She whipped her head around. His face had gone pasty again, but the sharp look in his eyes said he'd read her thoughts.

"Hungry. Yeah." She jammed her hands into her coat pockets. "We gonna get lunch sometime today?"

He gunned the engine, and the tires spun. Another try, same result. "Huh. Looks like we're gonna need a little push," he said, "if you wanna get that lunch." He jerked his thumb toward the back end. "Get out."

"What? You're the big macho man. You get out, and I'll steer."

Zach's left hand came around and fastened onto her chin before she could block him. He pulled her face so close to his she could smell his teeth rotting. "Give me a good reason to keep you alive," he said. His right arm shifted, and she heard a click near her waist. "Or do we end this here?"

She still hadn't healed up from the last time she heard that click. "Okay, okay," she said through her teeth.

He shoved her back against her door and made a show of folding his knife. "That's more like it."

Suddenly Zach reached across and opened the door, sending Tanisha tumbling onto her back in the deep snow. He laughed as she struggled to her feet. She thought about slamming the door but left it hanging open instead. That boy needed to cool off.

Gripping the truck as she high-stepped through the drifts to the back bumper, she squinted back the way they'd come. How far would she get if she ran now? Not very. Except for the occasional clump of trees, it was just miles and miles of open country. Just heavy white snow cut by two deep ruts. Cold soaked into her shoes and the wet seat of her pants. Resigned and shivering, she turned and braced her feet in one of the ruts, her bare hands pressed against the frosty tailgate.

"Okay!" she yelled.

Zach gunned the engine. The tires spun, flinging ice in her face and inside her coat through the open zipper. Tanisha swatted it off. Cold, cold, cold. She stepped to the left and pushed again while he prodded the gas. This time, the flying slush missed her. The truck rocked forward, then back, then gained a little traction. It lurched ahead. It was rolling.

"Hey!" she shouted. The truck kept rolling. Tanisha scrambled after the pickup and finally grabbed the inside door handle. "You idiot!"

Zach laughed again and gave it gas. The door swung inward, pinching her arm. Tanisha held on, clutching both straps of the seatbelt with her left hand. Her legs fought against the dragging snow to stay even with the rest of her. She hated this dude—him and his squeaky, mocking laugh.

The pickup hit a bump and bucked. That jerked the door open and gave her a chance to swing a leg up to the running board. From there, she leveraged herself onto the seat. Now she slammed the door. "You think you're so funny." She glared at him, panting.

"Not me. You were the one doing the crazy little dance." Again with that annoying squeaky laugh of his. "Too bad I didn't have my phone out. Coulda filmed that."

Tanisha slouched in the seat, her arms crossed tight across her chest. She could put up with a lot, but mockery? No way. This was ending. She just needed her phone and some of Zach's gas money. Something buzzed on Zach's side of the cab. Without looking at him, she said, "Your phone went off."

Zach laid off the creepy laughter to ask, "What?"

"Your phone. A text or something."

Zach patted his coat to find the right pocket. He dragged the phone out, read the screen. With a shout that made Tanisha jump, he pumped his fist in the air. "Do I have connections or do I have connections! It's my man Kyle." He started to text back until the truck took a dangerous slide to the right.

"Here, let me do that," Tanisha said, holding out her hand.

He passed her the phone. "Ask him where."

The message was from some contact Zach had labeled "KM." When she read this Kyle's message, the words frightened her as much as Zach's switchblade.

Hey man. Saw your redhead girlfriend. You in town too? Im in need man. Bad.

Hovering over the screen, her finger refused to move.

Zach smacked her with a backhand. "C'mon, stupid, don't you know how to spell 'where'?"

She rubbed her cheek. Then, one letter at a time, she typed the word. Maybe if she just deleted it, only acted like she sent it.

Zach growled slowly, "Hit send. Or I'll send you out the windshield."

She sat frozen. Zach grabbed the phone out of her hand.

Tanisha couldn't bear to watch him do it. She turned her eyes toward the window. *Sorry, Maddie. I am so, so sorry...*

One tap. With a whoosh, the word was on its way.

Maddie noticed Nick's strange expression when he entered the cafeteria. Flora did, too, judging by the look she gave him. But he merely stepped to the counter and picked out a granola bar and a banana, then ate without saying a word. He was just finishing his quick breakfast when Nurse Jenny walked up to Maddie at the table.

She said simply, "Dr. Murphy would like to see you in his office, Ms. Clouse. He said there is room for your whole party there."

Maddie shot a quick look at Chris. His bloodshot eyes and the stubble along his jawline told her how tired he was.

"Are you up for this?" he asked.

Maddie shook her head. "First, I thought the results would never come. But now I wish I didn't have to hear them." She pressed her lips together and focused on Lucas. He gurgled at her. He even seemed to return her smile. If only he could go on acting normal like this. Forever.

Lena collected Maddie's diaper bag and gave Maddie's arm a gentle squeeze. Maddie followed Chris and the nurse toward the elevator to Megamind Murphy's private lair.

When the nurse opened the door for them, Maddie stepped through first. Outlined against the clearing sky beyond a huge window stood Dr. Murphy, on the far side of his desk. His gaze fastened on Lucas. Maddie shuddered. Was he already planning the surgery, calculating where he would make the first incision?

Then, as if startled out of his thoughts, Dr. Murphy motioned her to a soft armchair that faced his desk. He even turned it so it was easier for her to sit down while holding the baby.

"Ma'am?" he said, positioning a second chair for Lena. She accepted it graciously. Chris stood behind the two of them. Flora and Nick filled in on either side of him.

Maddie had never seen an office like this one. Her mother's oncologist always met with them in an exam room. But this room was decorated with a thick patterned rug, a big leather sofa, and bookshelves. No pictures, though. Not even on his desk. He had lots of degrees in frames on the wall, some kind of little coffee machine on a side table, and—Dr. Bair, back in the corner. The younger doctor sat on a tall, padded stool, one foot on the floor and his hands clasped around his other knee. He smiled and nodded when he caught Maddie's glance. Maddie swallowed down a feeling of dread. Calling in more doctors always meant more bad news.

Dr. Murphy glanced at Dr. Bair and cleared his throat. Eventually, he seated himself on a corner of his desk. "I apologize for keeping you waiting so long. It, uh, must have been a bit nerve-racking for you. The truth is, Lucas' scan was the first of its kind for me."

Maddie shook her head in confusion. "Wh-what do you mean?"

"I mean this." He turned his computer monitor around so they could see the screen. Maddie could make out two x-ray-like images of a head. Lucas' head. Dr. Murphy pulled his shiny stylus from his chest pocket and pointed to the picture on the left. "This," he said, gently tapping a rounded shape near the base of the brain, "is the medulloblastoma detected on the MRI you brought in. Clearly impacting nearby structures. And causing buildup of CSF—cerebrospinal fluid—as seen here and here."

Maddie cringed as his stylus tapped multiple places on the scan. She had googled all this stuff before they left Sargent. The words were all terribly familiar.

Dr. Murphy's stylus lowered, and for a moment, he just stared at the screen. Then he shook his head and went on. "And this," he said, resting his hand above the right side of the screen, "is Lucas' brain today."

Maddie leaned forward, narrowing her eyes at the screen. Then she realized Dr. Murphy was looking directly at her. She met his dark eyes. Was the man... smiling?

He said softly but firmly, "Ms. Clouse, your son no longer has a tumor."

Maddie gasped. "What did you say?"

Dr. Murphy laid down his stylus. "Your son's tumor has vanished. It's not there anymore."

Chris's hand grasped her shoulder. Flora and Lena cry-laughed at the same moment. Maddie blinked, numb, watching all of them in slow motion. She turned back to the newer scan. No more round blob, no more spaces where the doctor had seen fluid. It looked like one of those pictures on Google of a normal baby brain.

He's been healed. Laughing and crying at the same time, she folded herself over her precious baby and rocked with him back and forth. When she could speak, she sat up and held him out so she could see him—her healthy baby boy. He was contentedly rubbing his little fist against his gums. His shining deep brown eyes seemed to ask her what all the fuss was about.

"Lucas," she told him, "you're fine! God healed you! He did!" She hugged him to her heart and cried some more. Chris was hugging Lena, and Flora was crying on Nick's shoulder, and everyone was talking at once.

She almost didn't hear Dr. Murphy's next words. "I was wrong in not respecting your wishes," he said. "Apparently—Well… Ms. Clouse, I offer you my sincerest apology. Please…forgive me."

Her eyes met his. She could do nothing but nod. He bowed his head slightly, then stood and moved toward the door. Maddie tried to think of something to call out to him but could only follow him with her eyes. He stopped a moment next to Nick, long enough to shake his hand and say something in his ear. Nick nodded, reached into his back pocket, and worked a business card from his wallet. Then Dr. Murphy slipped out, closing the door softly behind him.

Now everyone crowded around Maddie, touching Lucas as if he were a new and unusual creature.

Over all the chatter, Chris said, "I think this calls for another prayer, don't you? We've got a lot to be thankful for!"

The others agreed and crowded in closer.

Maddie held up a hand. "Wait. I've gotta stand up. I'm getting claustrophobic down here."

Everyone laughed and moved back to help her to her feet. Someone shoved the chair aside, out of their circle. She cradled Lucas against her chest, facing outward, and each of his friends reached out to rest a hand on him.

The words they prayed came swirling through Maddie's hearing like a song she had always wanted to sing. And now, even though she was too choked up to speak, her heart sang it with them.

God, I don't know what you did, but I know this was all you. Lucas' brain is changed. Even Mega—I mean, even Dr. Murphy is changed. Maybe he is healed, too, somehow? You did something here I did not expect. And probably even more than I can see. I can only say thank you, God. Thank you, thank you, thank you.

The prayers trickled to an end, and her friends looked at one another as if unsure what they should do now. Maddie turned to see Dr. Bair, still in the corner, sweeping his thumb beneath his eyes.

He smiled and rose from his stool to come closer. "I am so happy for you, Ms. Clouse. And happy for Lucas, too. This is one of those days doctors always hope for. Sometimes we have a part in bringing them about." He cupped his hand around the back of Lucas's head. "But for Lucas, God had more spectacular plans."

Maddie smiled down at her happy baby again. "I still can hardly believe it." She shook her head and took another deep breath, feeling steadier by the minute. "I didn't really say thank you to Dr. Murphy. He left so quickly."

Dr. Bair nodded, aiming a secret little sideways smile at the door. To Maddie, he said, "Dr. Murphy—Well, this was a miracle. Dr. Murphy has never seen one so clearly before. It rocked his world... on a lot of levels. But he asked me to stay and answer any questions you may have."

Maddie couldn't think of anything much, let alone questions. "Your support was a big encouragement to me, Dr. Bair. Thanks."

Dr. Bair ducked his head briefly. "Glad I could help."

Chris stepped forward with similar words to say and shook Dr. Bair's hand. Then he said to her, "Hey, Maddie, this news is too good to keep to yourself. You've got to call your friends at Dos Almas. They'll be blown away."

Maddie's smile grew larger. "Oh, definitely, yes!"

Dr. Bair leaned forward. "I'm sorry, Dos Almas?"

Maddie said, "Dos Almas Pregnancy Center. It's in California. It's kind of a long story, but…"

Dr. Bair rested his hands on his waist. "Strangely enough, I've heard of Dos Almas Pregnancy Center. A colleague of mine just called me about the center. I wouldn't mind hearing your story if you don't mind telling it."

"Not at all." Maddie shook her head and smiled down at Lucas again. Then she told Dr. Bair how Lucas came to be and how her life had been changed by this little baby and a stranger with her mother's name and a group of people who cared what happened to her.

Maybe she was babbling, but she couldn't help it. Dr. Bair didn't seem to mind. Laying out the whole story this way just made it seem more awesome. She'd never seen any of this coming.

Maddie straightened then and finished with, "Everyone you see with me today is part of this story because of God and Dos Almas."

Dr. Bair looked at each of her friends one by one like he was taking a mental picture. Then he turned back to her, shaking his head and smiling. "Amazing how he works, isn't it?"

For some reason, the words gave Maddie the funny feeling this story wasn't over yet.

CHAPTER 15

Tanisha had to admit it: Zach was right about the highway into town. A snowplow, spewing snow aside, might as well have laid out a red carpet. All Zach needed was Kyle's reply, and Maddie would be doomed. Up ahead, Tanisha spotted the "Welcome to Jefferson" sign rising from the roadside like a giant headstone.

As they rolled past the headstone, Zach started grinning. This was it. Next chance she had... Her hand wrapped around the door handle.

"Place looks different covered in this much snow," Zach said, slowing.

Tanisha followed his line of sight. They were passing through a kind of industrial area. No homes, just big warehouse-type buildings, but farther apart than in any California industrial park she'd ever seen. Beyond them, those other buildings had to be in the downtown area. A pair of golden arches poked up out of the snow across from a red DQ sign. Her mouth watered. Could she put off the inevitable a little bit longer, give Maddie even a few more minutes of freedom? "So, are we gonna grab some lunch while we wait for your man Kyle?" she asked, trying to sound like it didn't really matter.

Zach checked his phone again and shook his head. He tossed it onto the seat and drummed his fingers on the steering wheel. His stomach growled so loudly Tanisha could hear it over the engine.

"Hold onto your panties," Zach said, his eyes scanning the intersection ahead. "Without Kyle making contact, I gotta do a deal to get us some lunch money. Then you're going in to place our order. I'm not showing my face too soon."

Tanisha pulled her coat tighter around her. So, Zach needed her to do the public stuff for him. Maybe he still thought the cops were following them. Seemed unlikely they'd find him now, though.

"Can't you just use the gas money?" she asked.

Zach fired a look at her. "You just let me manage the money, stupid."

As Zach steered the truck into an alley behind one of the warehouses, she tried out escape scenarios in her head. Zach gives her the lunch money, she goes inside alone...

"Man, where is everybody?" Zach's frown said he'd expected to find easy customers back here by the dumpsters and freight docks.

No point reminding him there'd just been a blizzard. The drifts the truck dove through in this back alley should have proved that.

"What about the cash I earned by 'working' back at the truck stop?" Tanisha couldn't keep the acid out of her voice.

"You paid for my motel room. And our breakfast. The guy didn't have much on him."

Tanisha rolled her eyes and watched the blank walls pass her window. Never had her life felt like such a dead end. She wasn't worth more than a cheap motel room and a couple of doughnuts.

The alley dumped them out onto a street lined with little shops. Zach turned right, back toward the main street, passing a man in a parka shoveling the sidewalk in front of a bakery. The guy looked up and waved. Zach scowled at him and drove on.

Tanisha's head turned to watch the shoveling man. Her stomach rumbled. The idea of sticking with Zach just long enough to get the free food was growing less appealing by the minute. What if people in Jefferson were all like that friendly guy with the shovel? She could take Zach's money, walk into McDonald's, ask the person at the counter to call the cops—

"Cops," Zach said under his breath.

Tanisha gasped. But Zach hadn't read her mind. At the intersection ahead, a patrol car rolled across their path. The cop turned and stared at Zach.

"Watch this," he said to Tanisha. He lifted one forefinger off the steering wheel and nodded at the cop. The cop did the same then cruised on by. Zach grunted. "Maddie called it the 'one-finger wave.'"

He muttered something about a different finger and pulled up to the stop sign. Looking along the entire street, he frowned. "C'mon, folks. Storm's over. There's gotta be someone outside..." He turned onto the main drag and kept driving, his head making a slow sweep from side to side.

They passed the McDonalds, with its cloud of steam billowing from the roof. Juicy, grilled burgers... salty fries... Tanisha launched a remark, but Zach's own stomach growled as he growled at her. Better not push her luck.

A woman in a deep teal parka stepped out of McDonald's with a bag in hand. Before she pulled up her hood, Tanisha caught a glimpse of long red hair. Maddie? Tanisha bit her lip and turned her eyes in another direction, hoping Zach hadn't seen her. But he had. He leaned forward to get a better look. Tanisha's heart was pounding so loud she almost didn't hear what Zach said to her.

He backhanded her arm. "Check her out, I said! Is that her?" He leaned way back in his seat, hiding his face with his right hand.

Tanisha made herself look at the redhead. Just then, a little girl came bouncing up to the woman, followed by a man. Obviously, a family. When the woman turned to talk to the girl, her face looked forty-something.

Tanisha swallowed and faced forward again. "Nope. Not her."

Zach shook his head. "That would have been too easy."

And too soon, Tanisha thought. *I've got to get out of this truck.*

Just then, Zach suddenly took a left. The truck slid halfway across the intersection on the layer of snow under its tires. Tanisha braced herself, jamming a couple of her fingers into the heater vent.

"Ouch! Would you quit—?" She twisted her fingers free.

"Oh, shut up," Zach replied. "I just found the kids who are gonna buy us lunch."

He drove along a snow-covered lot surrounded by a chain-link fence. From the basketball hoops and baseball backstops sticking up through the snow, Tanisha guessed it was a school yard. Outside the far end, three teenage boys leaned against the fence. Zach drove past slowly, easing the truck around the corner, where some tall, bare trees provided a little cover from the sun overhead. For the first time in hours, she didn't have to squint against the glare.

Zach waited a moment, watching the boys, then reached behind his seat into the duffel he kept there. After rummaging around in it, he came up with two baggies that he stuffed into his inner coat pocket. He gave her his spooky Twilight look.

"Sit tight," he said. "Or I'll be on you so fast you'll never feel it coming." He flashed his blade and clicked it shut again. Then he climbed from the truck, pulled his shoulders back, and swaggered toward the fence.

Tanisha watched. She wanted to yell at the boys, "Clear out! Get away while you can!" But she could tell the moment they noticed Zach, the moment they got curious and came closer. She cringed, remembering the slimy way he wormed into her mind that night at the bar, the night that ended her up here, on the road to selling out her best friend.

She had to look away. On the dashboard, down where the windshield met the defroster, lay her cell phone. Zach wasn't watching. Tanisha grabbed the phone.

She breathed faster. Stole a look at Zach. Still busy with the kids. She had the phone. Now, where was the gas money?

Zach's phone buzzed. KM had answered. *St. Olafs childrens hospital. Meet me at—*

Tanisha didn't wait to read more.

One eye on Zach, she flung her left arm over the seat. She could just barely touch the duffel. Pushing up with her feet, she grabbed hold of the open zipper. But she couldn't reach into it with the same arm. She checked again: Zach wasn't looking. In a flash, she knelt on her seat and plunged her hand into the duffel. Stinky clothes, a couple more baggies, and a wad—

Her eyes caught a car's motion through the back window. Cops. Her chest clenched as tight as her fingers around Zach's money. She couldn't breathe. Should she dive out the door and beg the cops for help, or—

The patrol car stopped several yards behind Zach's pickup but close enough to read the rear license plate. The California license plate.

Zach wrenched his door open and bulldozed into Tanisha. Before he'd even slammed his door, he had that pickup fishtailing around the corner. A siren started wailing.

At the intersection, he spun to the right onto the main drag. The cops followed, doing a little sliding of their own. Zach gunned it and headed for the edge of town. Back toward open country. And all that snow.

Tanisha braced one hand against the dashboard, and the other clung to the armrest. "Don't be an idiot, Zach! You can't outrun these guys! They drive in snow all the time. You're just—"

"Shut up!" He gripped the wheel with both hands, squinting into the glare.

Tanisha pressed back against her seat. Buildings passed in a blur. A hospital. The warehouse. Back the way they came. She wouldn't need McDonald's people to help her now. The police would catch them at last, and then she could tell them the whole story. If she could just remain seated until the ride came to a complete stop...

Zach laughed, mocking the siren. "Their cruisers can't clear these drifts like I can."

Tanisha looked back. The cops did seem farther behind than at first.

Zach yelled at the rearview mirror. "That's right. You're losing. Eat my snow!" He grinned like a shark.

He stomped on the accelerator, and the truck fishtailed momentarily, sending Zach's phone sliding into Tanisha's leg. She glanced down. *If Zach ever sees that message...* Closing her eyes against the painful white glare, Tanisha let the chase go on without her. All went silent. She breathed slower now, calm with absolute certainty. She lowered her left hand from the dashboard and let it cover Zach's phone. Her right hand crept up the armrest to the power window control.

Be free, Maddie. Be safe.

One push of the button, one fling of her arm, and the phone flew glinting through the sunlight.

Zach did a double-take. "What did you just—?" Arm outstretched, he lunged toward the window.

The world tilted, and Tanisha heard herself scream. Zach's body smashed hers against the door. They were falling. She couldn't breathe. Glass shattered. Sharp pain slammed her head and neck. Then a sudden stillness and the whiteness beside her began turning red.

Chris stood beside Chuck, the hospital's head of maintenance, each of them armed with a snow shovel.

"Ready?" Chuck asked.

"Let's do this," Chris answered, yanking his parka hood over his head.

Chuck activated the hospital's automatic front doors, which swooshed open for the first time in hours. A flat wall of snow three feet tall stood before them.

With a whoop of released energy, Chris drove his shovel into the drift and flung the first scoop aside. Chuck, grinning, knuckled down on his share of the job. Together, they had the opening cleared inside of fifteen minutes. A whole platoon of wheelchairs could easily make it out the doorway now.

Nick walked up just as they finished. "I see I waited long enough to miss the fun," he said, pulling on his coat.

"Welcome to the fresh air," Chris said, his nostrils flaring. He planted his shovel in the pile he'd made and sucked in a deep breath.

Even with the bright sunshine, the temps bit at his nose and lungs. *Ah, winter.*

"Well, Chris," Nick said, "we should be able to go home soon. Looks like the city's made a good start on plowing the major roads. Highways are opening up too."

Chuck nodded. "We get cleared pretty quickly around here. Over at Jefferson Regional, it takes a little longer. But after a storm, everybody's anxious to have access to a hospital ASAP. So, we get Regional's overflow until they're open."

As if to back up Chuck's statement, a siren split the icy air, and an ambulance pulled into view, followed by a police car. When the vehicles slowed to turn toward the side emergency entrance, Chris recognized the ambulance driver. Brent. Which meant Sean was probably in back with the patient.

Chris gave Chuck a clap on the shoulder. "Thanks for letting me help. I was going stir-crazy all cooped up here."

Chuck's grin returned. "I don't often get offers for help." He surveyed the hospital's snow-covered grounds. "You wouldn't want to stick around a little longer, would you?"

"Maybe next blizzard," Chris said, laughing. "Hey, Nick, I'm going to tuck around and see my friends, those EMTs that just came in. What a night they must have had, huh?"

Nick nodded and turned to accompany Chris into the lobby. "Sounds good. I think Maddie will be with Dr. Bair for a few more minutes. Then we can go into town and find something hot to eat before we go our separate ways."

"Great. I'm ready for a real meal." His smile felt a little hollow. The going-separate-ways part wrenched his heart. These last twenty-four hours plus had only welded him to Maddie more. He thought she might be feeling the same way. But knew he couldn't push her. He'd tried that years ago. Epic fail. At the moment, he had to remember, Maddie still had that drug dealer hounding her. For now, then, his job was to do all he could to protect her and support her through this.

Wet boots squeaking on the gleaming floor, he and Nick followed the hallway until red letters pointed toward the emergency entrance. Chris peeled off to the right, telling Nick, "I'll make it quick."

Following the signs to the farthest wing of the building made for a long trip, it turned out. Finally, Chris arrived at a pair of wide doors labeled Emergency. They opened easily when he pressed the round metal button. He entered and spotted his co-workers inside, beyond the reception desk.

The woman at the desk lifted bloodshot eyes to him and asked if he needed help. She seemed relieved when he told her why he was there. "They should be done shortly," she said. "Feel free to wait over there."

No way was he about to sit down again in one of those hospital chairs. But he did move away to go flip through a magazine.

Halfway through an article on waterskiing, he saw his buddies emerge, pulling on their coats.

Sean spotted him first. "Look what the cat dragged in," he said.

"Sean. How'd you get stuck working with Brent?" he teased, tossing his magazine back on the table.

Sean snorted. "Drew the short straw. Again."

Brent punched his partner in the arm. "Short suits you, midget." He shook his head at Chris. "Stuck at the company overnight, then we get called out first thing for a car wreck."

Chris frowned. "Bad?"

"Single car," Brent said. "A pickup, out in the country. Took the cops on quite the joyride. Ended badly."

"Oh. Casualties?"

Sean nodded. "One. Died pretty much instantly. The other one coulda walked away but had to be pried out of the wreck by the rescue squad."

"Crazy how that goes sometimes," Chris said. Just being with these guys made him itch to be back at work. He rubbed his scalp. Fact was, he itched all over. A good shower would sure be welcome.

Brent patted his inner shirt pocket. "Hey, mind if we step outside? I've gotta have a smoke."

Chris noticed Brent's hands shook when he reached for his coat zipper. For a guy as tough as a bulldog and big as a bear, Brent was still a puppy at heart. Chris moved toward the door, saying, "Yeah, let's get some fresh air. Rough one, huh?"

Brent grunted and swatted at the sensor to hurry the door open. Outside, he lit up downwind from the emergency entrance and began puffing away. Chris zipped up his own parka, taking a moment to pull back the sleeve and check his watch. He should probably head back in to join Maddie soon.

Just then, Sean pointed out a tow truck passing the hospital. "That was fast. That's the pickup right there."

A crushed black Ford F-150 hung from the tow's winch. Chris whistled at the thought of anyone being trapped in that cab. "It's pretty banged up."

"Yeah. Driver probably didn't navigate snow much, being from sunny SoCal."

Chris flipped back the hood of his parka to hear better. "California? How do you know they were from southern California?"

Sean shrugged. "The plates. Plus, Benson and Mackay said they were looking for this one. Their radios were full of chatter."

Chris's mental calculator kicked in. From Tanisha's text to Tricia, then Tricia's call to Maddie... That would be California to Minnesota in just over two days... in a blizzard...His heart sped up. What were the chances?

Brent blew one more cloud of smoke toward the blue sky. "I know we're not supposed to talk about our patients—" He threw his cigarette to the icy ground and stomped on it. "But creeps like him make me want to toss them in a ditch myself. The dude was wanted for trafficking and drugs in Cali. Cops said the Black girl with him was one of his victims. Somebody reported him for trafficking just last night near the Iowa border—even took down his plates. Our guys spotted him dealing drugs to some kids right here in town around noon."

Sean finished for him, "He tore out of there and ended up rolling into a dredge ditch."

Trafficking. Black girl. Chris kept himself from grabbing Sean by his coat collar, but he did get in his face. "Sean, you said there was one casualty. Which one died?"

Sean leaned away from him. "Chris, buddy. Chill. What's up with you? You know we can't give out names."

Chris took a step back. Took another breath. "I don't need names. Just—was it the male or the female who died?"

Brent was staring at him. "Chris, you don't think… I mean, was this your girl's…?"

Chris closed his eyes for a second, then spoke as calmly as possible, "Could have been. He was headed this way. Hunting her down." He stopped. The outdoor temps weren't causing the chill that now rippled up his neck. Was Maddie's nightmare over? Had it just ended in some ditch out there?

Brent made an awkward grab for Chris's arm, then drew back.

Sean looked back and forth between them, clueless. Only Brent knew a piece of Maddie's story, wrenched from Chris on one of the longest shifts the two of them had ever worked together.

Chris bent and braced his hands on his legs, breathing hard. "Guys," he said. "Please. Which one died?"

Brent jerked his chin toward the emergency entrance, just then sliding open. "There's your answer."

Two uniformed officers escorted a handcuffed individual from the building. Chris's knees buckled. Brent had to hold him up. Next minute, he had to hold him back.

Jarvis had survived.

Maddie left Dr. Bair's office feeling she could fly. When she had mentioned Lucas' heart condition, Dr. Bair offered to review the files that Dr. Balinga had sent over. Maddie had traveled so far, he said, and his appointments for the day had all been canceled. After studying the files, Dr. Bair said Lucas had "a mild pulmonary stenosis." Maddie liked the word "mild," especially since Dr. Bair said it meant that no surgery was needed now. He agreed with Dr. Balinga that it could be monitored and operated on when Lucas was older and stronger—just the way things had gone for Maddie. Another load lifted for the time being.

Just then, she spotted Chris coming down the hall. Light from a distant window shone all around him. If this had been a children's movie, there would have been birds singing overhead and dropping petals along his path. Maddie left Lucas in Lena's arms and practically ran to meet him. But the instant she reached him, she knew something was wrong.

"Chris? What—"

He gestured toward the others. "Let's talk all together."

Maddie's heart plummeted.

As if on second thought, Chris paused his determined stride and looked directly into her eyes. "Just for the record, everything is pretty much okay right now." Then the rigid line of his mouth softened. "In fact, when I'm standing here with you, things are way better than okay."

She gave him a cautious smile. "Way better," she said. Maddie placed her hand in the crook of his arm, and they continued their walk to Lena, Flora, and the miracle baby, Lucas.

Chris scanned the lobby and beckoned Nick over. Everyone drew in close to hear what he had to say.

Maddie folded her hands in front of her, listening to each sentence. She tried to keep fear off to the side. Tried to remember her safety was settled in God.

Zach had, indeed, come to Jefferson. But there had been an accident. Zach had been arrested. He was in police custody now.

That was what Chris wanted her to understand most: Zach was under lock and key. Probably awaiting formal charges as they spoke.

Maddie nodded. Chris repeated: Zach couldn't reach her. He hadn't seen her. He had only been patched up and then dragged off to jail. She could safely relax, eat lunch in Jefferson, then head home with Nick and Flora whenever she was ready.

She nodded again, stunned and numb. So much to process in so short a time. The tumor, the blizzard, the long dark night, the healing... Now this. Her head reeled. Yet a piece of the puzzle seemed to be missing. What was it?

Chris continued. "Now, Maddie, while that is all relatively good news, there's a part of this that's very sad." He held out his hand. She unclenched her hands and placed her fingers across his palm. He laid his other hand on top like a protective covering.

Maddie's throat tightened. Against the back wall of her mind, a wind began blowing. She could feel it coming, feel it driving in on her. Her fingers closed around Chris's hand.

His eyes were deep and concerned.

"Go on," she said.

He parceled out his words, "The sad part is that, in the accident, your friend Tanisha was killed."

Maddie's face crumpled, and her tears broke loose. Someone's arms steadied her. *Tanisha.* Maddie's whole body rocked with her sobs, and she didn't care who heard her. Her best friend—her wild, stylish, street-smart, brassy friend—was gone forever. And now, Tanisha would never know that Maddie understood how trapped she was. *Tanisha...*

The sorrowing wind blew hard against Maddie, gusty and strong. But this time, Maddie opened her heart's door and let it blow on through. It carried away the debris of decades. It winnowed the clutter of the last two days. She felt it all lift and twist away, faster than her mind could have sorted treasure from rubbish. She couldn't think now. She could only feel. Layers of fear and pain ached, peeled back, ripped loose, and blew far, far away.

And then, it subsided. She blinked, straightening, only to discover it was not Lena's shoulder she had been crying on. It had been Chris all the time. His arms still supported her.

Chris loosened his hug and started to step back. "Sorry—"

She managed a bit of a smile. "No. It was... all right."

Chris's eyes brightened. Then he ducked his head and stepped away.

Nearby, Lena, her face streaked with tears, held Lucas. Maddie reached out and stroked his back. He gurgled at her. Her friends chuckled, an awkward, relieved kind of sound.

Another storm had come and was going. And she was still standing. Thanks to all these wonderful friends. And the One who kept her safe.

Lena asked softly, "Are you going to be okay?"

Maddie nodded and hugged her and Lucas together. This faithful friend, this precious baby. They filled her arms, a strong, warm, living gift from God. He was here with her. Even in the storm, she was safe.

"I am," she said. "I am going to be okay."

CHAPTER 16

Chris reached for the tripod and turned off the camera on his phone.

Across the Dahlgrens' kitchen table from him, Maddie laid down her notes and sank back in her chair. She covered her eyes with her hand and exhaled heavily. "All done." A moment later, she peeked between her fingers. "Was it... too bad?"

"Bad?!" Chris shook his head but found he couldn't say more. *Try "heart-wrenching," plus a good dose of "inspiring" and "amazing."* He adjusted the tripod to hide his wordlessness.

Maddie leaned toward him. "What is it? Do we need to record it all over?" Her eyes watered like she might cry.

"No, no. It's perfect." Chris just looked at her. She was so beautiful. This glow she had taken on since January made her more lovely than ever. He cleared his throat. "Maddie, I am so proud of you."

"Why in the world?"

Chris gave up pretending and set the tripod aside. "Two reasons. One: You've just told your story, so—I mean, the way you talked about both the hard parts and the awesome parts... It'll have people at Tricia's banquet sitting on the edge of their seats. And reaching for a Kleenex at the same time."

She frowned. "You mean it went okay?"

Chris smiled. "Way beyond okay, Maddie." A faint pink washed across her cheeks. His heart did that flip-flop it used to do back in high school when she looked at him with those same questioning eyes. He distracted himself by disconnecting his phone from the tripod. "Do you want to hear reason two?"

Maddie hesitated, then nodded, her eyes focused on her lap and her hands tucked beneath her legs.

"It's that you've already started moving on from that difficult story. You've begun to build a beautiful new life." He paused, only continuing when she looked up and met his eyes. "Maddie Clouse, you are the most courageous woman I know."

She seemed to be searching his face. How he hoped she found what she was looking for. One corner of her mouth lifted just the littlest bit. A good sign.

She turned her attention to folding her notes into a tight little square on the table.

He passed her his phone. "Want to watch the recording yourself?"

She shook her head quickly. "No. Maybe later. But thank you. Thank you for spending your day off to come record this for me."

"You bet. Happy to help." In the silent moments that followed, they couldn't seem to quite unlock their gazes from each other.

Finally, Maddie said quietly, "You know, seeing you behind the camera while I was talking about... that... made me think about how loyal you have been to me. All this time. And it just dawned on me: that takes a lot of courage, too."

Chris picked up his phone, turning it over and over in his hand. "I don't know, Maddie. Maybe it is courage. Or maybe it's just that... I can't stop loving you." He held the phone still. "You may not want to hear that right now, but it's true."

He looked up to find that she was watching him. And she didn't stop. In some way that he couldn't quite put his finger on, her face seemed softer, more expressive than he'd seen it since she came back. She was just a little more... Maddie.

She swallowed. "A couple of days ago, I decided something." She took another breath and went on, "I decided I would never again do anything that would make it hard for you to... be loyal to me."

Chris's chest clenched. Her warm green eyes seemed to say far more than those words.

Standing suddenly, Maddie said, "I think I need a walk. Want to go get the mail with me?"

He stood and followed her through the living room, where Flora sat reading a book with Lucas sleeping cradled in her arm. She smiled at them and returned to her book. Side by side, Chris and Maddie slid into their shoes and pulled on their coats against the February cold. Chris opened the door for her, and they stepped into the brisk afternoon air.

Once outside, Maddie flapped her open coat. "Who knew filming could make a person so warm!"

He waved a hand and faked a British accent to say, "But of course. All movie stars say the same thing, Darling." That got her laughing along with him.

Halfway down the driveway, Maddie paused to breathe deeply of the chilly air. Pulling her hood over her head, she said, "You were right, Chris. This is a beautiful new life. I can't remember a time I ever felt this free."

Free. Chris scuffed his foot across a patch of rough ice on the driveway, a cold sense of reality stealing over his thoughts. *Rein it in, Nelson. She said she wants you to be "loyal."* Her newfound freedom just might include staying unshackled to him. When he glanced up, Maddie's eyes were directed far down the street.

Shivering slightly, she said, "But about the other thing, I think you were wrong."

"What other thing?"

"I don't feel at all courageous. Of the two job possibilities I had, I chose the flower shop because I could ride the bus. I wouldn't have to take the Dahlgrens' spare car." Her voice went quiet. "Being in cars still freaks me out."

"Understandable." Chris stood beside her, hands captive in his pockets, letting his eyes follow her line of sight. "But still, it was you who chose that job—you, yourself. You picked the job you wanted, and for a perfectly good reason."

"Well... yeah. I guess that's true."

He turned to face her. Her shimmering red hair spilled from inside her hood. The pensive smile she wore made him curious. "Tell me what you've enjoyed about your first two weeks working as a florist."

A smile spread across her lips as she spoke, "I absolutely love the fragrances. All those flowers! I walk in, and I'm surrounded by beauty, even in the workroom. And did I tell you they'll let me bring Lucas to work on days I don't have childcare?" She paused, then added, "I enjoy feeling… creative again. I actually get to create things, things that lift people's spirits."

Chris smiled back. "You were always good at the artsy stuff. Even when we were kids, you were drawing landscapes while I struggled with stick figures. Do you ever think about going back to finish your fine arts degree?"

Maddie shot him a sideways glance. "I hadn't gotten that far yet."

"Oh. Sure." Chris wanted to kick himself. *Stop pushing her.*

"But thanks for planting that seed," Maddie added. "I'll think about it. Nick mentioned there's a community college in Sargent. Might be a good place to start."

Chris fell silent.

She murmured, "You've always been my source of inspiration."

"Wait, really?" Now he was the one searching her face.

"Who talked me into applying for a college scholarship? You. Who suggested I should audition for the school musical? You. I didn't believe I could do either of those things." Maddie zipped up her coat. Then she elbowed him. "Do you remember, when we first became friends, you set a cupcake in the doorway of your tree fort to encourage me to conquer my fear of climbing the ladder?"

Chris nodded, smiling toward his feet. "But you're the one who climbed the ladder."

"Only because I wanted to be as brave as you."

He looked up into her sparkling eyes. If she kept talking like this—

"Well, that, and I wanted the cupcake," she finished, giggling like a ten-year-old. "Come on, let's get the mail before we freeze out here."

At the foot of the driveway, Maddie pulled several letters and a sales flyer from the mailbox. "Hey, look!" she said, "Two of these are for me. One is from Emily Radner at the Harbor. And this one's from Dos Almas. Race you to the house!" She swatted him with her letters then sprinted up the driveway, laughing over her shoulder.

Chris ran ahead to open the door for her again, and they stumbled inside. Flora looked up, shushing them but with a smile. After shedding their coats and shoes, they tiptoed around the corner to the kitchen table. Maddie opened the letter from Emily Radner first. She read the card, then passed it to Chris, fingering the enclosed newspaper clipping.

Chris scanned the message. "Very nice. So, what was in the paper? She said it's good news."

Maddie lowered herself into a chair as she read the short article. Whatever good news it contained didn't bring a smile to her face. Chris waited. Finally, she laid the clipping on the table and looked up. "Zach's charged with criminal vehicular homicide and sex trafficking here in Minnesota. Then he faces more charges in California. He could be locked away for decades."

Chris gripped the back of Maddie's chair until his knuckles whitened. The memory of watching that Jarvis creep get ushered out of the hospital doors made him glad Brent had been there to strong-arm him that day. Otherwise, Chris would have wound up behind bars himself. This was far better. He could let the justice system drop the hammer on Jarvis while he got to be here watching Maddie come back to life.

"Well, then," Maddie said, slowly folding the clipping and tucking it back into Emily's card. "At last, he'll get what's coming to him. And I'm glad. For Tanisha's sake... and mine."

Maddie's hair swept over his knuckles as she turned to peer up at him. "Chris, you want to sit down? I feel like you're standing over me for my protection or something."

I am. Always will be, God willing. "Sorry," he said. He released the chair and joined her at the table. "What did Dos Almas send you?"

Maddie shoved Emily's card aside and slit open the larger envelope from the pregnancy center. This time, she smiled. "Oh, it's their banquet invitation. Wouldn't it be fun to—" A separate, handwritten note slipped out from behind the invitation card. Maddie read it and gasped.

When she showed it to Chris, he read aloud: "'Our dear Maddie, a group of anonymous donors have offered to pay airfare for you and Lucas to attend our banquet. Do you think you could come? Seeing and hearing you on video will be wonderful, but Paloma and I would love to meet you in person. You could stay in one of our homes if you like. Please think it over and give me a call when you can. Your friend, Tricia.'"

He didn't need to ask if she wanted to go. Her eyes sparkled like a sky full of fireworks. "March 21 is only a month away," he said, grinning. "Better start looking for tickets."

Maddie practically bounced in her seat. "I've never been on a plane before. Is it fun?"

"Oh, yeah, Maddie." His arm swept across the air in front of her. "Out the window, you can see across the tops of clouds, for miles and miles. They look like mounds of whipped cream floating in the bright blue sky. And you're floating up there among them, effortlessly. It's awesome. You'll love it."

"Mmm! And when I land, there will be Tricia and Paloma, the friends I never thought I'd get to meet! And they will get to meet Lucas too. And—" Her face fell.

"What's the matter?"

"I just wish… I wish they could meet you, too, Chris. You and your mother. Without you—both of you—I wouldn't have made it back home. And most of what I said in my video would never have happened."

She reached for his hand.

His pulse pounded in his head.

She leaned closer. "Chris, would you go with me? I mean, I'll understand if you can't. You have your job and everything." She squeezed his hand and then let it go. "But it won't be nearly as nice without you."

"Well…" Chris swallowed. He didn't even try to stifle the smile that rose with the heat in his face. "Maybe we could find a way."

Reece laughed when Tricia took her seat at the table for the fifth time in five minutes. "Trish, relax. Your banquet committee took care of everything," he said. "Look around you. It's gorgeous."

Tricia let her gaze roam over the banquet hall decorated in cream and sparkling gold, with sprays of elegant white lilies and pale yellow roses. Candlelight danced over white-linen tables and the faces of guests filling the slipcovered chairs. Their guest speaker for the night seemed to be enjoying himself, too. He stood near another table in friendly conversation with Mike Benson and his wife.

Tricia craned her neck to seek out the other board members. Kathy and her adult son were hosting a nearby table, already half-filled with a talkative group of women from her church. Paul and his wife escorted their guests to their seats three tables away. Tricia caught his eye and clasped her hands together in a gesture of gratitude for his efforts in planning this event. Two other board members sat laughing with several couples they had invited. Among them sat Alex Cortez, the major donor who had changed his mind in February and promised to renew his regular gifts. And Dr. Joe… Dr. Joe still stood at the entrance, welcoming visitors, keeping an eye out for his special guests. Just then, his face lit up, and he stepped forward, hand extended.

"Reece, they're here," Tricia said, rising. "Come with me?" In her haste, she slipped out of her high-heeled shoe. He gave her his arm to lean on so she could wiggle back into it.

Before she could hurry away, he lifted her hand and kissed it. "Right behind you, Cinderella."

She gave him a grateful smile. What a kind prince for such a nervous executive director.

As they wove among the tables in the crowded room, Tricia tried to guess which of Dr. Joe's guests was which. One was younger and balding. His smile was as broad as Dr. Joe's as they shook hands. The taller man with short dark hair, however, was the most intriguing.

When Dr. Joe spotted her and Reece approaching, he beckoned them closer. To his first guest, he said, "Keith Bair, I'd like to introduce to you our executive director, Tricia Prescott, and her husband, Reece."

Dr. Bair gave them a childlike smile, open and bright. He shook hands eagerly and thanked them for the invitation to this fundraising banquet.

Tricia liked him immediately. "Of course, Dr. Bair! We are honored to have you here."

"And this," Dr. Joe said, sweeping his arm toward the taller man, "is Dr. Jackson Murphy."

Dr. Murphy stepped forward, hand out already. "Mrs. Prescott. I'm so glad to finally meet you after all our phone conversations. And Mr. Prescott," he said, with a warm and friendly grip for each of them. He had the ease of a politician in a crowd.

"Thank you so much for coming all this way to join us tonight," she said. "And please, call me Tricia."

Dr. Murphy bowed slightly. "Then I'm Jack."

Tricia nodded. She could see why Maddie had once felt intimidated by this tall and stately man. His imposing figure, if coupled with an assertive self-confidence, must have hit the poor girl like a tidal wave. By his own admission, he had been "rude and pompous" toward her. But apparently, Lucas and Maddie's miracle had set off a seismic event in Dr. Murphy's life. And somehow, that had triggered the aftershocks that led him here this evening. Over the phone, he had been remarkably straightforward about his history of self-aggrandizement and painful personal regrets…and his dramatic desire to make up for it all. He seemed grateful that his colleague, Dr. Bair, had presented him with an avenue for doing so.

Dr. Joe motioned to the punch table. "Gentlemen, shall we get something to drink and find our seats?"

Tricia spoke up first. "I really feel bad that you two are seated so far in the back. Can't we give you our places closer to the front?"

Drs. Bair and Murphy exchanged glances. Dr. Murphy said, "That's very kind of you. But we would rather just blend in among your other guests, I believe."

Tricia bowed her head. "As you wish, gentlemen. We are just so overcome with gratitude—"

Dr. Bair smiled. "And you've expressed that so well. Which reminds me: Mrs. Prescott, in recent years, Dr. Murphy and I have spoken with many people seeking funds for worthy causes. But we both agreed that none of them ever showed the same passion for their work that you did. You make a very convincing case for the value of your ministry."

Tricia reached up to cool her cheek that had suddenly grown warm. "Why… thank you."

Reece squeezed her hand and placed it in the crook of his arm. "Thank you, Dr. Bair, Dr. Murphy. We'll talk again later." As they wound their way back to their table, he leaned closer and murmured in her ear, "As Joey says, 'Told ya.'"

Tricia shook her head, an irresistible smile growing on her lips. For tonight, it didn't matter what her salary was, only that she was making a difference where she served. Walking at Reece's side, she relished how her handsome prince of a husband made his simple navy blazer and tan slacks look like a tuxedo. Knowing how hard he'd been laboring to approach the level of income he once had, she was impressed with how naturally he relaxed into the evening's duties. He was going to make an excellent master of ceremonies.

When they reached their table, Paloma was there, her long hair shining silver in the candlelight and her ageless smile reaching from cheek to cheek. For right beside her sat a happy little redhead who just had to be their long-invisible, much-imagined friend.

Tricia's breath caught. "Maddie?"

As the girl stood, Tricia circled the table to hug her. From the sounds of sniffling going on, Tricia wasn't the only one tearing up.

She leaned back for a moment, drinking in the girl's features. Beautiful long, copper curls framed her slim face with its delicate nose and deep green eyes. She stood shorter than Tricia's chin, more petite than she would have dreamed such a strong young woman could be.

Maddie laughed. "Tricia! This is you! I never guessed you were so tall!"

Tricia giggled herself. "I'm much shorter on the phone."

Meanwhile, the muscular young man beside Maddie stood and gave Reece a hearty handshake. "Chris Nelson," he said.

"You two have made our whole night," Reece said after introducing himself and Tricia. "Tricia has wanted to meet you two for—well, for months!" The men chuckled and moved to take their seats.

But Tricia couldn't yet let go of Maddie's hands. She looked deeply into those green eyes whose expression she had so often longed to read during their long texting exchanges and phone calls. "Maddie, I'm so glad to finally see you. After your long trip out here, how are you doing?"

Maddie's smile widened. "I am happier than I can say. Just to finally get to meet you and Paloma—Can you believe we're all here together?"

Tricia squeezed her hands. "Oh, I have something for you. Something I wanted to give to a girl named Lizzie. But now I can give it to *you*." She slid a basket out from under her chair.

Maddie reached inside and pulled out Chocolate, the teddy bear. She hugged it and smiled at Tricia. "It's adorable! Lucas's first teddy bear!"

At that moment, Avery Caine and her husband Rocky joined them, along with a slender blonde woman holding a baby with a full head of dark curls. "Hey, everybody," Avery said, "this is Lena Nelson. And Lucas."

Tricia and Paloma erupted into what Reece liked to call "mommy noises" and rushed to greet Lucas. Paloma reached him first, so Tricia contented herself with meeting Lena and showing her to a seat while Paloma held the baby.

If Paloma's flow of Spanish greetings took hold, Lucas would be bilingual by the end of the evening, Tricia thought. She had to laugh at the pair of them, making noises to each other. She finally got a turn to hold him about the time Reece climbed to the stage to welcome everyone to the banquet.

Over dinner, as gentle classical music floated around them, the strangers-turned-friends never ran out of stories to tell. Then Lena's camera came out. "Baby pictures!" she announced. The camera traveled around the table multiple times. Tricia's smile muscles grew delightfully tired.

The evening flew by in a way Tricia could never have anticipated back in January. Who could have known there would be not just one but three young women, including Maddie, willing to record their stories of transformation? Watching the videos now, with Maddie and Lucas sitting directly across from her, Tricia felt profoundly privileged to have played a small part in all that God had done.

Before Tricia knew it, the guest speaker neared the culmination of his remarks, and her turn to take the stage with Mike Benson drew closer. She took a last sip of water, wiped her mouth, and reapplied her lipstick. From his table, Mike caught her eye and gave her a nod. She smiled back hopefully.

Applause rose from the crowd, the speaker left the stage, and Reece called Tricia and Mike to the podium. She rose to her feet, grateful that this time her shoe stayed on. Mike followed her up front.

She adjusted the microphone with a quick glance at Reece to soothe her jitters. The audience appeared so much larger from the stage, so much larger than she had expected two months ago. Her gaze swept the applauding crowd, and the room fell silent as she began.

"Ladies and gentlemen, I imagine right now you're feeling as I do: amazed by the stories we've heard tonight. One, the story of a brave mother who made an adoption plan to give her child a bright future. Another, a story of discovering the courage to avoid quick fixes that would have led down a path of compromise and regret. And finally, a story of finding freedom from trafficking, to discover that a child never asked for could become the best gift ever."

The crowd sent up murmurs of agreement and some scattered applause. Over at their table, Paloma patted one of Maddie's hands while Chris held the other.

Tricia went on, "And the Lord has done all this through a loyal team of volunteers, led primarily by our fearless Client Services Coordinator, Paloma Cisneros. Paloma, would you please stand up so we can express our appreciation?"

Paloma shot her the "you-know-I-hate-this" glare, but she stood anyway as Tricia and the guests honored her with applause. In the candlelight, it was hard to be sure how deeply she blushed before bowing her head and sitting down again.

"The Lord has done all this without a headquarters, without a home to call our own," Tricia went on. "For months, our Mother and Baby Boutique items have been scattered across the city, requiring our teammates to spend countless hours collecting and delivering the things parents needed. For months, we have traveled to meet clients—sometimes in their homes or our homes. We have met with women and men in library study rooms, churches, the park... In short, our team has been everywhere except together.

"Sadly, we sometimes heard that potential clients did not come to us for help because our disjointed arrangements did not inspire their confidence. How many stories like those we shared tonight have ended differently because women couldn't or didn't find us?"

An uneasy quiet settled over the audience.

Then Tricia continued, "Tonight, however, as our speaker hinted, you have an opportunity to help write happier endings for the stories to come. Here's Mike Benson, chairman of our board of directors, to explain how."

Tricia stepped away from the podium to stand by Reece. Mike took center stage then with all the aplomb of a seasoned public speaker. Tricia tipped her head to listen to Mike but occasionally let her gaze wander across his listeners below. She prayed that these supporters would catch the vision for all that Dos Almas could do with its own building, and specifically with the building it hoped to purchase.

Mike gestured toward the schematic diagram the guests had strolled past upon entering the banquet hall, now filling the big screen behind him. He described the different rooms, along with the center's dreams for each one. Tricia worked to keep her face pleasantly neutral, but in her mind, she was walking through the building, peopling it with women seeking pregnancy tests and options information, young families choosing needed items from the spacious boutique, staff and volunteers working in the back office, and board members and supporters gathering in the meeting room. And someday, in that extra room, a nervous woman preparing for an ultrasound—her first glimpse of her precious baby.

Tricia snapped back to the present at a nudge from Reece's elbow. "Here it comes," he whispered.

"Tonight, ladies and gentlemen," Mike said, "I have the awesome privilege to inform you that our dream of owning that building has been placed miraculously within our reach. Through a series of events that stretched the influence of Dos Almas Pregnancy Center halfway across the country, two neonatal specialists have collaborated to offer us a matching grant. They have agreed to match all funds raised in connection with this evening's banquet…up to half the price of the building."

Mike's announcement created ripples of gasps, sudden murmurs, and spontaneous applause. People looked at one another and kept clapping. Never in the center's history had such an enormous donation been made. Tricia took Reece's hand as Drake's words echoed in her mind: "Ask, seek, knock, Mom."

O me of little faith.

In the dim light at the back of the hall, Dr. Murphy inclined his head toward Dr. Bair as if in private conversation. How Tricia wanted to call out those two doctors' names and make them stand and be recognized. But she had promised to respect their wish for anonymity, however difficult that might be.

Mike now held up a copy of the pledge cards that waited on each table. Tricia's heart beat faster. Before he had even finished explaining the various ways to donate, people started reaching for the cards and texting into their cell phones to give online. When Mike stopped speaking, he stepped away from the podium while the instrumentalists filled the air with music. That was Tricia's cue to leave the stage and return to her table.

Maddie reached out for her hand. "Tricia, is it true? Dr. Murphy and Dr. Bair are the ones who did this? And they're here somewhere?"

Tricia smiled. "Yes, it's all true. Because of you, two doctors from faraway Minnesota decided to pour their generosity out on Dos Almas Pregnancy Center."

Maddie and Chris looked at each other with wide, astonished eyes.

Watching Maddie's coppery curls catch the light, Tricia thought suddenly of Paloma's poppies, of a single seed, and of surprising abundance. Her heart swelled as she leaned toward Maddie. "Would you like to see them?"

Maddie was already on her feet. Lena and Chris, holding Lucas, rose to go along.

Tricia motioned for them to follow her. With Maddie's lovely hair shining like polished copper in the candlelight, Tricia wasn't surprised that the two doctors spotted her en route and stood to welcome her and her friends. They moved quietly to the very back of the banquet hall for their reunion.

Dr. Bair's boyish smile flashed in the soft light. "Ms. Clouse, how good to see you again!"

Maddie, beaming, stepped forward to shake his hand. "Hi, Dr. Bair." Then she shook her head and added, "I wondered why you kept asking me about this pregnancy center. Now I know."

Dr. Bair inclined his head briefly. "God makes some of the most astounding connections, doesn't he?"

Dr. Murphy, all stately charm earlier, stood back quietly while Dr. Bair did all the talking. Now Maddie moved toward him. "Hello, Dr. Murphy. It's nice to see you again."

Dr. Murphy's ruddy face deepened in color. "Thank you for saying so, Ms. Clouse. You are more gracious than I deserve. I am truly happy to see you, as well."

She glanced at Dr. Bair. "I guess I shouldn't be surprised that you two baby doctors would do something so... huge... to help pregnant women and their babies."

Dr. Murphy looked at his polished shoes. "Actually, you are right to be surprised, Ms. Clouse. Not at Bair's involvement, of course. But mine... Let's just say that even I am surprised at where I am now."

Maddie cocked her head like a little bird waiting for the next seed to drop.

Dr. Murphy looked up again, caught Tricia's eye, and then turned his gaze on Maddie with a warmth befitting a doting uncle. "You, Ms. Clouse, poked a hole in this old doctor's façade and let the Light come in. Joining my colleague in this endeavor was simply a long-overdue step in the right direction. The first of many, I hope."

Chris, who had joined Maddie, shifted Lucas to his left shoulder and reached to shake the doctor's hands. "Who knew our paths would cross here, right?"

Dr. Murphy's straight lips curved into a grin. "You are so right. Say, Ms. Clouse, would you do me the honor of letting me hold your son for a moment?"

Maddie's eyes opened wide. "Well, um, sure." She nodded to Chris.

Chris placed Lucas in the doctor's hands and stepped back. Dr. Murphy held Lucas beneath his little arms, close enough, so they were eye to eye. Lucas batted his cheek with a tiny fist. "I deserve that," the doctor laughed. "But I hope I never will again."

He laid the baby into the crook of his arm, where he could run a finger along his chubby cheek. "I owe you, Lucas," he said softly. In the candlelight, something glinted below Dr. Murphy's right eye.

Tricia, tearing up herself, noted the musicians' instrumental number had reached its final measures, and most of the guests were now quietly chatting with one another. She tore her attention away from Lucas and turned to face the stage.

Reece moved to the podium with Paloma's laptop computer.

Even this far away, Tricia could read the excitement on his face. Heart racing, she interlaced her fingers and pressed them to her lips.

"Ladies and gentlemen," Reece began, "Thank you for joining us tonight to celebrate God's accomplishments and to consider how we can all support his work through Dos Almas going forward. I realize that many of your gifts are still sitting in the envelopes on your tables, waiting to be counted. But before you go, would you like an update on the funds that have already been given electronically?" Reece paused, lifting his eyes to connect with Tricia at the back of the room. The air pulsed with anticipation.

Reece glanced back to the screen. "Those of you who gave online..." he paused and looked up, "have already donated... over half of the amount needed to make the complete match and buy Dos Almas this building!"

Giddy with joy, Tricia breathed in deeply and turned to smile at the two doctors, at Maddie and her friends, at anyone who was looking. *"Ask, seek, knock, Mom..."* She pressed her fists to her cheeks as tears trickled down them.

After a moment, she found Maddie had come to stand beside her, holding Lucas in her arms. Maddie looked up to meet her eyes. Neither of them said a thing. After all the words they had spoken without seeing one another, tonight it was enough to stand side by side amid wordless applause, all rising to the One who had walked with them in the storm.

THE END

APPENDIX

Learn more about helping women facing crises involving pregnancy using the following list of resources.

- **Heartbeat International** (https://www.heartbeatinternational.org): Worldwide network of over 2800 pregnancy help organizations, including medical clinics, resource centers, maternity homes, and adoption agencies. Provides training, networking, and support services.
- **Pregnancy Help News** (https://pregnancyhelpnews.com/): Free online news publication; subscribe to stay up-to-date on developments in the world of pregnancy help.
- **Worldwide Directory of Pregnancy Help Organizations** (https://www.heartbeatinternational.org/worldwide-directory): Locate a pregnancy help organization near you or near a friend in crisis.
- **Care Net** (https://www.care-net.org/): Network of over 1100 US pregnancy centers.
- **Be Charity Wise / Trauma-Informed Church** (https://www.becharitywise.com/traumachurch): Free book and several training options to help you create lasting change in your community by providing trauma-informed care.
- **Embrace Grace** (https://embracegrace.com/): Find or start a church-based support group for women and men facing unexpected pregnancy and/or single parenthood.

For information and helpful resources on countering human trafficking:

- **Polaris Project** (https://polarisproject.org/): Data-driven information to help you understand and respond to the realities of human trafficking.
- **Cry Freedom Missions** (https://www.cryfreedommissions.com/): Non-profit "fighting to eradicate sex trafficking through Reaching, Rescuing, and Restoring the lives of survivors." See also their survivor-made jewelry, home décor, and more.
- **Shared Hope International** (https://sharedhope.org/): Resources and trainings for responding to human trafficking and bringing restoration to victims.
- **Love 2 Hope** (https://www.love2hope.com/): Workshops for building human trafficking awareness and mobilization on behalf of trafficking victims. See their Resources section for an extensive list of must-read books.
- **Hotline to report potential trafficking**: (https://human-traffickinghotline.org/get-help): Call 1-888-373-7888.

ABOUT THE AUTHOR

As a freelance writer, ghostwriter, and communications manager for a Minnesota pregnancy center, Karen Ingle encounters inspiring individuals across the globe who are quietly igniting hope in others' darkness every day. Now Karen spins those hidden stories into novels for readers who may be—or become—some of those who dare to "Love. Real. Hard."

Behind all Karen's writing winds a life path that has (like yours?) led through some breathtaking ups and devastating downs. Love and joy came interspersed with challenges like widowhood, single motherhood, and adoption. She knows the power of being loved real hard by God, family, and friends.

Karen expected southern California to be her lifelong home until she met and married Dennis, who introduced her to the changing seasons of Minnesota. She has never regretted their move. Except during blizzards. A teacher by training, Karen homeschooled all five of their children. Everyone survived the adventure.

Would you like to connect with Karen? Find her at:
- Website: https://KarenIngleAuthor.com
- Facebook: https://www.facebook.com/kareningleauthor
- Instagram: @kareningleauthor

CPSIA information can be obtained
at www.ICGtesting.com
Printed in the USA
JSHW041951051222
34254JS00007B/11